DA

ANDREW VACHSS

URBAN RENEWAL

Andrew Vachss is a lawyer who represents children and youths exclusively. His many books include the Burke novels, the Cross series, the Aftershock series, and three collections of short stories. His books have been translated into twenty languages, and his work has appeared in *Parade*, *Antaeus*, *Esquire*, *Playboy*, and *The New York Times*, among other publications. He divides his time between his native New York City and the Pacific Northwest.

www.vachss.com

BOOKS BY ANDREW VACHSS

URBAN RENEWAL

ANDREW VACHSS

URBAN RENEWAL

A Cross Novel

VINTAGE CRIME/BLACK LIZARD
Vintage Books
A Division of Random House LLC
New York

A VINTAGE CRIME/BLACK LIZARD ORIGINAL, JANUARY 2014

The Library of Congress Cataloging-in-Publication Data
Vachss, Andrew H.
Urban renewal : a Cross novel / Andrew Vachss.
p. cm.
1. Gangsters—Fiction. 2. Chicago (Ill.)—Fiction. I. Title.
PS3572.A33U73 2014
813'.54—dc23
2013020579

Vintage Trade Paperback ISBN: 978-0-8041-6881-6
eBook ISBN: 978-0-8041-6882-3

Book design by Joy O'Meara-Wispe

www.weeklylizard.com

Printed in the United States of America
10 9 8 7 6 5 4 3 2 1

for Grizzly . . .

I wish I had known sooner
I wish I could have done something
By the time I did, already too late, I know
But I can still hear you, brother
Breathing out that gasoline mist
That always awaits my flamethrower
For structures that *should* have been condemned

URBAN RENEWAL

"THAT'S IT?" the radically contoured, raven-haired young woman said. Her once-sweet face twisted into a bitter grimace. *"That's* where I'm supposed to work? *That's* the place where you said I'd be so—"

"Safe? Guaranteed, honey. Twenty-four-karat, with a platinum cherry on top," a similarly structured blonde who looked too young to have a driver's license answered reassuringly. Her pampered hands rested possessively on the steering wheel of her azure-toned Mercedes two-seater, a hardtop-convertible she proudly referred to as "off paper, totally."

I earned this, ran through her thoughts. *It's mine, not some loan-shark "finance company's."*

"It looks . . . scary. Like someone dropped it into the middle of a junkyard."

"We work *indoors,*" the blonde sighed dramatically, not disguising her weariness of the brunette's nonstop fretting. "This isn't your first ride, girl. You know there's not going to be no free-peek windows, so what's it matter what's outside?"

"But . . ."

"Ssssh, now. If you don't like it, what would you be giving up?"

"If I don't bring home—"

"You're not *going* home, remember?"

"But all my things—"

"They'll still be there, don't worry."

"You don't know him."

"That's one thing *I* don't know. You just sit still for another minute or two and I'll show you a couple dozen *you* don't."

"THIS HAS to be a joke," the brunette whined as the little Mercedes wove its way past the gutted remains of vehicles ranging from motorcycles to semi-trailers.

"Ssssh," the blonde said again. "Girl, you have *got* to learn a little patience."

"Maybe that's my problem. Sometimes, I think I'm *too* damn patient," her passenger said, eyeing the motley collection of free-range dogs hunting the rats who were constantly in motion among the twisted piles of rusting metal.

The blonde wheeled her car past a fenced-in area marked "Valet Parking." The brunette got only a vague glance at neat rows of parked cars before the blonde abruptly turned left and rolled her little prize to the back of what looked like a long rectangular concrete bunker. Only a discrete band of blood-red neon spelling out "XX" broke the dullness of its appearance.

The back area was almost as wide as the main building, but no more than twenty feet deep. There were numerous individual slots, each marked with a letter above its door. The blonde tapped a key on her iPhone. *Brand-new—no more bootlegs for this little girl!* she thought, as she did every time she used it.

When an indecipherable grunting noise answered, she said, "Arabella. And a friend."

Slot J opened. Arabella drove in confidently, left her keys in the ignition, and climbed out as the door slid down behind her.

"Will you come on?" she snapped over her shoulder.

The brunette followed as the blonde stood in front of a mirrored door. An audible "click" sounded. The blonde strode inside, tugging her friend's hand, as if they were BFFs about to enter a club one of them wasn't so sure about.

An extremely large man stood behind the door, his upper body covered in Maori tattoos. His eyes were forced into slits from the compression of his eyebrows. It was a full ten seconds before he nodded.

"What was *that*?" the brunette asked.

"That's just K-2."

"Like 'Kato'?"

"No, like Kay-Two. Get it?"

"No. But . . ."

"But what? You think your 'man' is going to just walk past *him*?"

"Not without an elephant gun."

"Hold that thought," the blonde said, smiling.

"THOSE ARE the dressing rooms," the blonde said, "but we won't be going on for another hour or so. I thought you'd want to look the place over first."

"Uh . . . okay."

The blonde opened another door. "This is backstage. If you're going on, you walk up those stairs. If you're not, you just . . . Well, follow me."

The two women seated themselves at a small round table set against the wall, to the right of the stage.

"Mae can sure work that pole," the blonde said. "It's real brass, by the way. Used to be in a firehouse, the way I heard it."

"Everything's very . . . nice."

"Oh, it's the *best*. That's not some cheesy carpeted-over linoleum your feet are resting on, honey—that's deep-pile. Plush. Look around. Look anywhere you want—you'll see nothing *but* the best. Check out over there, way over to the other side. That section's for the paying customers . . . and I don't mean the ones who want to get close to the girls; the ones who want the girls to get close to *them*, right? And trust me, there's not a cheapskate in the lot."

"But we work for tips only, right? No—?"

"You don't do anything you don't want to do," the blonde assured her. "When I told you everything in here was the best, I was talking about the girls, too. Sure, there's a VIP Room and all that, but you can just work your shift, and anything they throw on the stage or stuff in your garter or whatever, that's what you earn."

"VIP Room? Does that mean I—?"

"Nooooh," the blonde answered, stretching out the word like a bratty teenager. "That 'Valet Parking' is just a shuck to make the marks feel like big shots—there's no *other* parking lot. But the VIP Room, that's . . . well, it costs whatever it costs, see?"

"No, I don't."

"Ah . . . look, honey, it's not that complicated. Some girls cost more than others, some girls will do some things other girls won't . . . and some girls won't work that room at all."

"How does the house make its money, then? All the watered champagne in the world wouldn't pay for this setup."

"You rent your spot. Three girls are always onstage: one on the pole, two up front. Costs you a hundred bucks for twenty-five minutes. Some trios do better rotating, some not. Doesn't matter—you take turns working whatever spots you decide, and you split up the tips at the end. Or you could even go it alone, but that's three hundred for the twenty-five minutes, so you'd better *really* work it, you make that choice. And, not for nothing, that champagne *isn't* watered."

"That's some 'rent' they charge here. Six hundred an hour."

"Which would be almost fifteen grand every day—they never close. But you can buy eight slots at a time—that's why it's twenty-five minutes, so you can take five for yourself if you're going right back on again."

"Jeez."

"Oh, you don't *have* to do it. They've got more girls who want to work here than they can take. But if you work, say, six slots, you should pull in well over a grand a night, net. *After* the rent, see?"

"Without ever leaving the stage? No lap dances, none of that VIP Room stuff?"

"Yep."

"But the girls who *do* . . ."

"Oh, sure. There's girls taking an easy ten G's a week out of here."

"Do you ever—?"

"Honey, what *I* do is up to me. Just like it is for you. And what you *don't* do, either. What *I* don't do is talk about what I do, you with me?"

"Sure."

"Okay. Now, glance—and I mean *glance*, no more—to your right. There's a man sitting in that far corner. That's his private spot."

"He doesn't look like much."

"He owns the place."

"Oh. Is he here all the time?"

"Not even close."

"Then who stops people from—?"

"Look at the door, baby. You can look *there* as long as you want."

"I see."

"No, you don't. You see one bad guy at the door. That's Bruno. And he *is* a certified killer, sure. Now look behind the bar. That's Gringo."

"Gringo? But he's—"

"You think a Mexican named 'Gringo' is weird, wait 'til you meet Princess."

"Are you serious?"

"Oh, yeah. He's not here now, but Rhino is. Look all the way down at the end of the bar. See him?"

"I see . . . Nobody's *that* size."

"That's what I thought, too. At first. But he's no thug. In fact, he's a real gentleman. There's something wrong with his voice, so it comes out like a squeak. But he's the only one that can do anything with Princess if something jumps off."

"Jumps off *here*?"

"Now you're beginning to get the idea," the blonde said, making a gesture of some kind toward the man seated behind a triangular table in the far corner, a man whom she knew only as "Cross."

"COME ON," the blonde told her friend. "He says it's okay."

The two girls sat, each on one side of the triangle table which had been fitted into the corner slot. The tabletop appeared to be a three-inch-thick slab of some kind of dull-gray plastic. Anyone who approached the table uninvited would quickly be treated to a head-on view of that slab—it was hinged to pop forward from the corner at the touch of a floor button. And would turn even a heavy-caliber round into a harmless *splat!*

"This is Taylor," the blonde said. "I already ran down the deal to her."

"And . . . ?"

"And I'll take it," Taylor said, quickly. There was something about the nondescript man. Something that warned her not to equivocate.

She dropped her eyes to the ashtray where Cross was grinding out a cigarette he'd lit when Arabella first pointed him out. Her eyes were drawn to the bull's-eye tattoo on the back of his right hand; she quickly looked away.

"Really?"

"I didn't mean like I was doing you a favor or anything. I just—"

"She's got a boyfriend who talks with his hands," the blonde cut her off.

"And you want that to stop?" Cross asked without inflection.

"Yes! He—"

"I'm not a social worker. You want him not to bother you *here*, that's covered by your rent. You want him not to bother you ever *again*, that's something you have to pay extra for."

"You mean . . . ?"

"Cash. In advance."

"But he takes all my—"

"We don't do labor bonds."

"Huh?"

"They don't take IOUs," the blonde explained. "I already told you, didn't I? You can stay with me until you build up enough to get another place. If you start here tonight, you won't be going back. And, from the money you'll be making . . ."

"But everything in that apartment is mine. I mean . . . I *worked* for it."

"Up to you," the blonde said.

"Could I . . . could I pay you to go and *get* my stuff?"

"No" was all Cross said.

"What am I supposed to *do*?" the brunette said, on the verge of tears.

"I'm on in ten," the blonde said. "You decide what you want to do, catch me on my break."

THE BRUNETTE looked at Cross from under heavily veiled eyelashes. That didn't work any better than the trembling lips, the tears, and her unvoiced offer of . . . whatever.

He might as well be a piece of furniture, she thought. *Arabella already told me that—but she's so damn dramatic about everything, I guess I don't pay much attention when she talks.*

"You want to work here—fetching your 'things,' that's on the house, too," Cross said, lighting another cigarette. "Call your boyfriend, tell him where you'll be working tonight."

"What good is that going to—?"

"Has he got more than one girl?"

"J.B. isn't a pimp," she said indignantly.

"Sure, he is. I was just asking about the size of his stable."

"I Am Not A Whore," the brunette said, each word a separate statement.

"You got a kid?"

"No."

"A dog?"

"No. Why are you asking me?"

"If you had either one, he could put you right back in line by threatening to hurt them."

"He threatens to hurt *me*," she snapped. "Isn't that enough?"

"He ever do more than threaten?"

"Yes. He once took my—"

"Doesn't matter," Cross said, stubbing out his cigarette.

Three drags and he's done? Taylor thought. "Why doesn't it matter?" she said aloud.

Cross looked at her. "If you hadn't got all huffy when I said 'pimp,' you'd be asking to work the VIP Room."

"And how do you know I *won't* ask to do that?"

Cross said nothing. Arabella was a good worker, quick to catch on. But she was always picking up strays. Touching the corner of her right eye had already told him all this new one wanted to do was dance.

He nodded his head, as if some agreement had been reached. "If he was a street-certified pimp, he'd know better than to come around this place. But he's some kind of 'boyfriend,' right? The kind who doesn't work. What'd you do, meet him in a club?"

"I . . . Yes, that's right. I mean, not a club like this one. A nightclub."

"Good-looking guy? Smooth, silky? Nice way of talking?"

"That's right," she said, already on the defensive from . . . she wasn't sure exactly what.

"Didn't take long before he moved in with you."

"Well, we were going to be together anyway, so—"

"So it just kept going in the same direction, rolling downhill. He was waiting on some deal to come through. Or he wanted to cut a demo. Or . . . whatever. No matter how he put it, he told you he was in some kind of bind, right? That's when you started dancing."

"So?"

"You first meet him, he pays for your drinks. Now you pay all *his* bills."

"I never thought—"

"You think you're the first girl to bet on the wrong horse? So what? It's only money—he didn't take anything you can't replace. How does he work it? Pick you up every night, make sure he gets his cash?"

"No. I mean, not every night. Sometimes he does, sometimes he doesn't. It depends . . . ."

"Then he won't know any better."

"I don't understand."

"You don't need to. Just give me a picture of him. You probably have one on your phone."

The brunette tried to work up a resentful look, but it wouldn't come. Finally, she reached in her clutch bag and took out a portrait-quality laminated color photo of a slim man in a beige sport coat that looked to be made out of some kind of velvety material, a black silk shirt with pearl buttons underneath. His face looked as if he'd never had to shave, with perfect skin accented by sharp cheekbones. Despite a Cajun complexion, his eyes were blue and his hair had a faint reddish tinge. The diamond studs in his earlobes flashed brilliantly, even in the photo.

"This is Jean-Baptiste," she said, unable to keep the pride out of her voice. "What happens now?"

"Depends on him."

"Meaning what?"

Cross lit another cigarette, blew a harsh jet toward the invisible ceiling. "It's not important. But *this* is, so listen close before you say anything. If he shows up here tonight, you'll be able to go back to your place. But I wouldn't do that, I was you. I'd make sure I worked until tomorrow. And then go spend the next night with a friend. Just get this straight: if he *doesn't* show, you *can't* go back."

"I can't leave Teffie."

"Your . . ."

"Cat," she answered Cross's question. "He was a rescue."

"So not declawed?"

"No!" the brunette said proudly. "He's, you know, spayed and everything, but he still goes out whenever he wants. There's a little slot in the window, and—"

The brunette stopped mid-sentence, as a pair of hands dropped lightly on her shoulders.

"Relax," a man's voice said. "I just need to talk to the boss."

"You mean alone?" the brunette said, without turning around.

"Always."

The brunette stood up. "I . . . I'm ready to work," she said to Cross.

"Get your shifts straight with Arabella. Then phone the pretty boy and tell him where you're working, what time you'll be getting off."

"He might come earlier. He does that, sometimes."

"Won't change anything."

"Oh."

"Uh . . ." the man behind her muttered, the thinnest thread of impatience surfacing in his voice.

The brunette got up and walked off, not looking back.

"WHAT'D HE do *this* time, Buddha?"

"This's got nothing to do with Princess, boss." The speaker was a short, pudgy man with pitch-dark eyes that were slightly corner-slanted. "It's So Long. She came up with a real moneymaker of an idea—"

"She ever come up with any *other* kind of idea?"

"You got any more potshots you want to take, or can I just get on with this?"

Cross scrubbed out his cigarette.

"Thing is," Buddha said, "she wants to meet with you about it."

"You inviting me over for dinner?"

"Come on, boss, you don't have to keep lobbing those frags my way. She'll come to the spot, how's that?"

"Sure. Couldn't bring her here, right? She'd want to look at the books."

"*Damn!* Lighten up, okay? You think I don't know what the deal is with my own wife?"

"No, brother—I think you do. So I'm puzzled—why would you want her in *our* business all of a sudden? Everything we own on paper, it's in your name and Ace's, joint owners. And it's a total tontine, so she's in for half no matter what. That makes her fifty-fifty to take it all."

"I don't get—"

"You go first, Ace's woman, she takes everything. You know Sharyn—she'd cut it right down the middle, give So Long her rightful piece. But if *Ace* goes first, it all goes to So Long. You saying *she'd* cut Sharyn in?"

"That's what she promised when we all made the deal."

"Yeah. And she's gonna *keep* that promise, because nobody's selling nothing off until we're *all* gone. So, if I'm still around—or Rhino, or maybe even Tracker and Tiger, depending—she's going to do the right thing."

"Or Sharyn ends up with it all, you're saying?"

"Do I have to?"

"Yeah. Yeah, you do, boss. Spell it out for me," the pudgy man said, comfortable in the seat vacated by the brunette. Nothing in his posture vibed "danger," but he wasn't a member of the Cross crew for his looks.

"Okay, brother," Cross said, not raising his voice. "There's a few of us. *Damn* few of us. None of us young, and none of us expecting to die of old age, either. Ace and Sharyn have been together a long time. Five kids."

"Two of them are old enough—"

"Five kids," Cross went on, as if Buddha hadn't spoken. "Sharyn may not know exactly what Ace does, but she knows he doesn't bring home a paycheck. Or any other kind of check.

"And he takes care of her. Of her and those kids. *Good* care. What So Long knows . . . well, let's just say that's one very curious woman. And a real smart one, too."

"Tell me something I don't know."

"I can't do that, brother. You just want me to say it out loud, yeah? All right, then: If Ace goes before you do, you'd be the only one who owns anything that we all put together. So Sharyn keeps right on getting whatever money she needs. We take care of our own.

"But So Long, she's got both smart and greedy in her. If the greedy part wins out, then Sharyn is gonna end up with it all."

"Because she'd be the sole survivor."

"Yeah."

"That's my wife, Cross."

"Right. *Your* wife. Ace and me, we partnered up when we were little kids. Had no choice. Rhino, me and Ace found him inside that joint. They had him down as a monster retard, a drooling idiot they had to keep chained up—they were afraid of what would happen if he ever got loose.

"Well, we got him out of those chains. And he got *me* over the wall. He got hurt doing that, but we came back for him, just like I promised. That was the core. The OGs. You were the first we brought in with us. And it was me who certified you—the skills and the mind, you had it all.

"Then it was just the four of us, for a long time. So you

know what happened when we went down south . . . and came back with Princess. You know how we added Tracker, but he only works with us when he wants to. Same as Tiger."

"Boss, you got any idea why Rhino pulled Princess out of that job we did down south?"

"Ideas? Sure. But I don't know. Not for certain. And I'm not going to ask. Princess, he's one of us. Who knows that better than you?"

"You're saying *what* with that? I was in before he was."

"I already said that," Cross said, his voice unchanged. "I don't know what you were doing in that jungle, but I know you were working. I was, too. When both of us decided we'd be better off working for ourselves, that brought you in. Before Princess."

"Then . . . Ah, hell. I only wish I knew why—"

"It doesn't matter. Nothing we put *behind* us matters. That's part of our deal."

"I know."

"I know you do. But you wanted to hear it spelled out, so here it is: Me, Rhino, and Princess, we've got nobody but ourselves. You've got So Long. Ace, he's got Sharyn and their kids. On paper, everything we own belongs to you two. Ace goes first, it's *all* yours. I know you'd do the right thing. We all know that.

"But, no matter how careful you are, things can happen. Say you and Ace get taken out together. So Long would end up with a *lot* of cash. Property, too. But they'd have to get us *all*, understand? If any one of us was still alive—just alive, even if we're locked up—Sharyn *would* get paid. Not some fifty-fifty thing—nobody's a damn CPA here—but anything she needs, Buddha. Anything."

"And if So Long doesn't t.c.b.—"

"It'd be on you to fix that."

"What if I'm not around, myself?"

"Like I said, Inside or Out, dead or alive, wouldn't matter. Sharyn's got a number to call. It's not going to change, that number. She only uses it if she asks So Long for some money and that money doesn't show up."

"That's cold, boss. Even for you."

"Cold? How much money could Sharyn ever need that So Long wouldn't have lying around in petty cash? Like I said, if 'smart' trumps 'greedy,' So Long's got nothing to worry about."

"Sharyn's not the brightest—"

"You don't even believe that, brother. But pretend you're right—how smart would she *have* to be? She knows all she has to do is call So Long when she needs money. And call another number if she doesn't *get* that money."

Cross lit another smoke.

Buddha waited the three drags before he spoke. "So Long, she can get crazy."

"Crazy enough to spend some of the money having Sharyn put down?"

The pudgy man hesitated a second. Then said, "Yeah."

"No surprise. That's why there's an insurance policy."

"Huh?"

"If Sharyn dies, So Long goes right behind her."

"But if we're all—"

"The policy's been bought and paid for already."

"Who did you—?"

"No," Cross cut him short.

"I can't know?"

"No. All you need to know is the target, not the shoot-ers."

"And I'm supposed to tell So Long . . . what?"

"Nothing. You don't need to. She already knows."

"You sure about that?"

"Dead sure," Cross said, softly. "I told her myself."

THE SHARK CAR—a three-ton monster, further encum-bered by all-wheel drive and air-bagged suspension—slipped through the Chicago back streets. Its city-camo splotches of black and gray left anyone who spotted it wondering exactly *what* they'd just seen.

Buddha was behind the wheel, playing the controls with his fingertips as deftly as a concert pianist. The back seat was three-quarters full. With one passenger.

"I still can't figure out how you get so much speed out of this thing," Rhino squeaked. "With the armor plating, it's got to weigh—"

"Six thousand, six hundred, and change. With a full load of fluids. That's without a driver, never mind weight like yours," Buddha said, without inflection.

"So you'd need at least—"

"An eight-hundred-plus Elephant, blueprinted, rail-injected, three staggered shots of nitrous—when they're all playing, add another few hundred horses at the wheels—and some other little tricks. This thing has to go in snow, and deal with these Third World excuses for streets around here, too.

"With all-wheel drive, eighteen-by-eights were as big

as we could go. They're run-flats—but not to save weight, although they do. They're so we can keep moving even if someone manages to put a round in one. The fuel cell holds fifty of av-gas—there's no way to get to that, either."

"Redundant all around?"

"Yeah. Just followed the computer model you made. Even with all the carbon fiber, just keeping this sucker's weight under seven grand wasn't easy."

"You're not going to—?"

"My house? Come on, bro. We're only about five minutes away from the pickup."

"Eight, then?"

"Eight-fifteen. And the bitch will *still* tell me I'm late."

AS THE SHARK CAR slid to the curb, a woman with long, straight midnight hair stepped out of a doorway. She was wearing a red beret and an ankle-length black alligator coat over three-inch spike heels in the same shade as her beret.

The back door to the car hissed as it slowly opened. The woman stepped in as confidently as a movie star into a waiting limousine. If sitting next to a behemoth bothered her, she gave no sign.

"Cross" was all she said.

"So Long."

"My husband told you I had this plan?"

"That's *all* he said."

"There is money to invest, yes? From the . . . different properties."

"No, there isn't. I'm not paper-hanging those deeds."

"I do not understand."

"Liens, mortgages, equity loans, cash-out re-fi deals . . . You know *exactly* what I mean, So Long. Nothing gets put against any property we own."

"Okay. But, still, there *is* investment money someplace, yes?"

"Some," Cross said cautiously. "Depends on how things are going, any given week."

"Okay, then," the woman said, as if an agreement had already been reached. "Plenty of houses for sale now. Fore-closures all over the city. Most of the time, trashed. People giving up home, angry at the bank, they take everything. Then the others move in. Squatters, gangs, crack dealers."

"Uh-huh," Cross half-grunted as he lit a cigarette.

"I don't have smoking in my house."

"This isn't your house, So Long."

"You do not like me still, yes, Cross?"

"You're not my business."

"My husband, he *is* your business."

"I'm not a marriage counselor," Cross answered, taking another drag of his cigarette.

"Not about marriage, about money."

"What else would you want to talk to me about?"

"Sure. I see. I know this. About you. Not from what my husband says—*he* says nothing. But you not change. Not ever, right?"

"Right." Cross took the third hit off his cigarette and snapped it out through the lowered front-seat window, just behind Buddha's left shoulder.

"I have this," So Long said, taking a thin sheaf of papers from inside her coat. "Five properties. Same block. Same side of street. Vacant lot between, so three one side, two the other. All like I say before."

"But . . . ?"

"The rest of the block, people *staying*. They own their houses. Take a long time to do that. Own them, no mortgage. So they are not moving. But always frightened. Things happen, but police never come."

"And . . . ?"

"Total price, all five houses, four hundred and seventy-five thousand. *Asking* price. On market for long time. Price keep dropping. All MLS."

"What's this 'MLS'?"

"Multiple Listing Service. So *any* broker that is licensed, if he finds a buyer, he splits the commission with the one who has the first listing. See, we don't want any *one* broker to have what they call 'exclusive' on the properties. That looks bad. So we want different brokers for each place, but they'll all be ones we . . . know, okay?"

"*That's* your big investment?"

"All houses *very* solid. Gray stone, brick; no wood."

"No wood out front, but plenty behind, right? No windows, no electricity, no plumbing . . . probably no roof on some of them."

"*Not* true. Thieves take copper, you think, yes? No. Gangs not let them."

"Stash houses?"

"No! Gangs on both sides of the block, but different ones, and they already have all the empty houses they need. Maybe three, four blocks away. One side doesn't come any closer, the other side doesn't do anything, see?"

"Okay."

"Okay? Cross, *every* house on that block worth four, five hundred thousand, easy."

"Sure."

"You think, market bad, right? No mortgages like before. But yuppies can always get mortgages. How you say, 'urban pioneers,' yes?"

"Yeah, that's how you say it. And so what?"

"That block, clean out the five houses, move gangs even further off, easy million dollars waiting."

"We buy the five houses for, what, maybe three-fifty total, sell them for five hundred each; that's the plan?"

"Sure. Probably more."

"Banks, lawyers, brokers, titles—that's all money going out. And it's a paper trail Ray Charles could follow in a coal mine."

"I have all that. No trail, no problem."

"Yeah?"

"I am licensed real-estate broker. I have lawyer. Lao lawyer. He has friend in bank. Cambodian. Title is no problem. All LLC."

"And you're the LLC."

"Sure. When sell, pay taxes, but not income tax, only on capital gain. Pay only on the *gain*."

"And you're the LLC," Cross repeated, lighting another smoke.

"Who else you want in it?"

"Buddha's got civilian papers."

"Sure, but . . . connected to you, yes?"

"Just like the Double-X. And Red 71. So?"

"Those *not* same. Double-X, that is regular business. Pay taxes, license fees, all that. Red 71, only property taxes—no business there. And no capital gains to show, either one."

"Because we're not selling them, ever. That's true enough. You're an accountant now?"

"No degree, but—"

"Yeah, I know. When it comes to money management, you're a genius, So Long. But what you're saying is just another chorus of 'trust me,' right?"

"My husband trust me. You trust my husband—he is your brother, yes?"

"That doesn't make you my sister. And trust *you* with our money? Move in, clean up the place, take all the risks, and you do . . . what, exactly?"

"My idea. My contacts."

"Yeah. And your *five* LLCs, right? You'd only be paying a gain on *each* resale. You really believe that's worth a half-share?"

"More."

"No," Cross said, hitting another cigarette.

"You not even *look*?"

"Not for that split."

"You want what, then?"

"A million off the top, split the rest."

"Crazy."

Cross took a last drag, snapped the burning smoke out the window again. Even in the dim light, the bull's-eye tattoo on the back of his hand was clearly visible to So Long. She had never seen Cross without it. "What's crazy, So Long? The split, or just me?"

"Maybe both."

"Been nice talking to you, So Long. Always a pleasure."

"We negotiate, yes?"

"No."

"Without me, you cannot do this, Cross. You don't even know where the block is."

"There's all kinds of blocks like that. 'Specially on the South Side."

"Maybe. But all the paperwork—"

"Lawyers are whores. Some cost more than others, that's all."

"You would not cheat my husband."

"Is that a question?"

"No. But . . ."

"Save it, So Long. Buddha gets his piece of *our* piece. And you get a big piece of *that*, too."

"More like all of it," Buddha muttered, but not so quietly that it was inaudible in the back seat.

"Ha! Very nice. I take care of—"

"Enough, okay?" Cross interrupted. "Look, the only reason I'm even here is because Buddha asked me. We wouldn't net five extra-large apiece, even if your numbers are right."

"Maybe more."

"You start a sentence with 'maybe,' anything you say after that is true."

"What are you saying?"

" 'Maybe more' is the same as 'maybe less.' "

"You don't like to gamble, Cross."

"Buddha's the gambler in our crew."

"Huh!" Seeing that her pose of being grievously insulted wasn't going to play, So Long went back to being herself. "Okay, here, then. You take a look. You decide we go ahead, you get a million off the top, I take half of what's left."

"That's what I said. Which means you're putting up the money to buy the properties. On this sure thing of yours."

"Me? No. I thought—"

"Come on, So Long. Telling me *you* don't like to gamble?"

The car was quiet for a long minute.

"Sure," she finally surrendered.

No words were exchanged on the drive out to the suburb where Buddha and So Long shared an unmortgaged house. The deed was in So Long's name.

"CAN'T HURT to take a look, boss," Buddha said on the drive back.

"How's it gonna help?"

"She wasn't talking chump change."

"She's a gambler sometimes, brother. But she's a thief *all* the time."

"Of course she is. How's that change anything?"

"The way she's got it rigged, all the money would go through her. We'd never know how much she really scored, just what she turned over."

"It's a mil guaranteed, boss. And half of whatever's on top. Sure, So Long's gonna graft off that, but—"

"We don't hold the trump, Buddha."

"I'm not following."

"That 'my English not so good' crap's just a front. So Long's *real* smart, Buddha. This wouldn't be the first time she cheated us. We can't do what we'd normally do, anyone else did that to us. And she knows it."

Cross lit another cigarette. By the time he was finished with it, he'd spun the roulette wheel inside his head.

"Rhino?"

"If the houses haven't been ravaged, it *would* be because no gang's claimed that block, but they're still close enough so squatters couldn't move in without passing through their turf."

"Maybe worth it, then?"

"Not worth dying over. But if it's surrounded and not occupied, it's not claimed turf, either."

"I get it. Okay, Buddha, let's roll by."

"STREET LOOKS decent. Could use some work, but it's not all torn up. Hydrants are still in place. Probably some homeless sleeping in that lot, but no point in lighting it up just to see. This late, who cares? But we didn't spot one whore, one dope slinger . . . and they work until it gets light, rain or shine. Nobody legit getting up for work this early."

Cross didn't mention that they'd only been a few minutes away from the block they were surveying when he'd told Buddha to roll by—they'd been heading in that direction from the moment they'd dropped So Long off.

"We can come back tomorrow night, boss. Better to have some cover if we want to look close, anyway."

"Tracker could ghost it himself."

"Probably could. The man don't even cast a shadow. And he works a strange place better than anyone I've ever seen. Those feds who wanted their 'specimen,' they may have been off-the-hook loony, but they didn't have no budget cap. So, hiring him and Tiger, you know they bought the best. But even if Tracker says it's clean, we'd *still* need to hang close, just in case."

"Sure. But . . . look, Buddha. Bottom line is the Law. We're not going to be some Neighborhood Watch. If we can send a message that'll keep the gangs out, that's one thing. But there's only way to do that. And if some of them don't survive the delivery, we can't leave their bodies in the basement of one of the houses—that'd make them kind of hard to sell."

"There's other—"

"Sure. But you know how it works: clearing territory might be hard work, but it's nothing compared to trying to *occupy* it."

"This ain't Afghanistan, boss."

"Yeah. But it's never enough to just kill rats; you have to make sure more don't come back. And rats don't get turned off by dead bodies."

"Didn't look like anyone's claiming the block. No tags. Or worse, overtags. No slot doors, either. So any crack dealers working that street in daylight, they're small-time slingers. They'll just move on—they're used to it."

"Let's see tomorrow, okay?"

BOTH MEN were silent for the next several minutes—in hostile territory, speech is a luxury no soldier enjoys for long. Once clear, Buddha asked: "The spot?"

Cross glanced at his watch, a rubber-strapped black disk that popped alive only when tapped on its face.

"It's not even four. Let's see if Condor has anything for us."

Buddha leaned the Shark Car gently around a corner and turned toward the Badlands—unoccupied acreage that various developers had tried to purchase over the years, only to learn that it was city-owned. And condemned. Apparently, some obscure ordinance prevented the city of Chicago from selling land once used as a toxic-waste dump unless it was first brought "up to EPA standards."

Since that last phrase was not defined, every attempt to purchase had gotten lost in the bureaucratic maze. More knowledgeable developers had sought to untangle that snarl with the one lubricant that had never failed them in the past. But, no matter how much money they threw at the machinery, it stayed stuck.

Several years ago, the Russian mob had hired Chicago's premier fixer to unblock the path. But the Russians' boss, Viktor, heeded the note attached to a razor-tipped arrow embedded in the back wall of their storefront headquarters. It came right on the heels of the silenced rifle shot which had punched an opening in the black glass.

The note's message was as clear as its delivery method, each Cyrillic character etched in a harsh calligraphy: "Tomorrow, call your lawyer."

That lawyer's unsolved homicide remained a mystery. Still, the Russians had only been deterred, not defeated. They were a tight organization, ruthless and patient. There was no shortage of ways to earn good money in Chicago.

And elsewhere. Some Japanese oyabuns believed that freshly removed bear claws would grant an elongated life span to their possessor, and had the cash to pay what such prizes were worth. Viktor had many contacts on the Kamchatka Peninsula. "Harvesting" bears was not difficult, and smuggling the claws into close-by Japan even easier.

The Japanese underworld's voracious appetite for animal parts, from powdered rhino horn to intact tiger testicles, was no secret. In Africa, the risk of taking rhino horn was worth the potential profit to some. In China, there was no risk involved—tigers were bred in captivity as a "conservation" project . . . and some males had to be neutered when judged to be inferior specimens.

The Chinese government had no objection to the sale of tiger parts, as long as the proper "taxes" on such transactions were paid. After all, this was nothing but the sale of a manufactured product. But the Russian government considered bears to be their sacred national symbol, and trafficking in bear parts was a capital offense.

A fatal synergy resulted. First, the controller of all Chinese crime in Chicago, an old man named Chang, accepted a contract from a nonexistent government agency to deliver Cross—dead or alive—to a certain address. Chang asked no questions—it was an unspoken part of the contract that the government would remain uninterested in any of his local operations, and that alone made the reason for the promised COD irrelevant.

A master strategist, Chang used his contacts in Russia to confirm the bounty on Viktor, then immediately hired Cross to put a halt to Viktor's trade arrangements. The crafty old man envisioned a war by which he would profit regardless of its outcome.

Chang had paid off, in gold, just after learning that Viktor's entire gang was literally ripped apart by . . . something not yet known. Within minutes of that exchange, Chang's own headquarters had been hit by several RPG rounds.

Cross got word to an ancient Cambodian headman that the destruction of his mortal enemy—Chang—was a gift. A gesture of respect, for which no payment was expected.

Later, a gift was delivered to Red 71, the crew's known headquarters. An elaborately carved ebony stick, whose characters Rhino laboriously translated: "We can redeem this for a body. Payable anytime. And it can be any body we want."

The failure to deliver Cross caused the disappearance of two members of the "government" team that had reached out for Chang. If a nameless blond man and an Asian cyber-expert called Wanda were still alive, it wasn't known to the Cross crew. The whereabouts of Percy—a human war machine who returned to an inert state as though someone had thrown a switch in his brain when he was not on combat assignment—were unknown. But he would always be a high-value asset to whatever part of the government had sent Cross after a "specimen" he had never collected.

Two members of the team the blond man and Wanda had assembled had been freelancers: Tracker, a Chickasaw who had no purpose other than to carry on the work of his ancestors, and Tiger, whose own tribe was either mystery or myth.

Neither had disappeared. Tracker signed on after a lengthy prove-in period. He had no interest in money, but considered the Cross crew to be the logical descendants of his own people . . . people who did not hunt, gather, or farm.

Tiger worked jobs. "I do out-call, you know," had been her parting words to Cross. But only when the objective suited her. Her loyalty would always be to her sisters.

THE ENTRANCE to the Badlands was clearly marked . . . to those who knew. Those who didn't became permanent residents. Land ravaged by toxic waste was always in need of fertilizer.

The Shark Car cut its lights and motored serenely past the rusted-out hulk of a semi-trailer, guided only by the thermal-image screen that had rotated to replace the instrument panel. The screen was bisected: one showing what was ahead, the other a rearview camera.

The city-camo car coasted to a stop parallel to a chain-link fence torn in so many places that even its ceremonial swirl of concertina wire couldn't actually keep anyone out.

Buddha touched a button hidden under the console. Three parallel laser beams of blue and orange shot from behind the grille. They passed over an abandoned gas station lacking signs, pumps, and windows. All that remained was a squat concrete structure.

Both front windows zipped down. Ten minutes passed. Cross did not smoke. Buddha held his custom 4.5mm semi-auto pistol on his lap, watching the screen.

A figure appeared atop the fence. A teenager with a bright-blue Mohawk, folding his body into the shape that had given him his name, "Condor."

"Any more surveyors?" Cross called out softly.

"Not since the last one," the teenager replied.

"You're doing good," Cross told him.

"How come you ask?" the teenager said. "You gave us that cell to call you on if—"

"It's machinery," Cross said. "You can't be sure it's working unless you test it regular, and—"

"You told *us* never to do that," Condor finished the sentence. "I get it."

"Yeah, you do," Cross said, flicking a thick roll of bills wrapped in rubber bands over the fence.

"VISITORS?"

"Mostly regulars," Bruno answered Cross on his cell. "But a first-timer's been sitting at the same table for over an hour. No dances, just buying booze. Asked one of the waitresses for powder. She told me. So I walked over and told him we don't do that here. And we don't *let* no one do that here, neither."

Cross described the man in the photo the new dancer had shown him hours ago.

"Yep," Bruno said. "That's him. And he's been drawing a bead on the new dancer—Taylor, right?—every time she goes up."

"He doesn't leave."

"Got it."

"UH, BOSS," Buddha said, "not for nothing, but Bruno's not what you'd call a deep thinker."

"So?"

"So, if this guy tries to leave, Bruno's likely to make sure he never does."

"So?"

"So Bruno can't take another jolt Inside."

"You think he doesn't know that?"

"Sure. But if this guy's carrying . . ."

"So much the better. Then we can hit 911 ourselves—

we're as entitled to police protection as anyone else paying them off."

THE SHARK CAR pulled up behind the Double-X, into what appeared to be a stack of double-height Dumpsters sitting in a pool of black ink.

The three men exited the car and approached the extended wall used to allow dancers to park privately. Cross hit a sequence on a tiny keypad and a door popped open.

The man Arabella had called "K-2" responded with a slow shake of his head to Buddha's shoulder shrug and spread palms. Nobody had left the club . . . at least not past the exit/ entrance the Maori guarded.

Rhino slid off down an unlit corridor. Cross and Buddha entered a narrow tunnel, walked its length, and let themselves into a room built behind the corner where Cross kept his personal table.

As they did so, the lighting in the club shifted subtly. Only a few inside would recognize the signal, but Bruno had been watching for it. Now his face was a synonym for "perplexed." He knew he shouldn't leave his post, but he also knew that Cross would be expecting a report. Only Rhino's cigar-sized finger, further distinguished by its missing tip, pointed him toward the correct move.

Bruno moved to the inset triangle table with confidence—if Rhino said it was okay, any worries he might have harbored about the front door being covered vanished.

"He's at fifty-four," Bruno told Cross, proud of his memorization of the seating chart.

"Still acting like he was?"

"No lap dances or anything like that, yeah. But I know he asked Brandi something. I don't know what, but I could tell she was saying she didn't know nothing about it."

"Good. When you get back to the door, tell Brandi to bring us something to drink."

"Uh, sure, boss. But shouldn't I tell her what you—?"

"She'll know."

BRANDI MOVED to the corner table without a hint of a wiggle. She was balancing herself on four-inch spike heels as smoothly as if she were still in the ballet slippers she had worn for years, before the constant pressure to lose weight had caused her to seek other employment.

Her job interview had been blunt.

"Would I have to—?"

"It's a waitress job," Cross told her. "The only difference is that you don't get to wear much. And the tips are really good."

"I heard . . . I mean, I asked around, and . . ."

"What?"

"In some strip clubs, the waitresses have to work *under* the tables."

"Not here. Turn your chair just a little. Watch what happens."

A few minutes later, Brandi asked, "You weren't kidding about not wearing much, were you?"

"No," Cross answered, as if the idea of him "kidding" was absurd.

"I'd get a W-2?"

"A 1099," Cross told her. "You're an independent contractor."

"So no take-out for—"

"No take-out for anything. You get paid by check. A good check."

"How good?"

"Good enough not to bounce. Pay here is ten bucks an hour. The tips, you keep for yourself."

"I get it. If I want to make heavy tips, I have to—"

"Don't act stupid. You *don't* get it. None of the waitresses here are *allowed* to do anything but bring whatever the customer orders. If he wants a dance, you tell whatever dancer he picked—*she* tips you for that. If he wants the VIP Room, you tell him to just walk right in, make any selection he wants. You'll get a bigger tip for that."

"I don't know . . . ."

"Okay."

"What does that mean, 'Okay'?"

"It means, if you make up your mind to do this, you do it. And if you don't, you don't."

Since then, Brandi had been working anywhere between thirty and fifty hours a week. The tax bite was close to nothing, despite her diligent declaration of her 15-percent tips. The job was a dream, especially because she was the sole provider for her boy, whose father was a lot better at promises than payments.

On a bad week, Brandi would pocket thousands in cash as well as her paycheck. Some weeks were much better. She'd been at the Double-X for almost three years.

"What did he want?" Cross asked.

"Wanted to know when does Taylor—the new girl—when does she get off?"

"And you said . . . ?"

"He'd have to ask the manager."

"And the manager isn't around."

"Yep."

"Good work," Cross told her.

The former ballet dancer spun gracefully, leaving a table for the first time that night without some patron's trying to squeeze one of her muscular cheeks.

"This'll be easier than I thought," Cross said, pulling a cell phone out of his jacket in response to Buddha's raised-eyebrow silent question.

"Get Arabella," Cross told whoever answered.

The wait was short.

"She know he showed?"

"Yes," Arabella answered him. "She's . . . kind of scared, I guess. But only about leaving. She knows she's safe here."

"Skip your next turn. You and her, both. Go out the back way. Drive over to where she lives. There'll be a truck and a few guys waiting. Tell her this is a one-and-only. Anything she doesn't take, kiss it goodbye."

"How much time will we—?"

"All you need. Ring back here when you're away. That means back in *your* place, understand?"

"But I'll never fit all her—"

"Her stuff goes to a storage unit. The guys in the truck will know where to take it."

"I'm going to miss the rest of the time I paid for. Three more turns."

"Sell your shifts; there's plenty of girls who'll buy them."

"Sure. But I would've made a lot more if I—"

"You brought her here. That's what it costs."

"Oh."

"Storage unit is five a month. You two want to look for a bigger place, we can find one for you. Or, if she wants to go solo, that, too."

"Really? In this town—"

"I know a real good broker," Cross said, and pressed the "Off" button on his cell.

"TWO, THREE of K-2's crew for the move?" Buddha asked.

"Sure."

"They get paid a lot more than movers."

"We'll cover it."

"All for this new girl?"

"She'll be good for it."

"Yeah" was all Buddha said, sliding off into the darkness.

IT WAS getting close to the time the club usually started to empty out when the solitary man who'd asked about the new dancer finally realized she was already done for the night.

He slowly got to his feet, casually tossed some bills on the table, and walked out of the club.

Bruno slid into position behind him. Cross waved him off.

The tall, slender man strolled past the "Valet Parking" area and kept moving toward the back of the building. A black man about half his height and twice his width stepped out of the shadows.

"No going around the back, pal."

"I'm just—"

"You ain't *parked* back there. Your car's over in Valet Parking."

"That's right. I just wanted to wait for my girlfriend, make sure she knows I'm here to take her home."

"You're saying *she* told you to meet her back there?"

"Not exactly. I mean, she wouldn't be going out the front, right? These kind of places, sometimes a guy will sit out there, waiting. You know what I mean."

"That don't happen here."

"Come on, bro. I know there's got to be *some* way . . ."

"Like, say, if I never saw you?"

"Yeah. Like that."

"Only shade that turns me blind is green, 'bro.'"

The slender man handed over a fifty-dollar bill.

"When I say 'green,' I mean a full glass, not a little sip," the double-wide black man said, crunching the banknote into a ball and tossing it back disdainfully.

"A full glass is—?"

"Ten of those little sips."

"Five yards?! Just to—"

"You can't pay the toll, you don't get to roll. 'Bro.'"

The slender man peeled five hundreds off the outside of a wad, reflecting that he couldn't go back much deeper without hitting the smaller bills at its core. *Bitch is gonna pay me for all this!* played in his head, like a jukebox with only one selection.

The toll-taker faded back into wherever he had come

from. The man who'd paid the toll slowly walked around to the back of the club.

The air of supreme confidence that he wore the way another might wear a favorite jacket vanished as he viewed the unlit slab of garage doors. He pulled his cell phone and punched a speed-dial key for at least the twentieth time that night. And once again got the robotic voice of a voice-mail system that told him nothing.

No way she got here on her own. Maybe she just called a cab . . . ? Maybe the guy on the door . . . ?

Reluctantly acknowledging that he was running short of bribe money, and not eager to have a conversation with the thug at the door, who had made no effort to conceal his shoulder holster, the slender man glanced at his wafer-thin watch.

I wasted the whole night on the bitch. Gonna be light, soon. Time to jet. Just wait for her back at my place. Where else she gonna go? Sooner or later, she got to . . .

THE CHARCOAL Lexus coupe glided through the West Side, but neither the layered aroma of its rich leather interior nor the muted mixture of Bird and Miles flowing from its sixteen-speaker system soothed the slender man as it usually did. Rap was a lot of things, but no one ever called it "sleek," and nothing short of that standard ever made his personal playlist. But now . . .

Even the knowledge that the car *belonged* to him was cold comfort against the heat-seeker thoughts moving inside his head.

Sophistication was his trademark, not flying colors or waving guns around. Those gang boys would never understand that you have to *slide* your way through this world. He knew how to act if stopped by the cops: "Always let *them* tell you what they want. Could be license and registration, could be that old 'busted taillight' game so they can search your ride, could be the tax for using their streets," the ancient pimp had schooled him, back when he was still in his early teens.

"How am I gonna pull any—"

"You *ain't* gonna be pulling no girls, son. That game is lame today. Oh, there's always gonna be girls working the streets. Looking for a daddy, too. But half of them are poison. Underage. Runaways. You get caught with one of those in your stable, you gonna see the Walls, and be looking at them for a long time. And remember this: a bitch on the pipe never made *no* man *no* money, *no* how. Used to be you could keep that under control: a little Boy-and-Girl, that can still be mellow. But meth is death, young boy. Turn a racehorse into a scaly-leg skank in a month."

The old man stopped to take a long, deep hit from the oxygen tank next to his bed. He knew he didn't have long, and passing on the wisdom of decades spent in The Life gave him a kind of satisfaction the silver-tongued devil could never put into words. He knew the rules, as they'd been passed on down to him: "You know why they call some parts of town— any town—the 'Red Light District'? That's because the Game is only played in the Fast Lane. Which means, sooner or later, you gonna run a red light. That means 'Stop!' Right? Thing is, you don't stop, you gonna *get* stopped."

THE OLD pimp knew his baby sister's son wasn't coming by to visit him every few days out of love . . . or even concern. He hadn't known the boy even existed until Lucy had told him he was an uncle. "His name's Lawrence, Samuel. I know what you are. What you did. But you can still get yourself right with the Lord."

"I'm too old to be going on *Oprah*, Luce."

"You can just stop your slick-talk, Samuel. You know I don't mean asking for forgiveness. You probably couldn't even remember all the women you wronged in your sinful life. But I want you to listen to me now.

"My youngest, Lawrence, he's way too pretty, you know? And I take some blame there. I tried, but without no man in the house, a boy *is* going to run the streets. And I spoiled him, too. Me and Marcella and Jessee Lynn, all of us. We even let his big sisters show him off. Do his hair, spend their own money so he could look fine. Like he was a pet.

"As if that wasn't enough, taking him to church didn't teach him a thing but how to sweet-talk. I don't mean the Gospel, I mean . . . Well, that boy could sell salvation to sinners if he wanted, but he says there's no money in it. Can you imagine?"

"Boy should take a look at what some of those Revs you like so much have put together for themselves. I don't know their game as good as my own, but I know even the holiest woman will give up her money to a honey-talking preacher."

"Yes, that is *exactly* how you'd see it. So what else is my boy going to be but a man like you was? You're out of that world now. And you're not going back, not with that TB killing you slow. Now, Lawrence, he's heard your name a thousand times. 'True Blue.' He says it like you a . . . legend or something."

"Ain't no 'or something' about it, Sis."

"You just *can't* get off that train, can you, Samuel? Even when you know it's taking you straight into hellfire. But you don't have to die here, not in this dirty place. I could take you home with me. There's a room we could fix up with all this same stuff. And—"

"What's the hook, Luce?"

"Always got to be a hook, Samuel?"

"Always," the old man intoned, as piously as his sister would have thrown a Bible quote at him.

Minutes of silence passed. Then his sister said, "The 'hook' is you save my boy's life."

"How am I gonna do that now? You gonna put me on exhibit, tell him, 'See what happens when you make the wrong choice? That wasted old man there, he was called True Blue back in the day. You heard his name. You know what he had. Cars, clothes, gold, diamonds. More women than you could count. But look at him now, what do you see?'"

"I don't mean *nothing* like that, Samuel. All I want you to do is school him. Tell him the *truth*. Not just one side of it, the whole thing."

"Pimping ain't the same as it once was."

"You be sure to tell him *that*, too."

"No Bible on the bedstand?"

"For what? It would just be wasted on you, Samuel. But

the truth can still set *some* free. And in the world my boy's gonna live in, it's not the Good Book that knows the Word."

AND THE old man had to admit that his baby sister—half-sister, really—kept her word. His room was always fresh and clean, the food was *truly* fine, and he even had a little TV of his own. So, every time the boy came around to pump him about the pimping game, True Blue always told him nothing but the truth.

Some of that truth would have caused his little sister to pull the hose out of his oxygen tank.

"THE MACK MAN had a *role* once, son. I don't mean a role to play. I mean, there was a need . . . and it was his job to make sure it got filled. But what you got in The Life now is some truly sorry stuff. Mangy dogs, not wolves. Simps, not pimps. They can't make it, so they fake it."

"There's plenty of them, still."

"Of them, maybe. Of *us*, not even a trace. Listen, now: I'm not saying there wasn't some gorilla pimps back then. Kind of man who'd beat a woman half to death if she didn't come back with the money. But how many church girls you think *they* ever turned out?

"As for girls that got pulled, they was *already* on the game. You pulled some, some got pulled from you. Never meant a thing, and you never took it personal. You miss one train, there's always another one coming.

"But snatching children and raping them? Making them work in some hot-sheet house, turning dime tricks? Calling themselves 'players' on that stupid Internet thing you showed me? That's not pimping. They should get shot just for calling themselves that name."

He never even took a hit off his oxygen tank, the young man marveled. The emaciated pimp's voice seemed to recapture strength as he went on.

"And why did it go that way? 'Cause, for the punks who could only talk with their hands, there wasn't no *other* way. And the top-drawer girls, they go into business for themselves now. Advertise on that same Internet, only for real. No more out-front working girls—they all 'escorts' now."

"Even those girls—"

"Got pimps, you're gonna say? Nah, they got 'managers.' And most of *those* are women themselves, how's that? It's about the money, sure. But this business of turning what you earned over at the end of the night, that's dead. The only cash they ever see comes in tips—and even that's no sure bet, no matter how good they are.

"It's all credit cards. Money transfers. Stuff like that. Fools—and *all* johns are suckers, boy; never forget that— leave a clearer trail to follow than if they was paying off in orange money."

"What's orange money?"

"Boy, sometimes I worry about you. When some fool robs a bank, the teller hands over banded stacks of bills. Idea is that some of those stacks, they got little bombs in them. Not enough to hurt no one, but they shoot this orange dye all over the money. You supposed to *burn* those bills, but . . .

"Anyway, just listen, all right? You just interrupting to

prove you don't know nothing. Now, those 'escort' girls, they fine, sure enough. But every one of them is stone treacherous. You think a street girl got her a little black book? You still *that* dumb, you probably think those escort girls *don't*.

"What you got on the street today is nothing but trouble. I mean *serious* trouble. In my day, a mack man could drive a Rolls with mink upholstery, be *draped* in diamonds. And his women, they'd be *proud* to see their man showing so fine.

"But what you got out there now? You don't be seeing a player riding around, checking on his string, making sure they working. He probably don't have the gas money for some half-ass ride he most likely don't even own."

"But if a woman wants to give you her money . . . ?"

"What *money*, son? Those sorry skanks couldn't bring you a yard a night. And even if they did, it wouldn't be for long. Think you could really protect them if that kind of talk wasn't just game? There's other cars trolling those strolls. Every night, they're out there. A girl gets in one of *those* cars, she's not coming back. And ain't nobody gonna come looking for her, either."

"I drive a Lincoln. Brand-new."

"And not paid for. You don't own it, so you can't . . . *personalize* it, understand? Somebody spots you behind the wheel of that Lincoln, you know what they see? Another nigger limo driver. Ain't *that* special? You got a girl, works in some hair place, makes the payments, right?"

The old man paused just long enough to glance at his nephew's face.

"Yeah, I thought so. Same for your fancy phone. You didn't pull that woman, boy—she pulled *you*."

"But if I had—"

"You ain't *never* gonna have enough legit women to put you where you want to be, boy. They don't sell steak in no fish store."

"So how could a man do it? Do it right, I mean."

"You already passed the first step, boy. The young man who think he know it all shows he don't know nothing. But you sitting there, paying attention like you was in school. And you know I earned heavy back in the day. I got paid. So I'm worth listening to, and you already done that math in your head.

"Okay. First, you don't even *think* about cutting into one of those escort girls. They all got connects. Some of them got brands on them, too. Mess with one of those girls the Russians own, you gonna have yourself a real bad accident—like if you fell into a chainsaw, face-first. No. Where you go is the clubs."

"I go all the time. I'm even known in some of them."

"Known for what? You're not in the dope game, and you're not a shooter. You're known because you throw money around. That's gonna bring some girls close, and you can stand that kind of inspection—you a pretty thing, sure enough.

"But you need a lot more than that to close the trap. Unless you want to live off some heifer—maybe even a couple, three, four of them—you need a ride that's worthy. And you need a place to park it."

"I told you—"

"Yeah. You told me. That rented Lincoln. And I told *you* that's not gonna get it. I know you got a whole closet-full of threads. How I know that? 'Cause you still living in your mama's basement, boy."

"Well, I got plans."

"No, you don't, boy. What you got is dreams. You wanna make them come true, you got to listen to Mr. Blue. Those clubs, you looking for the kind of girl that wouldn't get near anybody without *real* coin. What you want is a stripper, son. Sure, she's making money on that stage, but she looks around every night. And you know what she sees? Younger stuff than her already coming up. How many years you think a girl can work that pole?

"If she's an independent, what *she's* looking for is some stockbroker, some politician, some fool with a credit card. And a wife. She don't want no wannabe rapper, no man-sized baby, no horse that can't run on the fast track. She wants to be a rich man's pet."

"A rich man? How am I going to come across like that?"

"You *already* all that. A born-pure con man. A hustler. That don't mean a gambler—that's not professional. A hustler don't play with dice. He don't work for nobody; he works the marks.

"So you need a racket where you got to have a lot of pure, sweet *smooth* to get over. If a girl believes you working on some million-dollar score, she'll *wait*, you with me? And while she's waiting, she's earning. Earning and turning, okay? She's gonna understand how a for-real, don't-have-to-work-no-more score can take a long time to put together. She's gonna understand how you got partners she never gets to meet. And she's gonna understand how, some nights when she comes home, you ain't gonna be there.

"Start her off like you training a dog. She gets home by six in the morning, you not there. But a couple of hours later, just when she's starting to get thinking you gone for good, you roll in. So she never knows.

"Got to give a girl one night off. Take her someplace nice. Throw some money around. But no more than that one night. And you make sure it's not the *same* night every week. Make it so she can count on you coming back, but not on *when*, understand?"

"So she's off balance?"

"No, boy. So she's *confident*. You and her, you're in it for the long haul. Together. Soon as this big score you're working on comes through, you can't be hanging around—some very bad people be looking for you. You not gonna put your own woman in the crosshairs, not the woman you love.

"She's gotta understand that. Accept it. Believe you're gonna send for her when you get settled in . . . I don't know, place like Cleveland. Not out of the country, but not next door, neither."

"But with just the one girl, I'm always on the bounce."

"First of all, I never said nothing about *one* girl, did I? That's why you make sure the girl can't count on any particular day of the week. You can run two of them like that. Not no more. Two is the max, understand?

"And you play it real, real careful. You need three phones. One for each girl—they *gonna* play detective on you, go through your phone while you sleep. And what do they find? *Their* number. *Their* picture. Load up the phone with anything else, don't matter. But only one *girl* on each."

"You said no more than two—"

"Two *girls*, not two *phones*. That third phone, that's for new stuff. You got to always be scouting."

"Ah."

"All right. If you play this correctly, you won't even need your own place. You tell them, ain't safe for them to come around where you live. Not 'cause of the neighborhood, 'cause of your partners. *They* can't have no woman in the picture. Bad men, these guys. They see a face they don't know, they might get suspicious. You got to sell it: girl wouldn't want *those* kinda guys getting suspicious about her."

"Because of this big score I've been scouting out?"

"Oh, yes! But, remember, the ride, that has got to be righteous."

"Can't do it."

"That's right, you can't. Way you're going, you getting older, not smarter."

"If I was smarter, what would I be doing?"

"Listening."

"I'm listening. I *been* listening. But—"

"How bad you want it, son?" the old man cut him off.

"How bad? If I had something that kept on making bank, I'd do . . . hell, damn near anything."

"I can get you a hundred large."

"Yeah? Who I gotta kill?"

"Boy calls himself the 'Chi-Town Terror.'"

"The rapper? Him? You got to be crazy, old man."

"What I got to be is what I am now: old. Get it? I buried a hundred men, and I'm not gonna die from no bullet."

"You were a killer?"

"No, fool. I needed that done, I always paid some sucker to do it. I mean, I've watched a hundred men go. And I'm still here. Did I roll the bones? Sure. Swig champagne? Snort some powder? Of *course*—that's what a mack man did then. I came up same way you should. By getting schooled.

"The man who taught *me* the game told me something I never forgot: The one thing you can't never pick up is the one thing you can't never shake. You know what that is? Worse than the clap, worse than a crazy whore who'll slice you in your sleep, worse than a prison jolt. The worst thing a man can pick up is a *need*.

"You never even go *near* anything you can't walk away from. That's the only law a pimp has to know. But he has to have it memorized and internalized. Down cold. A pimp on the spike is just a junkie with some nice clothes. A pimp on the bottle is just a drunk with a Cadillac that he's gonna drive into a wall. A pimp who can't stay away from the tables, he's gonna end up *under* those tables."

"I get it."

"Not yet, you don't. You understand, *maybe* you understand, you don't play a game you can't win. But you got to be willing to die before you even get to try."

"Come on, old man. That rhyme-time thing is too old-school for me. I can't break it down."

"Try this, then. This 'Chi-Town Terror' has made himself a mistake. The worst a man can make. When it comes to rap, there's East Coast and West Coast. That's it. There ain't no Midwest. And there ain't no 'neutral,' either. He thinks, okay, maybe he can't travel, but this town is big enough for him to *be* big in. See, he ain't signed. He wants to run his own show. Produce his own stuff. Sign up talent. Keep all the money."

"So?"

"So, if he pulls that off, gonna make a lot of people brave. You think they ain't got rappers all the way from Denver to Dallas? The way it is now, some go left and some go right. But who goes to the middle? Chicago, that's the middle. East and West, they go to the death to prove who's the best. Only thing they agree on is there can't be no *'rest'*—you see the picture I'm painting for you?" The old man sighed and took another deep inhale from his oxygen tank. "You surprised I know this, I can tell."

"I didn't think you even listened to rap."

"I don't. But I listen to the drums. Never stopped, even when they changed the beat. So—tell me, boy: you down with the whole rap scene, right?"

"Well, not—"

"Never mind. That ain't the point. 'Cause I know what you *can't* tell me. Who killed Tupac? Who killed Biggie?"

The young man said nothing, but his posture finally completed its gradual shift from half-slouch to full-attention.

"One hundred large for the Chi-Town Terror. All you got to do is walk up and put a couple in his head."

"Me?"

"You."

"I don't even have a gun."

"I do. And I got something even better. I got his crib."

"That palace on Lakeshore? How could I even get past the doorman, never mind his bodyguards?"

"Not his showroom, boy. His home-crib. When they tore down the high-rises, he moved his mother out to Chicago Heights. Ain't as nice as it sounds. Been a hard town for as long as I can remember. But it's a private house."

"Sure. Probably guarded around the—"

"Boy, *try* and listen! That house ain't guarded with guns; it's guarded with knowledge. Even his own crew don't know about it. When he comes over to see his mama, he goes Plain-Jane on the ride. And he goes alone."

"How did you—?"

"Stop acting the fool! I found out *from* a fool. You could torture that sucker for days and he still wouldn't say my name. He didn't even know what he was telling me while he was doing it."

"How could—?"

"Boy, how much time you think I have to keep filling in the blanks for you? The fool with the mouth, that's his mother's man. Younger than her, but he ain't nothing special, and he knows it. He's still in the saddle—he don't work for a living, but he's never broke. All he knows is that the old lady's son comes by, gives her cash. The rest I figured out for myself. And figured it was info I'd save for a rainy day. Check the weather out there, young boy—this is Chicago, not L.A. When it rains here, it rains *hard.*"

THE SLENDER man looked at his manicured nails, fingered the thin platinum chain under his royal-purple silk shirt. He'd been a good listener. And had become a good practitioner. The old man had been right: If a girl's fine enough to work the pole in a classy club, no reason to put her on the street, take all those risks. Dancing, she's going to make some *real* money. And bring it home to her man.

But no *man* spends all day playing with his Xbox. He doesn't act like a boy. He's got real game. Working on something big. Can't talk about it to his woman—he's got to protect her, and the less she knows, the better . . . for her.

He knows where she is at night. But she doesn't know where he is. Or what he's doing. Or when he's coming back.

But she knows this: when he *does*, there better be some cash on the table.

Trolling for new stuff is hard. Lot of competition out there. But when you got the goods, that stuff comes to you.

A man who understands The Life understands that it will always be there, but not always in the same form. "Evolution" is what the old man called it, and that sounded right.

So he knew Taylor would come back, sooner or later. After all, everything she owned, from her clothes to her jewelry to that stupid cat she was always fussing over, it was all back at his apartment. *His* apartment. His name was the *only* name on the lease. That way, she couldn't lock him out . . . and a bitch *will* do that, you don't plan ahead. Call the police, they'd never find a mark on her. And the cops couldn't even tell him to spend the night someplace else—they're not allowed to do evictions. They tell anyone to sleep someplace else, it'd be *her*.

As far as Taylor knew, her man was always on the edge of danger. The money for the car and the clothes and the bling—he'd *had* all that before they'd ever gotten together. It all came from working a robbery of some Colombians, down in Miami. *After* they dumped their powder, the way a real pro does—his crew wanted the cash, not the product.

The Colombians were still looking for him. That's why his next score had to be big enough to last them the rest of their lives. The rest of their lives *together*. No more dancing for her. He didn't like the idea of men looking at her that way. Not at *his* woman. But every time he hinted that he wanted her to quit, Taylor always managed to talk him out of it.

Naturally, his own crew was close by—you never pull a job in the same state twice. "You don't *want* to meet them," he'd told her. Promised they'd get this all sorted out pretty soon. Might be some blood spilled, but none of it was going to get on him.

In the meantime, she brought in the money while he worked the edges. Once he took care of the planning—that was his role; guns were for fools—the *big* job, that *last* job was going to go down. Taylor earned good, but she couldn't hope to make major bucks if she never left the stage. And he sure wasn't going to *make* her do anything she didn't want to do.

Yes, he had to slap her around every so often, but only when she got too pushy. "You hear the word 'When?'—don't matter if the next word out her mouth is 'Daddy,' you do what you got to do. But you never leave a mark." The old man had taught him both meanings of that last sentence, and Lawrence never forgot either one.

I'm the one holding all the cards, the player silently gloated, as he pulled *his* Lexus into the garage behind the building where *his* apartment was located.

All he had to do was wait. The same way he'd waited for Chi-Town Terror to visit his mother years ago.

"A MAN with style can't have all that 'MF' stuff come out his mouth," the old man had told him. "You don't need to sound like a preacher, but you got to have manners. Class. Always be professional. Don't show your cards on your face.

"Lawrence? That's the kind of name a boy gets from his mama. You got that voodoo blood in you, shows every-where. So you either a swamp nigger or a Creole prince. Which sounds better to you, huh? Try this one on for size: Jean-Baptiste. Nice, am I right? Okay, Jean-Baptiste LaRue. That's gonna be you. 'LaRue'—you know what it means in Creole? 'The Street.' Get it?

"Now, you practice saying that name, saying it the way I just said it. I know where you can get the right ID, match you all the way. But ID's like a custom suit—it's got to *fit* to be right. That name, it's special. You don't say it like you spell it, so you got to know both. Cop looks at your ID, asks you your name, it got to come out like you been saying it all your life."

True Blue had passed on, but not before Jean-Baptiste had learned it all. Now he was as smooth as ice, and patient as a glacier.

BUT WHEN he walked into an apartment that had been stripped to the bare walls, he could barely suppress the urge to go out, get a gun, and teach that bitch . . .

Teach her what, fool? True Blue's voice echoed, as if the old man were right there with him, both looking at the empty space. *Take a half-dozen men to pull off something like this. You think that bitch got friends that good? Nah. This was something that got paid for. Time for you to float, boy.*

Fighting for calm, he pulled the mate to Taylor's phone from the pocket of his russet suede jacket and hit her speed-dialed number. Number One, as he never failed to remind her.

"You know what to do. And when to do it." Taylor's sultry voice, followed by the beep signaling voice-mail was coming next.

Phone's in my name, he thought. *So she can't cancel the account. When the next bill comes, I'll know who she set this up with.*

Breathing deeply, as if preparing to dive off a cliff, Jean-Baptiste walked through the spacious apartment. Every room had been emptied.

Not my clothes! He fought off panic. But when he saw that his own walk-in closet was as empty as the rest of the place, he had to summon all his inner strength not to throw Taylor's phone through a window.

"HE SAID if J.B. showed up here, I could go home."

"Oh, honey," Arabella said, "you have to learn to really listen when a man talks. Especially *that* man."

"But I *was!*"

"Stop being a baby," the little blonde said. "Sure, you can go back to where you lived. Not 'home.' It's not going to be that, ever again. And he said 'sooner or later,' didn't he? That spells out 'not tonight' any way you look at it."

"But if I don't go back, he'll do something . . . ."

"If you don't go back, whatever that trash does, he'll have to do it to *himself*, honey. They even took your cat."

"Huh?"

Arabella expertly piloted her little Mercedes out of the safe zone and into the streets. "This is yours." She smiled, handing the brunette a folded piece of paper.

"What is it?"

"It's a rental agreement. For this huge storage unit—the address is on top. You paid three months in advance. Fifteen hundred, cash. The numbers on the bottom, they're for the combination lock."

"Fifteen hundred dollars?!"

"The unit's big enough to live in, girl. Had to be, to hold everything in that apartment of yours."

"It's been emptied out?"

"Are you really this thick? Yes, it's been emptied out. Right down to the walls. Check your phone, you'll see."

"But if—"

"If we're going to be roommates, you're going to have to learn to do what makes sense, honey. And what makes sense right this minute is for you to check your phone."

Taylor fumbled in her brand-name bag, pulled her latest-model phone from its slot, and saw she had a text waiting.

I FIND U. I WONT B ALONE. U GET *EVERYTHING* BACK
WHERE POS' 2B, OR *U* B 1 *VERY* SORRY HO.

"Oh my God!"

"Will you stop all the damn drama? What did he do, threaten you or something?"

"Yes! And he knows where to find me. I mean, if I go back to that club . . ."

"Oh, you *are* going back to that club, girl. Who do you think cleaned out your apartment?"

"But . . ."

"It's gonna be *your* butt if you don't, baby. You stay with me until . . . until we can find ourselves a nice little three-bedroom. I know a perfect spot. In Uptown. Second floor. We're going to be college girls, far as the owner knows. Old Polish guy, minds his own business. Last place that punk would ever expect to find you."

"But the club? I mean, he'll come after me. I know he will. And he's with this whole gang. Professionals."

"Sure, he is. And the Double-X, the people that work there, they're all amateurs, huh?"

"I . . . I guess not."

"Give me your phone."

"My phone?"

"Am I speaking a foreign language? That so-called man of yours, he has your phone on the same plan as his, right?"

"Yes. But—"

"I better not hear 'but' come out of your mouth again, girl. You make *any* calls on that phone, he's going to know soon as the bill comes. Why do you think I'm driving in circles? He's probably got his own chip in that phone, too."

"Oh."

"'Oh'? Oh, *what*? You just escape from a convent? Soon as you get new ID—"

"I *have* ID. 'Taylor' is just a name I made up."

"Really!"

"You don't have to sound so sarcastic."

"And you don't have to *act* so damn dumb. Who made up that 'Taylor' name you use? Yeah, I thought so. All right, like I *started* to say, you take your phone and throw it in the river when we go over the bridge. Then you take your *new* ID and use it to get yourself a *new* phone. What's the big deal?"

"I don't know where I could get new ID."

"I am *so* shocked to hear that! Look, honey, I told you that place was covered, didn't I? You'll have to pay for the ID, and they'll front it, same as for the storage unit. But you're not going to get cheated, and the *only* payment the man takes is cash, so don't waste your time trying to offer him anything else."

"The man with the tattoo on the back of his hand?"

"Bingo. I guess his name wouldn't mean anything to you. I bet you never even *heard* of Red 71."

The brunette just shook her head.

JEAN-BAPTISTE DROVE slowly to his other apartment. He was trying for that ice inside him that the ancient pimp had warned him he could never allow to melt.

Ronni was still asleep when he let himself in. She wouldn't wake up for hours, he knew—she always gobbled a handful of pills and washed them down with a double of Crown Royal just before she hit the sheets, never failed.

That one had been easy. Got too much weight on her for the best clubs, but a lot of men like their women thick, and she'd work any room he told her to, so she always came home with real money.

Dependable. That's what she had going for her. There was a neatly stacked pile of bills on the kitchen table. He riffed through them quickly—twelve big, one half, and the rest double sawbucks . . . all the way down to singles. Probably didn't keep a dime for herself. If she wanted something, she knew her man would get it for her. He paid all the bills, didn't he?

J.B. was still red-rage angry enough to wake the cow up and use the strap he kept hanging in the bedroom closet to remind her of . . .

Stop that, fool! his mind shouted at him. Ronni was a good girl. Not just that, until he could put another game plan together, she was his *only* girl.

He still had his ride. And half his wardrobe was sitting only a few feet away. He never left much cash lying around.

Not that any of his women would ever steal a dime, just playing it safe.

Speaking of which . . .

LESS THAN an hour passed before he emerged, wearing a subdued daytime outfit, but one that would scream "Money!" at any woman who was in the market for a man who could take her to the best places. And then take her away.

His mother had already left for her job, so he was able to get to the basement pad where True Blue had spent his last days. By then he was pretty much out of conversation, so J.B. had known it was coming.

The safe was hidden inside what looked like a drywall panel. He spun the combination without looking. About seventy thou in there. That calmed him down right away. As he knew it would.

Some other stuff in there, too. The old man had warned him to dispose of the pistol that had earned him his first new car and the extra custom touches that set it apart from the rest. But J.B. just couldn't do that.

His religion was superstition. Not only was that pistol his personal mojo hand, he wouldn't know where to get another one like it. The full magazine he'd emptied into Chi-Town Terror had been barely audible—no lights went on, no dog barked. Getting bullets was no problem—more 9mm rounds sitting in boxes on the West Side than there were roaches in the kitchens. But the pistol, that was special. Custom-made. The best.

And no cop was ever going to be searching his mother's

house. Even if he got dropped for—who knows?—the most they could do would be search any place he was carrying the keys to at the time. He never carried the key to his mother's house—that was under a back windowsill, on a magnetized strip even she didn't know about.

His mother's house. The one safe haven that would always be there for him. The parallel to the house of the Chi-Town Terror's mother had never entered his mind.

"Always make them underestimate you," he heard the old man's voice in his head, counseling him when he proudly returned with the news that he'd earned that bounty money. "Never carry, not even a blade. Only two people know you a genuine life-taker now: you and me. You keep it that way. Let them think, *Oh, that boy, he ain't nothing*. You don't want no street rep. Let 'em all sleep on you. That way, if anyone does come for you, they won't come prepared, see?"

When he hit that club where Taylor danced, she might have warned the bouncer to be on the lookout . . . you never know. So if he had to stand for a pat-down, he'd be clean. But once he got back to his car . . .

Besides, all he needed was to make certain she saw him. That alone might be enough to scare her into giving him back his things. *All* his things.

One thing he knew for sure: Taylor had a friend. A friend with enough money to hire that moving crew. So she might not scare that easily. It might come down to something else.

He'd been ready to take that big step-up once. And he was ready if it came to that again.

AS A rule, J.B. never touched powder. But every once in a while, he used it for what he called "boost." Sometimes, to work his game, he had to go without sleep for a couple of straight twenty-fours, and there was nothing like a hit of what the old pimp had called Girl to keep a man sharp and alert.

When the old man had first confided this, J.B. was less than eager to embrace it. He knew Girl was cocaine, just as Boy was heroin. And he knew the old man's core belief: women were both the most loyal and the most treacherous of all God's creations; to the pimp once known throughout certain parts of Chicago as "True Blue," it was just a matter of picking those from the first group. And it took more than knowledge to do that—you had to have that special instinct. Not something you could learn, no matter how well schooled you might be. This ability was a gift, like having an ear for music. Either you were born with it, or you weren't.

After the old man passed, J.B. moved slowly and with great care. But as the years went by, he came to believe that this gift had been implanted in him, as if the old man was schooling him from the grave.

So how could I have been so wrong about Taylor?

If she'd taken just her own things—especially that miserable, mangy cat—he would have chalked her up to The Life's Unwritten Law: They come, they go. The circle never breaks. But *his* stuff! The custom-tailored suits, the handmade shoes, his jewelry . . . Not irreplaceable, of course, but certainly a big hit on his wallet. Now, that was just plain evil.

In the past, women had cut up his clothes, or thrown bleach on them. And left some kind of note, too. Girls who did that, he knew he could expect them to come crawling back. And he knew they wouldn't even *try* that unless they came with enough cash to replace everything they'd ruined, and then some.

Yeah, this was different.

So it had to be dealt with. The word would get out, and his prestige—far more important than any wardrobe or car—would be damaged beyond repair.

Not going to happen.

Not to him.

Not ever! he thought to himself, not realizing that he was giving up the protective coloration the old man had warned him was a cloak of safety. The need to send a message to that bitch had overpowered the old man's warnings in a finger-snap.

Coke *might* kill you, if you didn't handle it correctly. But ego, no doubt about it, that *would* kill you. And the worst ego of all was the one you didn't know you had. The one that was sitting inside you, calling all the shots.

J.B. WENT through five of his one-time-use burner cells before he gave it up. Some of Chicago's *truly* bad men wouldn't accompany him to the Double-X no matter how much he offered. He couldn't even get the Motley brothers, twin gunmen who were reputed to have kept one undertaker in business for a decade, to come into the club by themselves and just watch his back.

"You know whose club that is?"

"What diff—?"

"The Double-X, even damn *winos* know it's run by the Cross crew."

"Never heard of them."

"Guess you never heard of Red 71, either."

"What's that, another club?"

"Yeah, man. Just another club. See if you can get a cabbie to take you there."

"I don't need a cab, man. I'll just go—"

"You know, me and my brother, we charge for what we do. But I'm givin' you this one for free: don't go near that place. You walk in with bad intentions, they turn you into dog food."

"That's just—" J.B. began, before he realized he was talking to a dead line.

RUMORS RUN through Chicago like white-water rapids. Anyone could watch them from a cliff, but trying to ride them, that was a job for an expert. The street racers worked on the fringe of the Badlands. No worries about the Law out there, but crossing the semi-trailer that marked one entrance was never done twice . . . not without permission.

The dope slingers wouldn't work a place where they'd never see a customer. Even the hookers who worked streets nobody should ever walk down gave it a pass. Some of the always-in-motion gambling houses had their own protection from raids, be it the police or some get-rich-quick boys who thought going in armed would change the game. But they never set up shop in the Badlands, not even for one night.

All Jean-Baptiste could learn was that Red 71 was supposed to be somewhere out there, at the other end of the marked entrance.

"If you don't know, don't go." The old man's words, still echoing. So this Red 71, whatever the hell it was, he'd leave that for some other time. But the Double-X, that was just another strip club. He'd been there before. Time to stop watching the rapids from a distance and climb into that kayak.

HE WAITED for a Friday night, when the place would be packed. Money flowing, waitresses always in motion, sometimes grinding it harder than the girls working the stage. Everybody was overworked, and the security staff would be no exception. "Take it outside!" was the only warning any patron would get. Once.

J.B. had to wait, but he made good use of the time. He did a pass-by in broad daylight, and was even less impressed than he'd been during his first visit. The building looked like a grayish concrete lump, casually dropped onto an empty prairie. It didn't have the class of clubs with canopies and liveried doormen, not even the grossly garish neon tubing twisted into the shape of impossibly endowed women at the other end of the scale.

He watched cars go in and out, using a small set of folding binoculars to distinguish patrons from employees. But there was no angle from which he could view where the entering cars were parked.

They wouldn't want the girls to have to walk through a parking lot. Not to enter, and sure as hell not when they were leaving. And there's nothing to see around the back of the place . . . .

Shrugging away insane ideas like underground tunnels, or a helicopter pad on the roof, he tapped one prominent cheekbone with a slender forefinger, a subconscious telegraph that he was trying to think a problem all the way through.

Behind the joint. That's got to be where the girls go. So damn dark back there, I couldn't really see much, but maybe they park in a far corner . . . .

Finally, he shrugged his shoulders in resignation and turned his custom Lexus coupe back toward civilization. Thanks to Ronni—now, *that* was one loyal girl—he wasn't short of money, and he could keep dressing to suit his role for weeks to come.

Maybe he should just let it go. Chalk it up to . . . whatever. But the bitch taking his property, that made it personal. And Jean-Baptiste was not a man you could do like that.

"WHO WANTS him?"

"You tell the man it's Howard and Harold."

"Funny, you sound like one man from here. You some kind of multiple personality?"

"Hey! I call the man to do him a solid, and you pull this—"

"Next time you see whoever sold you those calm-down pills, be sure and get your money back," Buddha said, gently replacing the handset of the pay phone in the basement poolroom of a building identified only by the number "71" graffiti-sprayed in red, with the "1" forming an arrow. An arrow pointing down.

The same red "71" was carelessly sprayed on the sides of various junked cars which surrounded the building. The stone structure was set in the midst of what looked like a scrap yard at first; but the carelessly scattered old appliances, chunks of unidentifiable machinery, and things that might have once been furniture combined to give it the look of an above-ground landfill. An astounding variety of animal life ran, jumped, crawled, and flitted in the shadows formed by the rusting metal: cats chasing mice while fleeing from dogs who lived on the plentiful supply of rats, snakes waiting for either prey to run past their ground-level hiding places. Crows and other carrion eaters perched, watched, and pounced when an opportunity opened up. Such movements always diverted the cats, and the high-speed evolution of new breeds of each species continued.

The vicious Chicago winters changed nothing but the hunting-and-hiding patterns. Snakes who would sun themselves on hot metal in the summer found hibernation spots without difficulty; the warm-blooded mammals still found live food, working very close to the ground. And the birds that frequented this bizarre collection of predators-and-prey were not the kind who went south for the winter.

The pay phone rang again. And it was answered the same way.

"What?"

"This is Howard Motley, okay? I want to speak to Cross."

"Then you know where to come," Buddha said, cutting the connection again.

THE PERFECTLY restored black 1973 Firebird Trans Am—"the last of the *real* ones, right down to the 455 cubes"—rolled slowly toward the scrap yard.

"I'm not so happy about this," the tall, rawboned man in the passenger seat said. He had a darkly shaded mark on his throat that looked more like a tumor than an Adam's apple.

"You ain't exactly a barrel of laughs most of the time," the driver replied. He was a mirror image of the first speaker, lacking only the purplish birthmark on his throat.

They were dressed alike, in long brown leather coats, heavy jeans, red corduroy shirts buttoned to the neck, and steel-toed ironworker's boots.

As if the pair of over-under .40-caliber derringers each man carried in the side pockets of his coat might prove insufficient, the console opened on a 12-gauge pump holding three-inch magnum shells, its barrel slightly cut down to sixteen inches. And the trunk held a pair of scoped M14s chambered for NATO rounds. Although those were not far removed from the .30-caliber slugs favored by deer hunters, no deer hunter needed a full-auto.

And no hunting license would keep ATF from seizing everything the twins carried, anyway. But the "going quietly" synapses had never connected inside their skulls. They could trace their lineage back to ancestors who'd mounted skulls of "strangers" on the walls of their cabins with great pride.

As the Firebird braked gently to a stop, the passenger said, "Don't we have to leave our pieces in the car?"

"Harold, I told you about fifty damn times. They don't care if you walk in carrying a damn bazooka. Nobody's gonna search us."

"That's weak."

"*You're* the one who's weak. Why they need to search us when we're walking into a place where we're in somebody's sights as soon as we start down the steps?"

"I still say this is weird."

"Lots of things are like that. So what? You and me, we're businessmen. We do business. We get paid. We got some info that's worth money, but the only way we turn it *into* money is face-to-face. Got to tell the man himself."

"Why?"

"'Cause that's the way they want it. And they the ones with the money."

"LOOKING FOR Cross," Harold said to a man who looked as if he'd missed his last appointment with the embalmer. The top half of his face was invisible behind a green eyeshade.

"Nobody here with that name."

"Look, old man, I was told—"

The light tap on his right shoulder cut Harold off. He turned, and found himself looking at a short, pudgy man with reflective black eyes slanted slightly at their corners, as if he had passed through more than one womb at birth.

"Just follow me," the man said, turning his back and moving away.

The two men trailed behind him, exchanging looks but not speaking. The poolroom was about half full. Most of the tables were being used for something other than their intended purpose. Some held a display of handguns, others were surrounded by men watching a dice roller throw against a board held in place by a triangular brace. Some tabletops were covered with cards, others with kilo-calibrated scales.

Every race, creed, and color was represented in some way,

as if this were the basement of the United Nations, with only practicing criminals permitted entrance.

The short man with the inanimate eyes led them to a table in a far corner. A man was seated there, the bull's-eye tattoo on the back of his right hand clearly visible as he held a cigarette to his lips.

In response to a silent direction, the twins took seats to either side of the man they had come to meet.

The man took another drag on his cigarette, ground it out, and looked from one twin to another, still saying nothing.

"We got some information we think you might be interested in," Harold said.

The man with the tattoo on the back of his hand still said nothing.

"Information that's worth money," Harold continued.

"Okay," Cross said. "What is it?"

Sensing that a lengthy conversation wasn't part of the package, and no drinks were going to be offered, Harold got right to it: "Guy tried to hire us. To hit someone who works at that club of yours."

"What guy? What club?"

"The club, that's the Double-X. The guy, that's what you're gonna pay us to tell you."

"Pay you how much?"

"Say, five grand?"

"Say goodbye."

"No, you don't understand. We can tell you more than the name he goes by. His car, what he looks like, you know—so you can see him coming."

"Tell me what you have. I'll tell you what it's worth."

"That's not how it works."

"That's how it works *here*."

The twins exchanged a quick look, telepathically communicating: *We came here for money. We call this guy's hand, get up, and walk out, we walk out with nothing.*

"Guy calls himself Jean-Baptiste. Some kind of pimp. Drives a charcoal Lexus coupe with matching wheels—big, but not stupid-big. Got that black fine-lining, too."

Cross said nothing.

"There's a girl works in your club. This Double-X. Just started. Name's Taylor. Black hair, maybe twenty-five years old, built like you'd expect. That's who he wanted us to take out."

"For how much?"

"We never got there. Soon as he said 'Double-X,' we knew better. But he was . . . desperate, like. So we figure, sooner or later, he finds *somebody* to take the job. Just follow her to wherever she's staying, drop her soon as she gets out of her car. No big job, but he sounded like he was willing to pay big money to get it done."

"Five grand."

"That's what *I* said," Harold replied. "Info like this is—"

"Five grand would be what you'd charge to do the job," Cross said, his voice a blend of mild and menace. "One grand, that's how much what you just said is worth."

"Hey!" Howard protested. "You don't know what we charge for—"

"You're Uptown guys, so you've got kind of a limited range. Twins, people tend to remember that. And your car, too. I can tell you half a dozen jobs you've done in the last couple of years. And your price for each one, you want me to."

"Go ahead."

"Okay. But, like you said, info is worth money. So, for every job I name, two hundred comes off the grand. You want to play? Or you want your money?"

The twins again exchanged looks, this time not attempting to hide their silent communication.

"We'll take the money," Harold said.

"It's at the front desk," Cross told him, lighting a cigarette in a clear gesture of dismissal.

The twins rose from their chairs as one, and walked all the way back over to the desk. The old man was still there. And a thin stack of hundreds was there, too.

Harold swept the money into his coat pocket without counting it, and the twins walked back up the stairs.

"WHY DID you—?"

"Because the grand isn't all we got," Harold cut off his twin.

"Yeah?"

"Yeah. See, if Cross didn't think we were coming to him straight, he wouldn't have paid us a dime."

"So?"

"So Cross, that's a man you never want thinking you're not playing straight with him. You remember that little guy? The one who took us over?"

"Sure."

"That's got to be Buddha."

"Who?"

"One of that crew. I heard he once won a ten-thousand-dollar bet from some sucker who thought no way a man could ever *shoot* a damn bumblebee at twenty feet. Hell, you can't hardly *see* one at that distance."

"And he did that?"

"With a *pistol*! That's what people say."

"Real people?"

"Oh yeah."

"Damn."

"I know. I just wish *we* knew someone who wanted that pretty boy killed. He's as good as dead anyway."

"I guess," Howard replied, already back to his normal state: total indifference to anything except a threat or a target.

"YOU THINKING what I'm thinking, boss?"

"It was a mistake to bring So Long back with you?"

"Hey, brother! There's no reason to be banging on me. Anyway, we haven't laid out dime one, so why even go there?"

"You're right, Buddha. Sorry."

"Huh!" the pudgy man sniffed, brushing aside an empty apology for something that hadn't remotely offended him in the first place. "What I was thinking was, if that new girl at the Double-X, if she wanted her problem taken care of . . ."

"Because we got no choice anyway."

"That's how I see it. You?"

"Yeah. He's crazy enough to try and hire the Motley Twins, he keeps on trying, he's gonna find someone crazy enough to take the job."

"So? Only place he knows to come is the club. He shows up, we just—"

"Wait! Hold up, brother. Your idea, it's actually not a bad one. Not at all."

"I thought you said—"

"Money's money, right? So, if that bottom feeder *has* some, why shouldn't *we* get it?"

JEAN-BAPTISTE DRESSED carefully, checking his reflection in the three-panel mirror he'd told Ronni she needed to have. "You got to be able to see what *they* gonna see, baby. Always keep your edge."

Oh, he looked *fine*. Not flashy, not like some pimp on the prowl, more like a successful businessman out for a little fun.

And he was every bit of that. *All* that.

Jean-Baptiste pulled his custom ride inside the chain-link fence surrounding the Double-X. As he knew from his previous visit, the gate would swing open automatically as a car approached.

He braked to a stop just past the front entrance. The Maori known as K-1 to distinguish him from his look-alike cousin, K-2, moved as slowly as a man slogging through quicksand, but he somehow managed to block the car from proceeding any farther.

"Valet parking only, sir."

If the man at the door recognized J.B., he gave no sign. J.B. palmed him a fifty, said, "A single, okay?"

In unspoken acknowledgement of the driver's bribe-request to park the Lexus where it would be in no danger of being dinged, the doorman pointed to his right. J.B. walked toward one of the few unoccupied single tables in the place.

But before he reached his destination, he felt a . . . presence of some kind behind him, herding him toward a larger table, using the air compressed between them as a push bar.

Some dark figure pulled out a chair, and J.B. found himself seated across from a man with unremarkable features. On his right, a real-life Indian. Like an Apache or something. On his left, a pudgy man with dark hair and darker eyes.

An instinct he trusted told him not to look around. He watched as the man facing him opened his left hand. A small flame leaped from that hand to the cigarette in his right. As he lit the smoke, J.B. noted the bull's-eye tattoo on the back of the man's hand.

In a voice as unremarkable as his facial features, the man said, "She'll be coming on soon. Working the pole first. The lighting in here—I can see her, she can't see me. That's the way we set it up."

"I don't know—"

"Don't be stupid," the man said. "You're here for Taylor. She cleaned you out. Told every girl in the place a couple of nights ago. So you need to do something to keep your face. And you need to come here to do it."

"Bitches run their mouths, so what?"

"So this: When she finishes her set, she goes back to the dressing room. For the right price, she never gets there. Never comes back."

"What about my stuff?"

"It's in a storage unit. You got the coin, you get the key."

"How do I know this is all legit?"

"Two reasons: One, you tried to hire the Motley Twins, but they know better than to touch anyone who works here.

Two, you come back here tomorrow night, that girl won't be here. You have my personal guarantee—you are never going to see Taylor on that stage again."

"What's that's supposed to mean, your 'guarantee'?"

"Think about it for a second. The Motley Twins turned you down, am I right? Everyone knows those two psychos would hit the Pope on St. Patrick's Day if they got paid. So I figure they probably said something about Red 71."

"Yeah . . ."

"And you didn't have a clue. Not your line of work. When you want something done, you *pay* people to do it for you, whether it's shining your shoes or sending a message."

"Now, *that's* true."

"Well, what else are we talking about here? You got a gun on you?"

"No, man. I don't mess with—"

"All right. You can rent one from us. Cost you five bills. You take the pistol, walk on back, shoot the bitch in the head, walk back out here, hand over the piece, and keep on walking."

"In front of all those—?"

"Why not? If anything, it'll just make you look even bigger. Nobody's going to talk. Nobody wants to be a witness. We'll throw in the body disposal, no charge."

Jean-Baptiste was tempted. But, this time, what he'd been taught overcame his ego.

"How much for me to walk out now?"

"Still five. Only five *large*. I know you paid more than that just for the suit you're wearing. So . . . ?"

LESS THAN an hour passed.

"Thirty-five and change!" Buddha gloated. "Didn't I say this was a beautiful idea?"

"He had that much left?"

"About ten on him, and twenty-five in a hideaway behind the glove box."

"I guess you never know," Cross said, his tone indicating that at least one person did. "Go back and find Arabella, you mind?"

"WHAT'S UP?" Arabella asked Cross, who was seated in his usual triangle spot.

"Your new girlfriend's ex-boyfriend."

"That boy's nothing."

"His money's just as good as anyone else's."

"Meaning . . . ?"

"Meaning he's putting out a contract on Taylor. Ten for a kill, double that for a splatter."

"A contract with who?"

"With the first person to snatch the offer."

"So you're saying . . . ?"

"You know what I'm saying, Arabella. You think wearing that little schoolgirl outfit is going to stun me blind? You've got an angel's face, and a scheming heart. The way you played this, Taylor's *got* to be living with you. No way she ever had a good experience with *any* man, so . . ."

"Who said that about me? Some dyke at Orchid Blue? Maybe your little pal, that crazy Tiger?"

"What's it matter? True is true. And something else is

true, too. Taylor's apartment was cleaned *out*. Wall to wall. Not just her stuff—his, too. All sitting in some big storage unit."

"So?" Arabella pouted.

"So *his* stuff, nobody's gone through it. And there's money in there, somewhere."

"And you want what?"

"Stop playing, Arabella. I look like a mark to you? You think I don't already know where the storage unit is? Whose men did that work, anyway?"

"So you could just go and take it, that's what you're telling me?"

"No. I'm giving you another chance to come to her rescue. Figure an easy ten to take him out. Maybe twice that, depending. You know he was here, earlier. What do you think he was here *for*, a lap dance?"

"He wanted to hire *your* people?"

"Yep."

"Oh."

"You just tell Taylor the truth. Believe it or not, that actually works, sometimes. There's only one way out for her now. We take the unit. You never go back there. The rent's paid out ninety days. You just let it go. The contents, that's a gamble. But I'll gamble on him having something worthwhile stashed there. And he'll never be a problem for Taylor, never again."

"You're going to—"

"That's enough. You're going back there and telling Taylor you just saved her ass *again*. For that, she should be letting you play with it a little."

"That's cold, Cross. Even for you."

"You ever hear anyone say, 'Okay, I'm going to give you the warm, soft facts,' Arabella?"

"BOSS, THOSE vines are fine. We could get an easy—"

"Trip to the Walls," Cross finished the sentence. "Guy like that, he was flash. Probably got monograms on everything, even places you can't see. Cash, sure. Jewelry that can be busted up, yeah, we can do that. But the clothes, they get razored—he could have cash sewn inside—and then they go into the fire."

"This is *real* nice," Princess said, holding up a lilac silk shirt with deep-purple collar and cuffs. "Can I have it?"

"Princess . . ." Rhino began, but Cross cut him off, saying, "Tell you what, Princess. If it fits, you can keep it, okay?"

"Sure!" said the hyper-muscled man with the heart of a child. A beast who always wanted to make friends.

The attempt was futile. Princess couldn't even get one of his anaconda arms through a sleeve. Even though he persisted—maybe it could be a short-sleeved shirt?—trying to close the front of what was left turned it to tatters.

"That's not fair!"

Rhino's turn: "Princess, you know well enough that one size never fits everyone."

"But it's so pretty. Maybe a . . . scarf or something?"

"There's money in here, Princess," Cross said. "So you start ripping it all apart, okay? The first piece of money you turn up, you can go out and buy yourself a whole new outfit, how's that?"

"See?" the armor-plated child told the one man who dwarfed his size. "Cross always figures out something."

"I know," Rhino said, barely suppressing the sigh of resignation that hovered near his lips whenever Princess turned intractable.

"HE HAD a fine little piece in that car," Buddha said to Cross and Ace, as the three men stood outside the storage unit. "Kind of old-school, probably put together maybe thirty years ago, but the workmanship was all top-drawer. The whole thing was built for quiet. Just a Beretta nine, but it was cut down some, and the whole barrel was baffled. The magazine was all standard stuff, but if you took some of the powder out, and reworked the bullet tips, all you'd need would be to get close before you cut loose. Nobody'd hear a sound."

"What, now *you* want to keep some of his stuff, too?" Ace half-laughed.

"Just saying."

"Uh-huh," Cross muttered, lighting a smoke.

"I mean, you wouldn't think a guy like him would carry a piece like that."

"So what?"

"So . . . maybe he got it from somebody who knows what he's doing. And knows who he sells his stuff to."

"And you think—what?—this gunsmith stays in touch with his clients, checks out how good his stuff is working?"

"Come on, brother. I was just . . . curious, like. There's all kinds of losers dealing hardware, but not many who can custom-build. Guy like that, he probably knows who we are."

"I thought we were real-estate investors."

"About that, was I right or was I right? I *told* you this job was gonna be pure money! If there's one thing So Long knows—"

"Yeah. You got rid of the car?"

"And him. The ride got the crusher; then it was torched into slices, and each slice got recrushed along with the other two. The punk himself, he got the acid bath, and then the grinder."

"That's good. Nothing like bone meal for fertilizer."

"Fertilizer? Boss, sometimes you—"

"Princess loves flowers. Planting things. We're going to turn those houses around, can't hurt to have them look nice. Anyway, recycling, that's the hot thing now, right?"

IT WAS still dark when the truck pulled out. Rhino used a bleach sprayer on the walls and floor of the storage unit, working backward, a gas mask protecting his face and eyes.

"There's still the other one," Cross told Buddha, speaking from the back seat of the Shark Car. Princess rode up front, the irony of calling "Shotgun!" lost on him.

"The girl Tracker found?"

"Yeah. Thing is, this guy wasn't working a street-girl game. He was a 'player,' not a pimp. The 'boyfriend,' right? So this other girl, she wouldn't know about Taylor."

"So? What difference, then?"

"Remember how the pistol surprised you, Buddha? I

think this boy was full of surprises. Probably has the same kind of stash he kept at Taylor's place over at this other girl's."

"Why is that bad for us?" Rhino asked, in the high-pitched, squeaky voice. For a man who weighed somewhere around five hundred pounds, a voice a couple of octaves below bass was the expectation.

"Surprises are always bad for us, brother," Cross said. As if the word "surprises" triggered a cinematic thread, the man-for-hire reflected that Rhino hadn't been born with that voice. None of them had been born to be what they had become . . . a no-limits unit every gang in the city feared.

For the thousandth time, Cross watched the tape replay in his mind.

Viewed from above, the institution appeared to be a huge starfish entangled in wire, its five arms radiating out from a fat central hub. This man-made starfish had a rapacious appetite. Teenaged boys entered at various tips of the arms and were pulled inside, to be devoured. Loops of razor wire coiled from one arm to the next.

Inside, a fifteen-year-old boy walked the full length of one of the starfish's long tentacles, his hands cuffed behind him. A burly guard kept one big hand on his elbow.

"Here," the guard said, stopping in front of a door marked

DIRECTOR

The guard opened the door, guided the boy inside, and pointed at a long wooden bench already occupied by a slender black youth.

"*Sit,*" the guard snarled, then went through the inner door that led to the office.

The two boys did not look at each other, did not speak. They sat uncomfortably on the front edge of the bench, keeping the handcuffs clear of their backs only with continual effort.

The guard reappeared and gestured for both of them to go into the office.

The office was carpeted and air-conditioned, dominated by a large wooden desk. On that desk, a brass nameplate:

PAUL T. LANDERS, DIRECTOR

On the wall behind the desk were various framed photographs, certificates, placques . . . and, hanging from an embedded brass spike, a thick, heavy, well-worn leather strap.

Paul Landers was a big, beefy man with small blue eyes set close together. His brown hair was cut in a military flattop. He wore a short-sleeved white shirt and a narrow dark tie; his thick wrist sported a gold watch with an expandable band. He pulled a file folder to the center of the desk and opened it slowly, as if the contents were sure to be disagreeable.

"*Marlon C. Cain,*" he said, glancing up. "*Thief. Chronic criminal. Anderson Hall at age nine. Carleton Reformatory at age thirteen. Two escapes.*"

Paul Landers closed that file, opened another, glanced at the boy next to Cain. "*Vernon D. Lewis. Attempted murder. First offense.*" The director of the Sterling Youth Correctional Facility looked up at the guard standing behind

Cain and the other boy. "The little bastard stuck a butcher knife into his mother's boyfriend," he said, nodding his head at the black youth. "Damn near killed him."

Paul Landers put one finger under the expandable band of his wristwatch, stretched it, and let it snap! back into place. Neither of the boys reacted. This practiced move had always made frightened boys flinch. Or at least blink. Probably too stupid to get the message, he thought to himself.

"Well, Mr. Cain, Mr. Lewis, welcome to the big time. Take the cuffs off them, Sergeant."

The guard stepped behind the white youth first, removed the handcuffs, then stepped in behind Lewis.

"Face that wall," Paul Landers ordered, his voice suddenly metallic. "Strip down to your shorts."

While Cain and Lewis did as they had been ordered, Paul Landers moved in behind them.

"We don't take any nonsense here," he said. "None. No back talk. No escapes . . . no escape attempts."

Suddenly Cain felt the heavy leather strop placed on his bare shoulder.

"No stabbings. No shakedowns."

Paul Landers placed the strop on the nape of Lewis's thin blue-black neck. "That okay with you, ace?"

"Yes, sir," Lewis replied quietly. His voice was adolescent-pitched, but held as steady as a deeply driven tent stake.

"Good. Then we understand each other. Isolation. Fifteen days," the director said to the guard. "Let them get the feel of this place."

Cain glanced out the director's window, taking one last look at the sunshine he knew he would not see again for over

*two weeks. Through the heavy steel bars, in the yard out-
side the fence, he saw the institution's twin flags, American
and state, on separate tall poles. As he looked, he saw the
other boy watching him. They locked their glass-reflected
glances. In that thin, ghostlike reflection, each recognized
in the other the hard, hypervigilant gaze of an unbroken,
still-dangerous POW.*

*The guard handcuffed the boys again, then walked
them up one arm of the starfish and down another, parad-
ing them barefoot and in their shorts in front of the other
boys. Unconsciously, Lewis imitated Cain's relaxed stride,
a silent communication to other inmates that he'd walked
this path before and knew it well.*

Months later, Cain walked onto the paved space between
two arms of the starfish, which the prison called a "yard."
His eyes darted back and forth, taking it all in: a basket-
ball game in progress, weight-lifting apparatus, handball
courts, a young boy plucking his eyebrows.

He did not acknowledge the greetings and glances
directed to him, walking straight ahead to where Vernon
Lewis was leaning against the chain-link fence. The slender
black youth had a dumbbell from one of the weight sets tied
to his side with a shoelace that ran across his chest. As he
spoke, he lifted the dumbbell and lowered it in measured
repetitions, using his free hand as cover, hiding his words
from any lip-readers who might trade information for a
favor from one of the wall-posted guards.

"They just brought in a real monster—I heard he hit
the scales in Processing at two ninety-five."

"Yeah, I heard that, too," Cain replied.

If Lewis was surprised that Cain already knew about the new arrival, he didn't show it. But he didn't doubt the other boy—Cain was immune to exaggeration, and would have triple-checked any passed-along word.

"We'll get to him later," the white youth went on, his eyes flickering across the yard. "Here comes company."

The youth approaching from across the yard was more man than boy, heavily muscled, broad-chested like a Rottweiler. He eye-locked Cain and moved forward behind his own stare. As he did so, two other boys fell in beside him.

Cain stood motionless, his eyes fixed on their approach.

Lewis continued his repetitions. Up, down. Up, down.

The three boys approached in a V-formation, the heavily muscled one at its protruding tip. When they closed to within a few feet, he said: "So, Cain . . . what's happening?"

Cain knew him only as "Bull," a blood-certified young man who'd swept into Sterling on a wave of respect because he'd killed a rival on the streets. But Cain had read the killer's eyes for an ugly mixture of bluff and cruelty. He did the math and came up with the one record that would never make the charts at Sterling.

Weakness.

"Fresh fish," Bull went on when it became apparent that Cain was not going to say anything. "Three of 'em."

Cain acknowledged that with a slight nod. He was always the first to get to any newcomers, always offering them protection. The mixed-race crew he and Lewis ran wasn't the biggest in the institution, but it was the most feared . . . maybe for exactly that same reason.

The price of protection varied. A percentage of any package the new arrival received from home, access to whatever he could steal from his institutional assignment, cigarettes, soft money . . . Some accepted. Some refused. Some said they weren't sure. And others said they just couldn't afford it. "Everybody pays, one way or another," Cain always told them all, something he knew for a fact.

Now Bull was showing respect, clearing the new names with Cain before he took the boys for his own. If Cain's crew had them covered, they were safe.

"Vincent Collona," Bull said.

Cain shook his head no. Collona had been assigned to the laundry and had access to spot removers such as naphthalene. More flammable than gasoline, and twice as handy.

"Joseph Clinter."

"Wait on that one," Cain said. "I'll tell you next week."

"Roland Spector."

Cain raised and dropped one shoulder in an I-don't-care motion, sealing Roland Spector's fate.

A slow smile crept across Bull's face. He glanced back across the yard at a slightly built boy standing off by himself. Bull's eyes were lit from within.

"I guess I'll go tell him to cut the back pockets off his jeans . . . . Better yet, I'll do it myself." Bull lifted his shirt to show his new toy, tucked into his pants. The shank was crudely notched for cutting, like a rip-saw's blade, each tooth razor-sharp.

Lewis did another repetition, slowly, almost casually. But not with the dumbbell.

"Maybe I'll just cut him a new—" Bull began. The words froze in his mouth when he found himself looking at

a short length of pipe taped to a piece of wood. Inside the pipe he caught the glint of sunlight on jacketed copper. A bullet.

"Whoa, Ace!" Bull said, holding up his hands, palms out, backing away.

"Don't ever show steel around us," Cain told him quietly. "I'll never say that again."

Bull looked into the eyes of the slender black youth who had taken the warden's racial slur as his name, symbolically returning fire. His were a light brown, almost tan, soft, with a gentle, liquid quality. And utterly devoid of bluff. "Man, I was just showing it off!" Bull said.

"One other thing," Cain added, ignoring the stupidity of that explanation. "The monster who just checked in, I'm telling you now—he's with us."

"Yeah, sure," Bull said. "You got it. He's not worth anything anyway."

Cain watched without interest as Bull walked away, happily slapping one of his flunkies on the back. The three of them went over to the slightly built boy and began to taunt him. Bull's two boys easily lifted him up by his back pockets, turning him around as they did so. The boy kicked and struggled. Bull made a quick move with his hand and suddenly the boy's pants were split, front to back. Bull's laugh echoed across the yard.

"Let's go," Cain said, ready to get on to other business.

"Since when did we take on this monster?" Ace asked.

"Since he weighed in at two ninety-five."

The huge, blank-faced boy was strapped into a wheelchair— the old-fashioned kind, made of wood, straight-backed, without arms, with a stabilizing set of little wheels behind the large rollers. Sometimes the guards released the straps long enough to allow him to use the nearby bathroom. Sometimes they didn't.

The boy had been in the chair for over four weeks, presumably so that the doctors could adjust his medication. There were festering sores on his buttocks and on the backs of his legs. He was not sure he could even stand unassisted, not anymore.

The shackled boy was sitting at the bottom of some deep lake, under its calm-looking but troubled top. The water and the thin, flickering light were always pressing down on him. Still, whenever a guard came to unstrap him or to force the plastic-coated capsules down his throat, he summoned the energy to speak.

"I never did a crime." His mantra: "I never did a crime." The one thing he clung to, no matter what new tortures were devised by his captors.

It was the truth. Repeatedly and violently abused as a small child, he had been removed from his parents and sent to a series of "homes." He was savagely beaten in some, sexually assaulted in others. One day, he screamed before he blindly struck out at his attackers.

That ended the "homes." As both his displays of temper and his physical stature grew, he was sent to ever-higher levels of institutional security. The doses of medication they originally administered to "calm him down" increased as he grew. Raging against the chemical bonds had the effect of a constant isometric exercise, turning the tranquilizers into red-zone levels of HGH.

He could hardly speak. One night, right after he had

first been strapped into the chair, a boy named Orville sneaked up behind him and held his nose. When the huge boy had gasped for air, Orville poured caustic drain cleaner down his throat. By the time the guards came the next morning with his medication and saw the chemical burns on his lips and his chin, the acid had destroyed most of his voice box.

When Orville passed by again, to laugh at the gobs of slapped-on salve intermixed with the drool, the huge boy had popped the first set of straps in a futile attempt to get to him.

The guards had come back with heavier straps—and more medication. Classification had determined that his "unprovoked attack" on Orville proved him to be as dangerous as others claimed. So the thirteen-year-old had been transferred to maximum security. The arms of the starfish had taken him in—he would not be disgorged until old enough for adult prison.

In Sterling's processing room, they helped him to stand on the scales.

Two ninety-five. And still growing.

"We call him Rhino," the guard who had driven the transfer van sneered, playing to his audience. "He gets six hundred milligrams of Thorazine three times a day— enough for a rhino. You figure the dosage by body weight, just like in the zoo."

When a heavy steel door closed somewhere behind him, Rhino tried to say, "I never did a crime." But his words came out as a slurred squeak.

"See?" the guard said. "It trumpets. Just like the rhinos on those nature shows."

Everyone laughed at that. Everybody except for one of the boys. That boy just looked at the monster, his face impassive, unamused.

"What are the marks on his arms?" Cain asked. "Some kind of drug reaction?"

"The boys where he came from," the guard explained. "They liked to see if they could get a rise out of him. It got to be kind of a thing—everybody did it."

Cain stepped closely enough to see the fresh cigarette burns and the scars from the old ones.

"What for? To use him as an ashtray?"

"The guy is a retard." The guard laughed it off. "He got no idea what planet he's on. He don't feel pain. Hell, he don't feel nothing."

Rhino moved his head from side to side. Even from the depths of the Thorazine lake, he struggled to register a protest. In the pre-violence stare-downs that characterized Sterling's processing room, his motion was barely discernible.

But Cain saw it.

Later on, he returned to where Rhino was strapped down. He went back again and again, seeming to come and go without regard to the time of day. And soon the monster realized something was different—for the first time he could remember, the other boys left him alone.

"I have a plan," Cain told him one winter afternoon, "but you have to play along for it to work."

Late that night, he loosened Rhino's straps, then sat on the floor next to the wheelchair. He knew the monster couldn't speak, but that didn't mean he couldn't hear. And if the drugged boy was surprised at a prisoner roaming free, he gave no sign.

Some nights Cain read to him, usually from a book of poetry he'd traded for. In an environment where a porno paperback cost a minimum of three cartons to "rent," the poetry was a one-pack purchase.

Other nights Cain just talked, his voice pitched very low.

"The way I figure it, you're in there somewhere," the gang leader said quietly. "You, the real you, whatever that is. If you ever want to get out, we got to change your medication." Cain reached into his pocket and took out two bright-blue capsules marked "T69" that he had "obtained" from the inmate-clerk who worked in the dispensary. "We'll start you on these. I fixed them myself, replaced half of that tranq-out crap with Contac—that's a cold medicine. We reduce your dosage gradually, okay? It could be a hard ride—let me know when you're ready."

Cain put the capsules back into his pocket and opened his book to read aloud from a collection of haiku.

The next night, when Cain opened the book, Rhino opened his hand, revealing the capsules that had been put into his mouth that day. Capsules he had tongued to the side instead of swallowing them.

Cain looked at the capsules. His nostrils flared slightly—the closest he got to a smile.

"Good!" he said, standing up to give Rhino the reduced dosage. "Payback's coming. Just be patient."

Cain opened the book on his lap, and spoke as if reading from it, "The time does itself—we just have to stay alive inside it until we can make our move."

Even after he was released from the chair, Rhino was careful to slump around as if he was both profoundly stupid *and heavily drugged. Once he became able to stay awake nights, he worked as Cain directed him.*

First the gang boss braided a string of dental floss. Then he wet the woven string and spun it slowly and carefully through an abrasive cleanser before setting it aside to dry. The string itself eventually became as sharp-edged as a piece of hacksaw wire. Inside Cain's cell, the monster used his enormous strength to saw tirelessly, night after night. "We need them all sawed through," Cain told him. "I could maybe get through with just two, but you'll need them all."

Some nights Cain read to him. Other nights he worked silently, braiding a much thicker rope from dental floss, or writing in some code he had devised. Cain's cell held a large volume—a dictionary and a thesaurus bound as one, stamped "Property of Sterling YCF." Although it was stolen from the prison library, its absence had gone unnoticed.

Ace passed by regularly but kept his distance. A model inmate, he was too close to parole to attempt an escape.

Cain was still reading aloud when Rhino finished—the bars were sawn through.

"I like that one," Rhino whisper-squeaked.

Cain looked up in amazement, even more astounded at Rhino's words than by the fact that the bars were already cut through.

Another week passed. On the yard, Cain said to Ace, "See you in a few weeks, right?"

Ace nodded solemnly.

Later that night, Cain said to Rhino, "Let's do it."

Rhino pulled the sawn-through bars aside as if they were strands of spaghetti.

Ace, watching, touched two fingers to his right eyebrow, brought them to his heart, tapped twice, and left the cell as silently as he had entered.

Cain secured the rope he'd fashioned from endless strands of dental floss and threw it down. He rolled a blanket lengthwise and tied it across his chest—even if he made it to the ground, there was still the razor wire atop the fence to negotiate.

"I'm going down first because I'm faster," he told Rhino. "If I don't make it, you get back to your cell—they'll never figure out how I got through the bars, and nobody's gonna suspect you. Ace is still here, so no one's gonna rat you out, either. But if you see me start up the fence, then make your move. Time you get to the fence yourself, I'll have the blanket draped over the wire."

Rhino put one huge hand on Cross's shoulder. "Later," he said, his voice a painful rasp.

Cain put his hand over Rhino's. "If you can't make the fence, I'll come back for you, brother."

Rhino looked into the first eyes that had ever viewed him as human, and nodded his understanding.

Cain turned away, slipped through the bars, and swung out on the dental-floss rope. He seemed to dance down the side of the building. The grass was wet with dew, further silencing his rush to the high fence, where he started his climb.

Rhino watched. As soon as he saw that Cain had unfurled the blanket over the wire, he wrapped the rope through his fingers and moved ponderously out the window.

Cain scrambled over the wire on the doubled-up blanket, dropped lightly to the ground on the other side, and vanished.

Rhino felt the makeshift rope stretch with his weight

even before it snapped. He felt the ground rush up to meet him. He hit hard on his back and just lay there, unable to move, his head lolling to one side, seeing only darkness where Cain had been.

For a few moments Rhino looked up at the stars, the same words playing over and over again in his mind: "I'll come back for you, brother."

The empty darkness behind the fence seemed to answer him with a vast internal echo. Rhino felt himself slipping back to the bottom of the familiar lake. He felt the weight of the water and the thin, flickering light pressing down on him. He never felt his own tears as they welled up and coursed down his cheeks.

Seven weeks later, Ace's things were all packed. He was ready to go, his get-out papers in one hand. Rhino was back in his chair, drool once again wetting his chin. Now they used a syringe—no more capsules for this one.

Ace stepped close to the monster's ear, speaking softly but in a voice devoid of doubt. "I passed it down. None of the punks here are gonna come near you."

After Ace left, Rhino's protection stayed intact. It wasn't long before some of the boys began the same games they had played before, in the other place. They urinated on him. They stubbed cigarettes out on his arms. They spit on him, and when they could, they tipped over his chair.

But before the week was out, every one of those boys met with some sort of prison misfortune. Two were stabbed, one was clubbed with a battery-loaded sock, and another woke up to find himself in flames.

"Word better be around by now," a Puerto Rican with two tears tattooed on his right cheek told the group of five youths as they stood together on the yard. "Ace passed the reins to me—you all know that. That means we got to carry it on if we want to keep what's ours. Anybody messes with that thing in the wheelchair, they messing with us. And nobody gets to do that, am I speaking the truth?"

Five fists came together in unspoken agreement.

And no matter how deeply he sank into the Thorazine lake, no matter how many times they injected him, Rhino heard the same words, over and over. "I'll come back for you, brother."

Months passed. Cain was officially listed as an escapee still on the run, although a better description would have been "vanished."

Ace had abandoned any hope of earning an honest living. But prison had taught him a trade. A well-paying one.

"I made sure nobody would mess with him, but I could give a fat rat's ass about that monfucious, whale-scale pal of yours," he sneered. "And this deal you got . . . it's gonna cost us, big-time. You want to explain that to me, my brother?"

Cain nodded slightly, as though pondering the question. In reality, buying time. The bottom line, he concluded, was simple enough: he had to go back for Rhino. In some part of his work-in-progress mind, he understood that he had no choice.

Just as he knew that Marlon C. Cain no longer existed, he knew that the freshly minted assassin standing before him wasn't bound by any promise of his own. But even as a teenager, the man who would be known as Cross for the rest of his life had known what buttons to push. He'd spent his whole life learning the lessons. And paid an immeasurable tuition before he passed the course.

Cross had already paid a well-connected lawyer to track down Rhino's institutional history. The monster had told the truth—he had never even been charged with a crime. The lawyer had told Cross that springing Rhino was a piece of cake—no court was going to tolerate what had been done to that "child." But that could take years. And even though a much faster route was available, it would take a lot of cash to grease those wheels. More cash than Cross could hope to accumulate by his low-level, low-risk thefts.

He had stared flat-eyed into the face of a lawyer who made his living representing truly deadly men. And the lawyer blinked. Obliquely, he told Cross that he was about to start trying a big criminal case. A mob guy was accused of shooting a rival. The mobster had a dozen people supporting his alibi, but there was this one pesky witness, a civilian who had been walking past when the street-side killing went down. If something were to happen to that witness, the case would collapse. And the lawyer then would have time to work on poor Rhino's case. Pro bono, of course . . .

"When I first started to cut down his Thorazine, it was—"

"Yeah," Ace interrupted. "I got that part. You needed those humongous arms to saw through the bars."

"I told him," Cross went on as if Ace hadn't spoken, " 'I know you're not a retard, and I know you're not crazy. Just nod your head if you understand me.' And he did. He nodded his head."

"Ain't that special?" Ace remarked sourly.

Cross continued to hold Ace's eyes, going on with his story. "So I asked him, 'Do you hate them?' And he nodded again."

Ace didn't say anything to that, keeping his silence because he knew what was coming next, the same question Cross had asked him during those first long nights in the Isolation Unit.

"I asked him, 'Do you hate them all?' And Rhino nodded again. That's when I said, 'Then you're my brother.'"

Ace looked away, then looked back at Cross, pursing his lips thoughtfully.

"You got the address of that witness?" he asked. "Man like that, he's probably fool enough to step on the third rail when he could have just taken a cab, specially with all that rain coming down like it is."

IN THE back room of Red 71, the one shielded by a thick curtain made up of carbon-black steel ball bearings on wire strings, Cross spoke to the assembled crew. "This Ronni girl, we'd never have a problem with her, not if things weren't all messed up by that punk. *He* was the problem. But now *she's* the one who's dangerous to us. She's not on our side of the law, which means we can't know what she's going to do next. We don't know when he told her he'd be back. She's probably used to him lying, so that's no big deal . . . for now. But he didn't take any of his things—that's the clear message to this girl that he *expected* to be coming back. She's going to wait, but not forever. Then she goes down to the precinct and reports her boyfriend is missing."

"The police ain't gonna give a damn," Ace said. "Especially about no fancy-dress nigger."

"And he's an adult, they're not married, and there's no proof of him being the victim of foul play," Cross agreed. "But he wouldn't have been with her at all if she wasn't bringing in money. If he's not there to *take* that money from her, she's going to have a pretty nice pile. More than enough to pay some PI to have a look. We don't want that."

"She is not a wrongdoer," Tracker said, solemnly.

"That's right," Rhino chimed in.

Princess didn't say anything, but Cross knew setting him in motion was ruled out as soon as he'd heard Rhino cosign Tracker's statement. Sensing the atmosphere in the room, Cross smoothly changed direction. "But I've been thinking. You guys're probably right. It's not like she *knows* anything."

Cross and Ace exchanged the same look they had just before Ace blew away that pesky eyewitness so many years ago.

I still don't get it, Ace thought, as he had many times. *The man didn't look like anything special when we was just kids, and he paid all that money for plastic surgery to look like* another *kind of nothing?*

BUDDHA DROPPED Tracker off, leaving just himself, Ace, and Cross in the car.

"If she gets hit outside her place, no way the cops don't toss her apartment," Buddha said.

"Probably divide all that punk's stuff up between themselves, too," Ace said, more to voice his opinion of police ethics than with any actual hope there would be nothing left that traced back to the "player," whom nobody but his mother would miss.

"Tracker said it was just one of those cheap condo-conversions. No doorman, no security, no cameras."

"So we can get in and—what?—carry all his stuff away?"

Cross just shook his head at Buddha's sarcasm.

"Come on, boss. He's probably got some kind of record, and even if we took every single thing of his, there'd still be his prints, his DNA . . . ."

"Man, you in *love* with that big-bang stuff, huh?" Ace said.

"The right tool for the job, that's the rule," Buddha defended himself. Lamely.

"What we need is a fire," Cross said.

"*And* a homicide? Yeah, no way the cops ever make *that* connection."

"You guys want to let it go?"

"Damn!" Ace snapped. "You know we can't do that."

"So . . ."

The car was quiet for several minutes.

"If she was *in* the place when the fire started, and she couldn't get out . . ."

"The whole building? We can't—"

"Tracker said it was really a bunch of two-flats, in the shape of a horseshoe. And she's got one of the end units."

"Still. Pretty hard to contain a fire that tight," Ace said.

"No reason to," Buddha answered. "So Long says that most of the people who bought into those crappy condos would *love* it if they burned down. Some of them have already walked away. The others, even if they're *not* upside down on their mortgage, they'd have their units insured for way more than they're worth."

RONNI CLIMBED wearily out of her leased Camry. Another miserable night. She still hadn't heard a word from Jean-Baptiste. And . . .

Her thoughts were cut short by the neatly dressed white man. And anything she was about to say stuck in her throat when the man said, "Jean-Baptiste wanted me to come by and give you something," as he took a small, neatly wrapped box from his coat pocket. "But you have to promise you won't open it until later—he wants to be there himself, to watch you do it."

Oh God! That's the right-size box for a ring, Ronni thought. Her mind was still swimming as the man accompanied her to her second-floor unit. He placed the little box on the night table next to the cordless phone, and turned to leave.

Ronni followed him, so she could close the door after he left. Suddenly the man whirled and drove a fist deep into Ronni's abdomen, taking the breath from her lungs.

When she came around, she was seated, handcuffed to a chair, and gagged with duct tape carefully circled around a thick pad of gauze.

Another man was there, too. A short man with dark hair and dead eyes. He tied off a vein in her left arm, and smoothly injected a go-home shot of damn-near-pure heroin. As soon as she slumped, he began to create a series of injection tracks, not only in both arms, but even between her toes, using a needle designed to create scarring. The police autopsy would note the track marks as "aged."

The two men removed the duct tape and handcuffs, gently placing Ronni under the bedspread, her head on a scented pillow.

"The people downstairs gonna be leaving for work in a few minutes."

"I know," Cross said. "And it'll be light soon, too." He lit a cigarette from the pack he found in Ronni's handbag. Then he spilled an entire can of Roach-Murder so that the trail ran from the half-kitchen to the bed. Leaving the can where it had been, under the sink, Cross distributed the contents of three more throughout the closet, leaving the door open. Those cans went into a black plastic bag.

As the two men slipped away, the flame trail had already begun.

"Let the marshals look for some 'accelerant' now," Buddha said as they drove away. "Ace was right—this one's gonna be written up as just another dope fiend who fell asleep with a cigarette in her hand."

"Yeah," the man in the passenger seat said. "Accidents don't make decisions—they just happen."

THE SHARK CAR slowly crawled the length of the block. Guided only by its running lights, mufflers on maximum choke, it was a barely discernible presence.

"Black on one side, Latin on the other," Ace said.

"But not *one* gang, either side?" Cross asked, in the manner of a man who wanted to make very sure a jury-rigged "bridge" of slatted timber would hold his weight.

"Not even close, brother. The blacks all the same tribe, but what they know, they don't show. Fools no different than they was back in the day—all about colors they wearing, not the color they *are*."

"Latinos even worse," Buddha added. "Even if all the PRs could get it together, they're out of luck now that MS-13 is supposed to be setting up shop. Those locos get their supply straight from the Zetas. And La Eme is sticking a toe in the water, too. Now, that's just business—so why get into a no-win war with the Norteños when they could just roll west?"

"So this block is, what, like some kind of neutral turf?"

"Worthless turf," Ace corrected. "There's no shortage of spots to sling dope in this town, so who needs *this* block, all full of civilians like it is? And if any pimp put his girls out here, the first condom some housewife spot in the street, you *know* the mayor's phone gonna be ringing off the hook."

"And that's *taxpayers* calling," Buddha echoed. "Which means voters. Which means trouble."

"You think So Long's play would work?"

"Why not?"

"Man wasn't asking you, bro," Ace said to Buddha. "You not exactly what us colored folk likes to call 'unprejudiced,' you see where I'm going?"

"She fronts the money," Cross said to Ace. "Every dime. And even with that army of crooks she calls brokers and lawyers, there's no way to record a deed in this city without leaving a trail."

"True."

"And she can't even cut the price she says a buyer paid—nobody's going to be buying for cash in this neighborhood, so there'll be recorded mortgage liens on everything."

"So what's the problem, then?"

"We know where to find people for just about anything in Chicago, right?"

"Sure."

"Yeah? You know where we could find an honest contractor?"

"YOU SAID I could have a dog!" Princess said petulantly.

"A dog, sure. But that . . . thing is insane," Cross answered, tilting his head in the direction of a huge white Akita with a black head who was doing his best to rip his way through the bars of a heavy-gauge steel cage.

"You want him, he's yours. No charge," said the outlaw who specialized in training attack dogs for those who were always expecting unexpected visitors. "Some security-guard company had him. He tore three of them *up*. He's probably been shot with tranquilizer guns more than all the psychos running around inside Kankakee put together."

"And you took him why, then?"

"Well, *look* at him. That's damn near a hundred and forty pounds of muscle. He's faster than a cobra, too. Problem is, he's ten times as mean."

"He's beautiful," Princess said.

The trainer said nothing. He hadn't stayed alive all these years by opening his mouth. Despite four grand juries, each of which had granted him full immunity, not a word of actual testimony had ever passed his lips. And he'd seen Princess walk over to one of his assistant trainers who'd just hit a Doberman with a "control stick." A few seconds later, the assistant trainer was out of breath. Not from running, from the punctured lung, already pooling with the blood that would soon choke him to death.

"He started it!" was all the maniac with the pansy paint had said. The trainer didn't know exactly what that meant, but he wasn't about to ask. That was one of his specialties, not asking. The unremarkable-looking man who occasionally visited always brought a big supply of bone meal with him. "A donation" was what he called it.

"Rhino . . ."

"Just go and *talk* to him, Princess. Don't touch him. Don't go in the cage. Just talk to him and—"

"See if he wants to be friends, right?"

"Right."

The bodybuilder's arms were so overmuscled that he couldn't walk without holding his biceps away from his body, giving him a rolling gait that didn't affect his balance. The closer he came to the caged Akita, the quieter the dog got.

Princess squatted down so his face was right against the chain link, level with that of the dog's, who was now on all fours.

"*¿Quiere usted ser mi amigo?*" Princess asked. As he had asked every man put against him in that cage in Central America years ago, ever since he'd been captured as a child. The snare was supposed to hold a jaguar, but the boy had almost torn his way free by the time the rifle-bearing killers reached the scene. They weren't certain exactly what kind of feral beast they had snared, but they immediately realized it was worth more money than any taxidermist's creation would be.

Princess had endured what followed. Finally declared "*¡Listo! ¡Listo perfecto!*" by the sadists who were "training" him—anything to avoid actual combat with their own creation—Princess was thrown into the cage while still a boy.

But Princess never wanted to fight—he wanted only to be friends. That wasn't an option in a world where the only law was Inevitability. So, when the other fighter—fully aware of the rewards of victory and the price of defeat—would launch into an attack, Princess would overcome his disappointment long enough to fracture a skull, or snap a spine . . . whatever it took to make the fighting stop.

"He started it!" began as his internal cue to create instant mayhem. Later, it became his war cry. Still later, his explanation. The only thing that remained constant throughout all those years was the final result.

Princess didn't like what he called "mean people." Captured as a child, trained by bloodlust savages, he still had a child's innocence. That changed forever one night. He had been riding next to Buddha and seen a gang of thugs attack a couple who had left a gay bar and went down the wrong street hand in hand. Princess relentlessly questioned the crew's driver, repeating, "But *why*, Buddha?"

Once he understood what Buddha had been telling him—that those men had been attacked simply because they were homosexuals—Princess asked, "But how could they tell? That gang, I mean?"

Buddha patiently explained that the gang needed some visual cues, the more outrageous the better.

From then on, Princess out-flamed Little Richard. It didn't always work, but quite a number of gay-bashing gangs had overlooked the man's obvious size and power under the instantly erased assumption that "fags won't fight."

After that, it was the hospital for the lucky ones. Once they learned what had happened to the *unlucky* ones, silence was the survivors' only option. They'd never seen *who* jumped them, but it had been at least a dozen of them.

Word got around. Not only to the gay-bashers, to the police. That's when Detective Mike McNamara, the man other cops called "King of the Confession Coaxers," was brought in. "We need to know what's happening to these gangs," the chief had told him.

"Why?"

"It's a *crime*, goddamnit! And we've had a lot of citizen complaints about it."

Some politician's son must have gotten himself crippled for life, McNamara thought, but kept his face expressionless.

"Look," the chief said, "you know we've given you a *long* leash, Detective. You don't share your informants. You don't even register them. You roam around Cook County like you don't even have a precinct. One day it's Stony Island, the next, you're in the projects. You snatch cars out of the asset-forfeiture pool whenever you want. We don't even say a word when you go all over the damn world to fight in those tournaments—"

"The International Police and Fire Games."

"Whatever. Those are supposed to be for amateurs, and you fought pro for years while you were on the job and never said a word to anyone."

"I always used my vacation time. And the Games aren't

for amateurs. The Russian team does about as much police work as I do competitive crocheting. All they do is train."

"Look, all I'm asking you to do is find out what's going on, okay? I know you can. So let's just say I'm asking you for a personal favor."

"I'll do my best," McNamara said. And walked away before he said something he'd regret.

USING HIS single-malt voice—that uniquely Irish way of speaking that could sound so lyrical and carry so much threat on the same breeze—McNamara succeeded in piecing together a description of a man who would be too overdeveloped for a comic book.

One visit to Red 71 had answered the question McNamara had been planning to ask Cross when he spotted Princess shooting pool with Rhino. *Good Sweet Jesus!* McNamara thought. *That's got to be him.*

Recognized by Rhino, McNamara crossed himself as if entering church, and was rewarded by a nod. In the back room, he found Cross, Ace, and Buddha. Whatever they had been discussing was of no interest to him.

"That guy out there, the one playing pool with Rhino?"

"What?" was all Cross replied.

"He's been ID'ed."

"By who?"

McNamara laughed. "Whoever's been busting up the gay-bashing crews, the chief wants them."

"DOA work for you?"

The detective moved his head a quarter-inch.

THE FOUR young men whose bodies had been unceremoniously dumped in a lot behind a Wilson Avenue flophouse were all known to the police. Records ranging from armed robbery to felonious assault.

"Why would *those* guys get into fag-bashing?" the chief asked.

"They probably got paid," McNamara answered.

It was the truth. The paymaster had been Cross. A meeting place had been set just outside the Badlands to lay out the job.

After that, the only thing left was transportation to the dump site.

And Princess was told he had to give up his hobby for a while.

"I'M NOT letting that damn dog ride behind me," Buddha said. "He decides the back of my neck looks good to him, then what?"

"Sweetie wouldn't hurt you, Buddha."

"*Sweetie!* You named that—"

"Don't hurt his feelings," Princess said, solemnly. "He's very sensitive. Besides, he's going to ride in my lap, so you don't have anything to worry about."

Buddha exchanged a look with Cross.

"Don't look at me," the crew leader said. "Remember, this whole thing was your wife's idea."

"THIS ONE," Buddha said, nosing the Shark Car into the front yard of one of the five houses So Long now owned. He kept rolling around to the back. "It's got the best sight lines."

"Now, me and Rhino—"

"Will you wait a damn second?"

"It's okay, Princess," Rhino assured the ridiculously over-muscled child, reaching a serving-platter-sized hand from the back seat to pat his shoulder. "We'll do it just like we practiced. But Buddha has to turn the car around first."

Buddha wheeled the Shark Car in a half-circle so it was facing out. He tapped one of the four parallel lines made up of different colored LED panels. A very faint hiss accompanied the trunk as it slid open a couple of inches. Only then did the two men get out.

Rhino grasped the handles protruding from a seven-foot-wide roll of CarbonSkin, pulled it free, raised it above his head, and snapped his wrists. The CarbonSkin—a carbon fiber product converted to a clothlike material—unfurled across the top of the car. Princess caught it at the front and gently lowered it into position.

"Damn!" Buddha said, impressed despite his natural tendency to belittle anything concerning his beloved street beast. "It's gone."

"The CarbonSkin is a light-eater," Rhino explained. "At night, even if you hit it with a flashlight, it would look like a shadow."

"But what happens if I have to blast out of here?"

"There's a tear panel right here," Rhino said, tapping

gently. "The car will go through it like an ice pick through tissue paper. And, no, it won't harm the finish."

"How many of these have we got?"

"A couple, just in case. But if you're not in a hurry, Princess and I can lift this one up high enough for you to back right in again."

"THAT MUCH?" Cross spoke into a burner cell, taken from the anti-magnetic locker in which several dozen such use-it-and-lose-it tools were stored.

"Yeah."

"Want to come to—?"

"No. Just this side of the border."

"One hour."

"Yes," said the one cop in all of Cook County who was guaranteed to lock you up if you offered him a bribe. The cop clicked off his phone—a heavy chromed job retrieved from a dope dealer's ornate SUV—and tossed it out the window of his white Crown Vic, the most unmistakable "unmarked" in the city.

THE SHARK CAR pulled up to the rusted-out semi-trailer resting on its axles that marked the entrance to the Badlands, then spun into a bootlegger's turn, leaving it facing any incoming traffic.

"How in hell can they *do* that?" whispered a kid whose Afro-Asian blood mix had guaranteed he'd never be adopted, despite the promises of the group home's social worker.

Another prisoner—which is how all the residents of that place thought of themselves—had told him where to find the Badlands, sealing a pact that they'd make the jump together.

But when the time to make a run for it came, the kid had found himself alone. Not for the first time. He decided not to wait for a bus he knew was never coming, and he'd been a permanent resident of the No-Name Crew ever since.

"That's Buddha," Condor said, using the voice of an experienced pro schooling an amateur. An amateur who'd already shown he had the guts, but was way short of the smarts he'd need to be a real asset. "He can make that monster car of theirs *dance*, A.B."

"I never saw anything like that, even in the movies."

"You're never gonna, either, little brother."

"I shouldn't ask?"

"Sure. You can always ask. That's the only way you learn. But that's *listen* and learn, understand?"

"No arguing, you're saying?"

"Right. Look, remember when Dino asked you where your name—'A.B.,' I'm talking about—where that came from?"

"Yeah."

"And you told him, right? You're Asian, and you're Black. So that would be 'A.B.' all by itself. But it's also two things the AB inside the Walls hate, so it's like a spit on them, too. Anybody ask you any more questions about your name after that?"

"No."

"Because . . . ?"

"Because they don't know how it is in there."

" 'They' is right. 'They' ain't *me*, see my point?"

Both teens immediately stopped talking as they heard another car approach. When the Crown Vic came into view, A.B. said, "That's a—"

"Not here it isn't," Condor corrected him, in an even lower whisper.

"Then what the—?"

"What did I just tell you?"

McNAMARA SLID out of the Crown Vic as smoothly as water flowing, the movement barely visible even to the watching teens.

The Shark Car's passenger door hissed as Cross stepped out. As he walked around to the front, McNamara said, "Buddha."

"Mac" was the driver's only response.

Both Cross and McNamara walked a short distance in the direction of the semi. As if by mutual consent, they stopped so they were close enough to one another for a side-mouthed whispered conversation.

"Your new dancer, she works for the feds."

"What?"

"You hard of hearing now? They popped her for moving weight almost four years ago. Been running her ever since. She's given them just enough to keep herself on the street and out of Wit Sec, but somebody high up is pulling the strings on this. They got bigger game in mind."

"Me?"

"Yeah."

"*Just* me, or—?"

"They figure, cut off the head, the snake dies."

"So now we're a CCE?"

"Yep. Continuing Criminal Enterprise—that's RICO to the max. But that's not her assignment. Ever since someone—more like some*thing*—turned the MCC into a slaughterhouse, they've been looking at you."

"They always—"

"Looking *hard*, okay?"

"I have to connect the dots on this?"

"No. Whoever's running her told your new dancer that if she got some *serious* info on you, she could walk. And keep walking. But if she didn't, she was going Inside. Looking at twenty-plus."

Played the player, Cross thought to himself. *And got him killed in the same move.*

"But she hasn't gotten enough yet?"

"Hasn't got a damn thing. Remember, we're not talking about crimes, not really. They could take you down anytime if that's all they wanted. And there's not exactly a lot of places to plant a wire on her when she's working."

"But if I was to see her outside . . . ?"

"Yeah."

"And she was to thank me for something . . . even something I didn't have anything to do with . . . ?"

"Bingo."

"That's a hard game, bingo. Lots of numbers to cover. Lots of cards, and lots of people playing. Besides, there's people I did work for—not in this country—that they wouldn't want to come out."

"You know a lawyer named Temestra?"

"Enough to know *he* knows some people."

"Yeah. About three years back, I got some maggot to confess to 'inappropriate sexual conduct with a minor.' "

"Nothing new for you."

"This is: the appellate court overturned the case. Said I had been 'overzealous.' You know what that sounds like."

"Sure."

"It wasn't anything *like* that. What I did was allow the scumbag to smoke in a no-smoking building."

"What?"

"There's no smoking allowed in the lockup. Especially not in the interviewing rooms. I could see the guy was climbing walls, and he hadn't lawyered up, so I just asked him if he'd like a smoke."

"And Temestra took on that guy's case? And *that's* what the appellate courts threw it out on?"

"Like I said."

"Could he have afforded a lawyer of Temestra's weight?"

"Not in a hundred years."

"So he had something they wanted. And he'd want more than just some cash in return."

"That'd be my guess."

"Nice talking to you," Cross said, stepping back.

The teens—by then, at least twenty of them were scattered behind the fence—watched as the cop climbed back in his car. As soon as he left, Condor called out, in a barely audible voice, "Buddha?"

"What?" the man behind the wheel of the Shark Car answered.

"Can I show my crew the card trick?"

"I only play for cash, kid."

"Just this once?" Condor half-pleaded.

"Do it," Cross said as he climbed in the passenger seat. "Give Condor some face—he's earned it."

"Ace of hearts," Buddha called out.

Less than two minutes passed before the setup was complete. Condor had placed a playing card in an open slot in the chain link, the heart symbol facing the Shark Car. And Buddha had smoothly assembled the perfect-tolerance .177-caliber single-shot pistol, its tiny night-beaded front barrel buried inside the heavy baffling that acted as the bedding material.

"Nobody being stupid?" he called out.

"Not a chance," Condor assured him, stepping up to the chain link so the playing card was about four feet to his left. "Everyone get off the side. Nobody behind the card. The shot's gonna *carry*, understand?"

No sound was heard, but the playing card flew off its perch, fluttering like a broken-winged bird.

"Dead center!" came a muffled call out of the darkness.

"When I tell you I know something, it *means* I know something." Condor, reasserting his authority, his voice still low but on full-carry.

The Shark Car glided off, as smoothly and deadly as its namesake.

ARABELLA ANSWERED the sequence of taps on the door to her apartment by blindly throwing it open. She knew that Cross wouldn't need a key to bypass the downstairs security camera, and that her towel-wrapped body wouldn't distract him.

But the woman who strode into the apartment was something else. In every sense of that term. Her height was exaggerated by blue stiletto heels, but her body needed no exaggeration, especially since it was wrapped in a single piece of same-shade blue spandex. But even the pair of throwing knives strapped to one muscular thigh didn't draw Arabella's eye from the Amazon's thick mane of orange and black stripes.

Tiger! ran through Arabella's mind. *So this is her, for real.* She dismissed the rumors that all the stories about her were just that . . . stories.

Tiger snapped her hip, slamming the door closed behind her.

"Your roommate won't be back for a while," she said, smiling.

"How . . . how do you know that?"

"Those FBI debriefings, they take a lot of time."

"She said she was—"

"Stop it, you silly little brat. She said her name was 'Taylor,' too. And her man had been beating on her so bad she just *had* to get away."

"She was lying?"

"You just get into town, or what?"

"But even Cross—"

"Was what? Fooled? Then what am I doing here?"

"I . . . I don't know."

"You know a lot of things, but you're good at keeping your eyes closed, aren't you?"

"I don't understand what you're saying. I never thought . . . I mean, when *I* came to the Double-X, I was running myself. That was almost three years ago. I heard word that if there was any safe place in Chicago for a strip-per, that was it."

"Uh-huh. And you heard it in the Orchid Blue, right?"

"Well . . . I guess so."

Tiger stepped to Arabella, snatched the towel off her still-damp body, and said, "You weren't running from any man."

"So?" Arabella snapped back. "How is it your business who I—?"

"Sit!" Tiger snapped at her, pointing to a leather couch.

Without knowing exactly why, Arabella did as she'd been told.

"Now, listen, because I'm only going to say this once. You can't be all sugar and spice unless you get paid. And it doesn't have to be in money."

"What—?"

"Shut your mouth," Tiger interrupted. "Unless you want it slapped. Or even if you do."

Arabella crossed her legs and threw the woman standing over her a little pout, running her tongue over the lower lip.

"You can tell when a girl's a true bi. And you already found out that this Taylor's not, haven't you? I know she'll do whatever you think she should be doing, but her heart's not in it. Tell me I'm wrong."

Arabella shook her head, as clear a "no" as she could manage without speaking.

"You thought—what?—she'd come around?"

Arabella answered the question the same way she had the last one.

"But she's kind of trapped, yeah? I mean, all her stuff's in some storage unit—it wouldn't fit in a little place like this. A one-bedroom, right?"

Arabella nodded again, but this time in the affirmative.

"One bedroom, one bed. And she even made the first move."

Another nod.

"You stupid little twit. Now the *federales* know everything about you. Where you live, where you work, the taxes you never paid, the nose candy you keep for special occasions, whose numbers are in your phone . . ."

Tears welled in Arabella's big eyes.

"Poor baby," Tiger sneered. "All you wanted was to be a friend to some helpless girl whose man was beating on her, and this is the thanks you get."

"What should I—?"

"You must have wanted that," Tiger said, as the sound of her slap was still echoing. "When I want you to speak, I'll tell you."

Arabella clasped her hands, looked down at her own freshly shaved triangle, and didn't make another sound.

"She played you like a piano. In your case, that would be a *baby* grand. No matter what you do now, she's going to keep that pipeline open. You kick her out, the next knock on your door will be men with badges. You can wiggle and jiggle all you want, they're still going to take you in. Anything happens to her, you're going to be on the hook for it. There's only one way out."

"What?" Arabella said, risking another slap. Or inviting one.

"You're going to die."

"No! I wouldn't ever—"

"You're a disgrace to lipstick lesbians everywhere, you know that? You're not *really* going to die, you little fool. But *she* is. In your cute little Mercedes. It's going to be blown up. All they'll find inside is what's left of two burned-out bodies. They can play CSI until their eyes fall out, but the skeletons are going to match. Yours and hers. Size, age, all that."

"When is this—?"

"She'll be back here by around five. You're both working the eight-to-four tonight. Just get in your car and drive over to the joint. Park where you always park. After that, you're gone."

"Gone to where? I don't have any—"

"The 'where' is Alaska. And you'll go back to being a redhead. With a surgical scar from when they took your appendix out."

"They're going to cut me?"

"It's called plastic surgery," Tiger told her. "The very best. When they're done, you'll look like you're sixteen, even up close. You get a good ninety days to heal up, make sure everything's just right. Then you get fifty grand. Not a penny more. Plus, transportation to Alaska. You spend three years working there, you'll be rich. You want to come back then, that's fine—nobody's going to be looking for you."

"I don't know what to say. Don't I have any—?"

"Other choices? Sure, you can decide if I leave now, or take you back to that bedroom first and show you a few tricks."

"EVEN LOW-GRADE morons would know they couldn't plant someone inside our crew. Or a bug inside Red 71. So the closest they could hope to get would be a dancer inside the Double-X. What they want is a better look at us—who's on our team, how we operate. People like them, they're always looking for a handle . . . so they can twist it."

"The feds?" Buddha asked, his slightly slanted eyes narrowing. "You think they're still after that . . . whatever the hell it was?"

"If *it's* not going to stop, why would they?" Rhino said, his tone as reasonable as his statement.

"It will never stop." Tracker spoke for the first time that night. "I hired on with that federal team for my own reasons. They needed my skills—that is what they said. But now I know what they really needed was a man with a direct connection to what they were hunting."

"That's why you went back to freelancing?"

"No. I left them because they lied. They wanted a specimen, they said. Because that . . . thing was a threat to our race. As you said, Cross: the *human* race. But it came to us that it was a threat to only that part of our race that we ourselves see as the enemy. They . . . it . . . I don't know: it is not a friend to us. But not an enemy, either."

"And that's why they wanted *me* in," added the man who had lived up to his name "twice over," unaware that he was lightly brushing his fingers across a tiny scar on his right cheekbone, just below the eye. An undecipherable mark too small to see in the mirror, it only glowed when it burned.

That symbol had been branded on his face as he and the first mixed-race army ever assembled inside a federal jail had battled together against . . . something. For most of the fighters, it had been a battle to the death.

Cross never questioned anything he knew would prove to

be beyond his understanding. But that very knowledge—that some things were beyond human understanding—allowed him to trust what others would call his "instincts." So he hadn't wasted any mind-time on why he had been spared by that . . . entity.

Something had been running amok inside a federal lockup, killing at will, never leaving a trace other than eviscerated bodies. But that was only the latest series of known attacks. The same method, and the same grisly calling card, had been documented all over the globe, going back at least as long as any records had survived. All the way back to cave paintings.

The government wasn't looking for a way to protect others—what it wanted was this supreme weapon for itself. Certain they could replicate anything they could study, the government-sponsored team had hired Cross to capture a "specimen." Their offer went far beyond money. Or threats. It was the promise of a Get Out of Jail Free card for his crew that had finally persuaded the master plotter to sign on.

It had been Cross's plan that resulted in a mob of prisoners ranging from white supremacists to black nationalists attacking an unseen enemy in the darkened basement where condemned men had once been led to their death. That gas chamber had been abandoned years ago, but its triple layer of protection against the leakage of the cyanide fumes was still intact.

The plan worked. A piece of whatever had been killing at will had been trapped inside the chamber. But even a capsule sealed so tightly that gas could not escape proved incapable of holding whatever had been locked inside it.

You can't kill "kill," Cross thought then.

And now.

So he didn't make any attempt to learn why that tiny blue brand burned at different times—he couldn't see it, but he could feel it. And he had come to trust it.

"Yes," Tracker said. "They knew a lot of information about you that they didn't share with me. But it wasn't you they wanted. Just as it wasn't me."

"Yeah," Buddha sneered. "We're just a pack of hired guns. Not like those holy government guys, serving their 'higher cause.'"

"It is not that simple," Tracker said. "After those who hired us did not succeed, they were . . . banished. Tiger and I, we were never part of them, so we simply got paid . . . and dismissed. They won't be using us again. But Percy, you remember him?"

Cross just nodded. That human war machine would never leave the no-uniform army he'd enlisted in for the duration . . . a volunteer for a life sentence that guaranteed he would never die of old age. But Percy was not one of "them," the core to the question Cross had asked Rhino back when they were still kids. Just kids, consigned to the hellhole where the system buried its own creations:

Do you hate them? Do you hate them all?

"I don't know where Percy went," Tracker went on. "But Tiger, she walked as I did."

"You think they know about . . . everything?" Buddha asked.

"I don't think so," Tracker replied. "But whatever they learned, they still know. It's in their system forever." The Indian took a deep, stabilizing breath, then summed it up: "Evil always casts its own shadow. It never occurred to them that the shadow they were seeking was their own."

"So what do they want with us now?" Cross asked the Indian. "We wouldn't take a job like that ever again. And if they wanted to erase us, how hard could that have been?"

"They don't want any of us to disappear," Tiger said. "We live where they can't even visit, so we're their only source of information."

"They want to *turn* us? Make us into a crew of CIs?"

"What else?" the Amazon answered.

"Confidential informants," Buddha mused out loud. "Only way you get on that payroll is if you can infiltrate. Or if you always *were* inside—like those CIA guys who handed stuff over to the highest bidder."

"There's another way," Cross said, very softly. "The cops—the detectives, anyway—they've all got CIs, too. But they don't pay them, not with money. It's more like a trade: they pass on a two-bit collar and just look the other way. So they might leave a dealer on the street, and the dealer feeds them whatever he picks up. Sometimes, it's just penny-ante stuff, but it's always got to be bigger than what the cop's letting slide.

"It's just return on investment. And if the potential return is big enough, a cop might let damn near *anything* slide. You know, something that gets him a promotion if the case is major—like nabbing a serial killer, or busting a prostitution ring with big-name clients—anything that gets the cop's name in the papers."

"Mac doesn't want his name in the papers," Buddha said. "And he's probably got more info coming his way than he can handle. But there's that one thing, that one card he always holds: you give Mac some info, you know he won't give *you* up."

"So they want to place this 'Taylor' whore inside," Tiger snarled. "And they use that dumb little cutie to vouch her in. Yeah, that *is* how they'd do it."

"She doesn't know anything," Cross said.

"Taylor? Or the little blonde?"

"Neither one. They come here, they dance, they get paid."

"Wrong," Tiger said, coldly.

When nobody responded, Tiger continued: "They weren't after information. What they wanted was leverage."

"What leverage?"

"I don't know. But Taylor, she was a probe, no doubt about that."

Cross felt the near-invisible brand burn again.

"What did you tell her? Arabella, I mean."

"Just what you said to tell her."

"So she's expecting Taylor to end up inside the charred wreck of her precious little car? And for another crisped-out skeleton that would match her own to be found there, too?"

"Yep."

"And Arabella, she's not going to run? She's ready to leave everything behind and end up in Alaska?"

"Absolutely," Tiger said, showing her brilliant white teeth in what didn't resemble a smile. "I think she even expects me to come visit her every once in a while."

Cross looked at his cheap, generic watch—the one that kept better time than any Rolex. "We've still got an hour before they're supposed to show."

"ARABELLA EXPECTS what, exactly?" Buddha asked Tiger.

"The same thing I told you the *last* two times you asked me."

"She really thinks we're gonna X-ray her, find a skeleton to match, put a driver in her car, and then blast it someplace far from here after she bails out?"

"Yep."

"All before her shift's over?"

"Like I said."

"We don't want to buy her play," Cross said. "She's a long way from stupid. The bug you planted isn't giving us anything but their blah-blah before they go to work, that's true. But if you know somebody's listening, you can keep them from learning anything."

"That's why Ace isn't here," Buddha said. "He's over there. Just outside."

"SO WE'RE down to two plays, and we got about half an hour to pick one," Cross said, holding up a cell phone to show the crew how the choice would be communicated.

"Put me down for Ace doing a double," Buddha said. "Couple of strippers dealing on the side. Didn't pay off, so the suppliers hired a hit man. He blows them both away, plants a quarter-key and a few grand around—anyplace that looks good, crib or car. Happens every day."

"Where's Princess?" Cross suddenly asked.

"He's out back. Playing with that psycho dog."

"Why do you have to be so nasty, Buddha?" Rhino suddenly squeaked. "They're . . . connected. Princess was caged, so he could fight while people watched. And Sweetie was caged because some people did some bad things to him, too."

"I stand corrected," the man with black-agate eyes said. "They're *both* psychos, okay?"

The gray jumpsuit that covered the mass that was Rhino twitched slightly. Unnoticeable, unless you were watching for it. Cross was. And Tiger was a step ahead of him.

"At least neither of them's on a leash," she sneered.

"What's that supposed to mean?" Buddha demanded.

"Ask your wife, sucker."

"Enough!" Cross said, without raising his voice. "I'm not exposing Ace like that unless there's *no* choice. And it's not the best way to cauterize this wound, anyway."

"So . . . ?" Buddha asked.

"So—we need somebody who can fit inside that little car, for openers."

"I am a *very* flexible girl," Tiger said, raising her right leg back over her shoulder and tapping the wall behind her with the toe of one shoe.

"And I'll have you covered," Buddha said, unable to take his eyes off Tiger's pose, which she apparently planned on maintaining for a while.

"Tell K-2 you're switching places with him for tonight," Cross said to Rhino.

"I don't want to—"

"How else, brother? We can't be sure what'll be left, and the last thing we need is for some eager beaver to find bullet holes in the skulls."

"It must be done," Tracker added. "And even my knife could leave a mark. . . ."

Rhino nodded his assent, his normally placid face now overlaid with an ineffable remorse.

"WHERE'S K-2?" Arabella asked, when she saw Rhino standing in the spot always occupied by the Maori. *This is the last time I'm going to think K-2's gigantic*, she thought, trying an experimental little pout without a lot of hope that it would have any effect. Normally a lot more bouncy and confident, Arabella had been feeling just a bit off center for hours. Maybe it was Taylor copping an attitude when Arabella said they didn't have time to play—being late for work wasn't an option.

Or maybe it was Taylor picking up on Tiger's scent—it hadn't come off, even in a half-hour steamy shower.

Whatever! Arabella baby-talked inside her head. *Deal with it: The "battered woman" you thought you were playing, "saving" her—sure, saving her for yourself—all the time, she was really playing you. Using you to get inside the Double-X, so she could spy on the Cross crew. You don't owe this whore a damn thing.*

The two women approached, holding hands, but were forced to separate in order to walk around Rhino's bulk. They had only taken a single step past him when they felt something like a giant crab's claw on the back of their necks. A claw that vise-gripped right through the flesh to the spinal column.

Before either could make a sound, their heads were slammed together hard enough to fracture both skulls into fragments.

Rhino released his hold, the women slumped to the floor, and Cross, Buddha, Tracker, and Tiger entered the area.

"Make sure Princess doesn't come back here," Cross told Rhino. It was a reminder, not an order—he didn't have to tell the massive creature how an emotional reaction was the last thing they needed right then.

Cross picked up Arabella's lifeless body; Tracker did the same with Taylor's. Tiger opened the passenger-side door of Arabella's little Mercedes. Taylor was bigger, so she got the passenger seat. Then Arabella was carefully placed on her lap before the seat belt strapped them both in.

Without another word, Tiger started the engine. Cross and Tracker went out the back door and into the waiting Shark Car. Cross took the passenger seat, Tracker the back.

This seating pattern had nothing to do with status—the rule was always to distribute their shooters to cover both sides, and only Buddha and Tracker truly qualified.

The Shark Car shadowed the Mercedes as it left the enclosed lot and headed toward the Badlands.

"Three-to-one that dyke gets stopped," Buddha complained.

"She's not driving fast," Cross said mildly.

"Man, any cop that *sees* her is gonna find some excuse to stop her—the way she's built, she could stop a damn clock. And with that hair . . ."

"Relax, brother. Tiger's been on jobs with us before. You ever see her not hold up her end?"

"Good one, boss."

"Cut it out, Buddha. Tiger knows this is business."

"Anyone behind the wheel can make a mistake."

"That would mean you could lose control of this car, then?" Tracker spoke from the back seat.

"Very nice," Buddha said. Whether he was addressing

Tracker's comment or admiring the short-barreled rifle Tracker had just unveiled wasn't clear.

Tracker touched a button, and his side window zipped down noiselessly.

"Acquired," he announced.

Neither man in the front seat said anything, their eyes riveted to the little Mercedes, now buzzing toward the outer edge of the Badlands like a bluebottle fly in pursuit of food.

The Shark Car kept pace, leaving enough room to maneuver should that become necessary.

Tiger went past the semi-trailer, caught the winking red dot out of the corner of her left eye, and kept going until she spotted another light. She pulled to a smooth stop in the middle of what had once been a paved street. Then she unsnapped the seat belt and, in a single motion, pulled Arabella behind the wheel and backed herself out of the little car.

Tiger moved into the passenger seat of the Shark Car as it emptied out; Buddha covered his side with his pistol; Tracker swung his scope in tightly controlled loops. Cross moved close enough to the "fence" to catch the whisper: "You move, you die," Condor warned his crew. "When they get gone, then we do, too."

Cross carried a FedEx box in both gloved hands. He placed it very carefully on the dashboard of the Mercedes and walked back to the Shark Car.

"Thirty seconds," he said as he covered the ground.

"Go!" Condor hissed at the nearest members of his gang, knowing the order would be passed along faster than anyone could run.

Just before the sound of the blast traveled several blocks

of wavelength and went audible, the azure Mercedes became a red-and-yellow fireball.

Metal, glass, wood, plastic, flesh, and bone all were reduced to the same color, that white-gray ash every crematorium worker knows by sight.

"Dust *that* for prints, chumps," Buddha said, smiling in what any street-level denizen would recognize as the "Step off or die!" advertisement of a man who didn't necessarily *like* killing . . . but didn't *mind* it, either.

ANOTHER WEEK passed before Buddha brought up what he knew would be a touchy subject. Looking around the table in the backroom office of the Double-X, he threw out a tentative probe.

"Boss, So Long says, if we don't get started on that rehab soon, we're gonna miss out on some real scores."

"This pie's gonna be sliced pretty thin as it is," Cross said sourly.

"Is that right?"

"Leave it, Buddha. Me, Rhino, Princess, Ace, Tracker, Tiger . . . Even if we pry another four hundred extra-large out of So Long, that's, what, two K for each of us?"

"Those houses, they don't need much work at all. Not to sell them, anyway."

"What does that mean?" Tracker asked.

"It means whoever buys those houses is going to have to put in a lot of work on their own. Inside work, I mean."

"You're an expert on contracting now?"

"I've done enough contracts to be," Tiger said, flashing her teeth in a sugary snarl.

"It would be fair to sell the houses pretty much as they are, provided the life-support systems are all in good working order," Rhino said, his high-pitched squeak not diminishing the seriousness of his manner.

"So Long says she can get just about anyone a mortgage."

"Probably can," Cross said. "But if we sell to people who can't make the payments, we're going to end up trashing the block."

"So?"

"So that's how this wonderful opportunity showed up in the first place. If we want to rob a bank, the time to do it is *before* they empty the vault."

"Speak English, brother," Ace said.

"Banks give mortgage money to people who they know damn well are right on the margin. Then they sell those loans the same day. Instead of risking, say, five hundred thou at seven percent, they take one point off the top and leave someone else holding the bag. It's harder to do than it once was—you know, that 'mortgage crisis' thing that still has the government printing money? It's not like Zimbabwe here, at least not yet. But I feel sorry for any chump who thinks he's going to live off his Social Security check."

"Tie it together."

"If we do like Rhino says, we're cutting the profit down so damn far we'd be better off with fire insurance."

"So Long could probably—"

"Paper fraud's not our game," Cross said flatly. "That leaves a trail. Always does."

"Then what's our move?"

"Let's get an inspector, let him check those life-support systems Rhino was talking about. If they're solid, then we can move them quick—lots of people are pretty handy with tools. But that still leaves us with those thin slices. And it doesn't do a damn thing about the *real* work we have to put in."

"What, the gang thing? If any of them try and—"

"We can't leave bodies in the street, Buddha. And we can't stay around and *patrol* the damn block, either."

"Then why did we take this deal in the first place?" Tiger said.

"Where's this 'we' stuff coming from?" Buddha snapped at her. "It wasn't your decision, you just hired on."

"I hired on for a *piece*, right? So I guess that made it my decision, too."

"Ice it," Cross said, knowing from experience how quickly Tiger could escalate. She had a temper, Buddha didn't; but either was capable of taking out the other. Like a drag race between equally matched cars—whoever got off first was going to win.

Tiger tried to cross her arms over her chest, but that was physically impossible. Buddha didn't bother looking daggers at a woman who needed little excuse to *throw* hers.

"Let me think this over for a little bit," Cross said. "Rhino, I need you and Ace for this idea I'm starting to get. So hang back, okay?"

"What am *I* supposed to do while you're having your little meeting," Tiger said, indignantly, "go work the pole?"

"You would be a *great* dancer, Tiger," Princess assured her. "You're so beautiful."

"You're not wrong about that, honey."

Princess beamed at the genuine affection he heard in her voice.

"What about us?" Buddha said, nodding at Tracker.

"You're going to the block, both of you. We're going to need to know who's doing business, and how close. If there's a buffer zone, we need to know that, too."

Without a word, Tracker stood up. Buddha followed his example, moving with a deliberate lack of speed.

"Come on, Tiger!" Princess said excitedly. "We've gotta get you an outfit."

"Princess—"

"And you can meet my puppy, too."

Tiger shrugged her shoulders, shot Cross a death-ray look, and followed the huge child out of the room.

AS SOON as the others had cleared out, Cross turned to the two men he had known since they were locked down together as juveniles.

"It comes down to this," he said. "If it's gangs that want to play turf war, there's no way we can hold that block. But if they're doing business that's too heavy for street-side, there could be a way."

"Tax," Ace said.

Cross nodded.

Rhino looked a question at the two of them.

"We could shake them down," Cross explained. "I've been thinking about this, and it doesn't add up. There's gangs on each side of that area, but none of them move in? There's only one thing that could mean."

Rhino's face showed he still wasn't following.

"The real businessmen aren't gang boys, they're mob

guys. Which means gambling. And everything that goes along with it. Bookmaking, numbers, loan-sharking, and whores anyplace they've got a casino or two. You know what I mean: looks like a low-rent dive on the outside, but it's all Vegas on the inside."

"Expansion wouldn't do them any good," Rhino squeaked, showing that he understood where this was going. "It would just spread them thin. But they're used to collecting tax, not paying it. So, if we make it hard for them to work unless they pay *us*, we could maybe negotiate some kind of deal."

"If we want them to stay where they are, we can't let them see what *we* want," Ace added.

"Yeah," Cross said. "It's just about that simple."

"There's black gangs on one side, Latinos on the other," the assassin who always checked for a pulse answered. "And you think the Outfit is cutting a few blocks out of each side? So that 'buffer' thing, it wasn't an accident?"

"The way I heard it from Mac—and the guy *he* heard it from was . . . reliable—in New York, the mob kept rolling in Harlem at least up to the end of Vietnam. They had a joint on Pleasant Avenue—some name, huh? What's important is this: Plenty of gangs in Harlem, right? They all knew what was going on, but none of them ever did anything about it. Never even *tried* to."

"Like a peace treaty?"

"Sort of," Cross answered Rhino. "But it was more about the pad than anything else. They were paying the cops, so any gang moving on them would be a suicide mission. And the gangs—black on one side, Spanish on the other, just like here—they were too busy fighting each other to really give a damn if some old white guys wanted to run a candy store.

Some of the candy the Italians kept there got so old it was rotting right on the shelves."

"Nothing like that around here," Ace said.

"You sure, brother? When the city took down the high-rises, they fractured the gangs, just like they wanted. Only thing is, they didn't break them, they just broke them *up*."

Rhino gestured a request for more information.

"Used to be—what?—five thousand Vice Lords? All under one command."

"True," Ace said. "But you coming up way short on the number. Could have been twice that, back in the day."

"And the Stones? They kept changing their name, but . . ."

"Not their game," Ace finished the line. "And most folks don't know that the Latin gangs ain't no new thing. Go far back as you want, they was organized. Zoot suits, pachucos, all self-defense. Between the cops—they had that Red Squad deal in the sixties—and the black gangs, they wasn't lying about this town, either."

"Red Squad?" Rhino squeaked.

"Sure. The Panthers and the FALN—"

"The—"

"Puerto Rican *independistas*," Cross told the giant. "They didn't get the press the Panthers did, but they were a whole lot more serious. Bombing was their specialty."

"And they didn't need to take no Spanish course when they got to Cuba," Ace added.

"Okay. But here's how it is *now*: instead of fighting over control of the South Side, or even just Englewood, now it's micro-gangs, fighting over blocks. No central leadership, no 'Main Twenty-One,' no leadership charts.

"In L.A., they break down into what they call 'sets,' but there's still some kind of broad allegiance: Crips and Bloods, La Eme and La Familia, like that. Not in this town. Nobody's taxing these little groups, and they're not paying the cops, either.

"Let me talk to Mike Mac. If I can reach him, I'll be back soon."

"WHAT?" A blunt question from a man who questioned everything. His face was a map of Ireland and told of a life spent in fight rings.

"I just want to check some things."

"Why?"

"Come on, Mac."

"I'll listen."

Cross briefly summarized what he'd told Ace and Rhino. Then said, "That about right?"

"Yeah. That's why the murder rate is so high now. One punk knows where he can get some coke—even *that's* easier now, with no one crew in charge of supply. You hear about *that*, too?"

"No," Cross said, flat-faced, ignoring that the cop had just told him he knew who was responsible for the disappearance of several local kingpins. And that those cases were never going to *be* cases as far as the police were concerned.

"Okay. It doesn't take a degree in chemistry to brew up some rock. Another punk, he's got some crappy TEC-9. Add three, four more, plus one car, and that's a gang today."

"Not looking to expand?"

"No. And that's your answer to the next question, too—they're too small-time to have anyone on their payroll. Even those killer-clowns know there's no point taking territory you can't hold. You'd lose more than the territory; you'd lose face."

"Then they're a lot smarter than—"

"Yeah. I know. Anything you want to tell me?"

"Not right now."

McNamara let out a laugh so short it could have passed for a snort through his broken-too-often-to-repair nose.

"What?" Cross said, knowing what was coming.

"Just over a year ago, a car got blown to bits out in the Badlands. Now we got another, almost the same place. Only difference was the size of the cars—and we could estimate that only because one was a stretch limo and the other was much smaller."

"Huh!"

"You think—this is just your opinion I'm asking for—those two could have been connected in some way?"

"I couldn't even guess."

"Yeah? See, if those *were* connected, it might make a little more sense. We'd have to figure it for someone trying to send a message."

"Beats a vat of acid."

"Or a river dump. And ever since the supply line got cut, all those Central American guys disappearing, the Outfit *could* decide it was time to go back into business."

"It's something they'd do. Greed rules."

"Uh-huh. I guess it's a job for the OC Unit."

"If the police figured that, I wouldn't be arguing with them."

"You're not giving me much."

"I didn't ask for much."

"You never do, Cross. But, somehow, every time I talk to you, I feel like a guy who got shorted on the split."

"I wouldn't do that. We're not on opposite sides of the table. Anyone asked, I'd say we were friends. You?"

"Depends on who was asking," the cop said. He turned smoothly and was back inside his unmarked car while his last words were still hanging in the air.

"DIDN'T TAKE long," Ace said.

"Wasn't a lot to say," Cross told the two men who had been awaiting his return. Then he quickly summarized what he'd been told.

"You think Buddha and Tracker can sniff that out?"

"If Mac said that was the scene, that's good enough for me."

Ace nodded. He didn't know how Cross and the cop they called Mike Mac had reached their détente many years back, but that glue had held for so long he'd taken it for granted that their leader could get the kind of information they needed—confirming that cops were on the take in a certain area wouldn't have violated McNamara's personal code. So when he'd said they weren't, it was taken for gospel.

"Can I ask something?" the assassin said.

Cross and Rhino reacted as one man: Why would Ace say anything like that? Ask a question? After all they'd been through. Been through *together*. What the hell was *that* about?

Ace looked from Rhino to Cross, then back again. Greeted with noncommittal silence, the man who had practiced his trade for decades, despite the short life span of others who had chosen the same path, took a breath. Then:

"I want to get Sharyn and the kids out of where they are," he said.

"Why?" Cross asked, genuinely puzzled. Sure, Ace's family lived in one of the few remaining projects in Chicago, but their safety was not at risk—nobody takes a long drink from a bottle with a skull-and-crossbones on its label. And the interior of the four-bedroom, top-floor apartment was beautifully decorated, from the plush carpeting to the sound-proofed walls. Even the inside-facing bulletproof door was a single slab of fine teak, and the Lexan windows each had a set of Levolor blinds between two panes of tinted glass. None of the kids had ever learned to sleep in the bathtub—there had been no need to teach them that basic survival skill.

"You know one thing my kids never had? A yard. I mean, a yard that was *theirs*, where they could play without some dirtbag watching them from the sidewalk. Or some punks throwing lead with their eyes closed. And my Sharyn, she's a country girl. Always growing things inside the place. But she never had what she really wants.

"She never said a word to me, but she don't have to—I know she wants a garden. Not for flowers, for food. Wants to grow her own corn, or potatoes or . . . hell, I don't know. And it don't matter. That woman deserves more than I ever gave her. She don't want diamonds and furs, you feel me? She wants some ground. That's what she always calls it, 'ground.' Wants some ground that's *hers*. Her people were sharecroppers, before I got her old man to take some cash and buy himself out.

"Now, her father, he was a *proud* man. Wouldn't touch charity, not from nothing or nobody. I had to tell him it would be a tax dodge for me, and it would belong to Sharyn when him and his woman left. All he wanted to know he already knew—I never made no baby-mama out of his daughter; I wasn't the kind of slimy punk who buys Pampers every so often and acts like it's *not* the Welfare who's feeding his own children."

Ace took a breath—for him, this was a very lengthy speech. "I want one of the houses. One of those five, I'm saying. I want Sharyn to have her garden. I want my kids to have a place to play where she don't need a damn telescope just to watch them from the windows. I don't care about no schools; Sharyn wouldn't let me send the kids to *any* public school in this town. I got the coin stashed. Maybe not the price So Long wants them to go for, but I damn sure got the price she *paid*."

"That won't work. Asking So Long for a discount would be like asking a whore for a free ride. Besides, it's too much information for her to have."

"I know," said the man whose business card was the ace of spades. His only jewelry was the 12-gauge sawed-off he always wore on a rawhide string necklace.

"How much can you put your hands on? Without going into your case money."

"Somewhere around one and a half. Damn, you know I *make* money, bro. But with all those kids . . . And if I check out before Buddha does, no way that evil little—"

"I can put my hands on two full," Cross interrupted.

"I can do better than that," Rhino squeaked. "And you only need around five."

Ace went very still. Then he held out his right hand, balled into a fist. Cross put his own fist on top. And Rhino's hand opened like a giant umbrella over both, repeating a blood oath they'd taken when they were all prisoners.

"Do you hate them?" Cross asked.

Rhino nodded.

"Do you hate them ALL?"

"Yes," Rhino said, so softly his squeak was barely audible.

"Then you're my brother," all three men said, together.

CROSS WAS on the middle drag of his third cigarette when Princess walked in, holding Tiger's hand.

"She won't wear what I picked out," the huge child complained.

"Princess," the deadly Amazon said, soothingly, "that's a Las Vegas getup. For a chorus girl, not a stripper."

"But it's so pretty!"

Cross shot Tiger a look.

"I am *not* going on any stage in a peacock-feather headdress!"

"Not tonight, you mean, right? Someday . . ."

Catching on immediately, Tiger turned to Princess. "It's a lovely outfit, baby. But it's the wrong crowd for it. Tonight, I'm saying. But for a special occasion . . ."

"All right!"

"A *special* occasion," she warned.

Princess grinned happily. "What are you guys doing?"

"Just paperwork," Rhino told him. "Ace is buying a house."

"Oh boy! It'll have a backyard and everything?"

Ace gave Rhino a look that would turn most men into jelly. "Yeah," he told Princess. "A backyard."

"Then I can bring my dog over to play with your kids! That'll be great!"

"You think I'm letting my children within a hundred yards of that—?"

"Oh, don't be such a fussbudget," Tiger said. "Sweetie wouldn't hurt a child. Would you, honey?"

For the first time, all three seated men noticed the black-headed Akita. He was in a sitting position between Tiger and Princess, as if he'd been valedictorian of his obedience-school class.

"He's pinning us," Cross said.

"Well, he doesn't *know* you, does he?" Tiger said. "Go introduce them, Princess."

The once-caged beast stepped over to the table. "This is Cross," he said, beckoning to the dog as he emphasized the gang leader's name.

When the dog approached, Princess said, "He's my *friend*. Like Tiger. And this is Ace."

As the dog was getting the scent of both men, Princess said, "And this is Rhino. You know him. He's my *best* friend. We even live in the same place. But don't worry, Sweetie. There's plenty of room for you, too."

The hyper-muscled man didn't see Tiger pull one of her throwing daggers from the sheath around her thigh, telling the others not to react if the dog growled—if anything went wrong, she had it covered.

"Go on, pat him," Princess told the seated men. "He loves that."

Cross reached down and ran his hand over the beast's head. Ace was a lot more reluctant, but he finally gave in.

"See?" Princess crowed, walking around to the far side of the three men. "Come on, Sweetie."

The monster's hand was about the same size as the dog's head, but his touch was gentle.

"I always wanted a dog," Princess said, unaware of the tears running from his eyes. "I love him."

"You should have told me," Rhino gently chided.

"I . . . I wanted to. Lots of times. But . . . I don't know."

"It's all right, honey," Tiger said, patting Princess on his right biceps. "I understand. Some things, they just take time."

At the word "time" all three seated men looked at Tiger. Her eyes widened in a deliberate parody of innocence.

"Please?" Princess said to Ace.

"That ain't my call, bro. That's up to my woman."

"Oh, Sharyn likes me," Princess said confidently. "We're friends."

"She likes her babies better, I promise you."

"That's only fair," Rhino put in.

"That's what a mother's *supposed* to do," Tiger assured him. "Protect her children, right?"

"I . . . guess," the man whose mother had sold him to a warlord at birth answered. The warlord knew the value of a baby who weighed thirteen pounds plus, but never lived to collect.

How that baby had survived for years alone in the surrounding jungle was a mystery no man was interested in investigating.

"I'm not bringing my kids to this place," Ace said, flatly. "And don't even *think* about the spot."

"Our poolroom? I brought Sweetie with me, and nobody said anything."

Cross and Rhino exchanged looks. The idea of anyone being stupid enough to challenge Princess *and* that killer dog, never mind *inside* Red 71, was too ludicrous even to contemplate.

"Okay, here's how it happens," Cross said, using a voice that accented every word with *"done deal"* italics. "After Ace gets his house, and everybody gets moved in, you bring that dog—"

"Sweetie."

"Sweetie, yeah." Ace jumped in, on the cutting edge of his patience supply. "You bring that dog over. If the kids like him, then we'll see, okay?"

"What if they don't like him?"

"Then he never comes back. One chance, that's all he gets."

"I guess that's fair. Right, Rhino?"

"Of course," the giant squeaked. "We wouldn't want anyone playing with Sweetie unless they liked him."

"Okay!"

"I'll be there, too."

"Well, sure," Princess said, not understanding what Ace had just told everyone else in the room. Tiger sheathed her dagger. Ace took his hand out from inside his coat.

A tiny orange fiber-optic dot showed above the door.

"They're back," Cross said.

BUDDHA SHAMBLED into the back room, a now habitual stride he had worked many years to develop. Anything that caused an enemy to hesitate even for tenths of a second could be a lifesaver. Or life-taker.

"I warn you, now," Condor had instructed his gang when he first took over, "their driver, this Buddha guy, he looks like a guy who don't even belong out here. And while you're still trying to figure out what he's doing, he's gonna do you, understand?"

"So he's KOS?" a tall, skinny black youth asked.

"No! Are you crazy? I'm just saying, Cross, he always gets word out to us. So we know he's coming. See that little lamp over there?"

"Yeah. Yeah, I see it, but so what? Damn thing don't work, anyway."

"Someone's always in this room," Condor said, patiently. "Not sleeping, on guard. They see that light go on, they pass word down the line."

"So how's this Buddha guy gonna fool us if we see him coming?"

Condor took a deep breath, then let it out slow. A demonstration that he was being really patient. "Buddha never gets out of the car, okay? He's the driver. So, if that Shark Car pulls up and Buddha does get out, something's wrong."

"And we do . . . what, then?"

"We don't do nothing," Condor snapped at the new member. "We wait. But we don't move. We don't talk. We don't make a sound. If Buddha's got something to say to us, he'll find a way to say it."

TRACKER SLID into the room behind Buddha, as soundless as a shadow flowing into a corner.

"There's nothing out there, boss," Buddha said. "Not on either side. Few baby-bangers, Latino to the north, Afro to the south. They're not moving on each other, so they don't need a pass-through."

"Neutral turf?"

"Nah. They ain't even *that* far advanced. Can't even throw their sign at a passing car without getting their fingers tangled."

"That all they threw?" Ace said.

"Yep."

"Maybe they didn't pick up on you," Cross said. "It's hard to see our machine at night, specially with all the streetlights busted."

"Could be they saw it coming. Even heard it. But it ain't got that right sound. That old-school rumble-coming one," Ace said.

"They are not coming for one another," Tracker said.

"How do you know that?" Tiger asked him, genuinely interested.

"We had to go several blocks *past* the one we . . . care about before there was even a sign of them. On both sides. That means it's not a neutral zone—it's like when two tribes are separated by a river too wide for them to see across. They may know an enemy is somewhere on the other side, but they have no way to get across. And if they try and fail, the river itself becomes their enemy."

"YOU TELL So Long yet?" Cross asked Buddha when they were alone.

"Tell her what?"

"That one of the houses is already sold. You've had a couple of hours. Tiger's still playing around on the damn stage, and we've got to get her home."

"Oh. Well, about that . . ."

"About what?"

"Well, So Long, she says the plan wasn't to take cash. She figured on making more out of the mortgages, I guess. You know, both ends."

"Yeah. And . . . ?"

"And she don't trust you, brother. The way she scans it, you put up the cash 'cause you already have *other* buyers lined up. For more gelt, see?"

"No, I don't see. The plan was to off-load each house for five, maybe a little more. She was supposed to take care of all of that. We just cut down her task. Squeezing extra points off the mortgages, that would be greedy and stupid. So Long's only half of that. We couldn't let her do it, anyway. Not with Ace's family moving into one of them."

"I guess that's right."

"Buddha, come on, brother. You think I trust *her*?"

"No."

"You think *she* thinks I trust her?"

"Oh, *hell*, no."

"She was going to jack us on five sales. We just cut her down to four. *That's* what she sees happening."

"Yeah, probably."

"She told us the deal. We took it. The deal was to buy the whole package for three-fifty and sell for a minimum of two point five, total. I didn't change *that* deal. And she's not gonna do it, either."

"What do *we* want one of those houses for? We already got—"

"I already told you. We don't want it. Ace wants it. And he's already put down the cash."

"Pretty risky," Buddha mused aloud.

"Buying the house?"

"*Marking* the house. Over where he was cribbed, wasn't a banger in this whole town insane enough to knock on *that* door. Word is out. *Way* out. Been that way since . . . a long, long time, boss."

"That crib's in the projects. What's left of them, anyway. This house, it's in a nice neighborhood."

"*That* block? Since when?"

"Since we started our own Urban Renewal project."

"Which we did when we made the deal, right?"

"Right."

"So Long's never going to stop giving me grief on this."

"Oh, that's just the way girls play." Tiger's voice, coming a fraction ahead of her body as she glided into the room. If she was wearing a costume, it was invisible.

"You want to get dressed, so we can roll?" Cross snapped.

"You're no fun. *You* want me to get dressed, Buddha?"

"Hell, yes! If I have to look at you for another ten seconds, So Long's gonna know."

A WEEK passed before the crew met at Red 71.

"You want to get the place all fixed up before Sharyn and your kids move in? Or . . . ?"

"You ever live with a woman, Cross? In your whole life?" Tiger said, hands on hips.

"What's that got to do with anything?"

"Sharyn's going to have her own taste. And she doesn't want to be running around like a lunatic checking on workmen, either. I'll give you ten-to-one she wants to get in the new place first, and get to the decorating later."

"Buddha could probably fit them all in one trip."

"How many you talking about?" Buddha asked Ace.

"Got two in college, three in the house. So, five, total."

"How does your wife plus three equal five?"

"You forget me, bro?"

"Yeah. Okay. Sure, that'd work. And—what?—you get the Maori Maulers to do the moving."

"Too many trips," Ace vetoed.

"So we get a big van, what's the problem?"

"Problem is, they got to go up and down a lot of stairs, a lot of times."

"Who's gonna bother *those* guys?"

"Some fool," Ace said, as if that explained everything any reasonable person could ask.

"Me, too!" Princess jumped up. "I can carry a lot of stuff."

"All right," said Rhino, before Princess could start pleading.

"I'd better go, too," Tiger said.

"You? What for?"

Tiger regarded Ace for a long moment before she said, "To make sure none of these ham-fisted males drop anything, or scratch it up, or . . ."

"I get it," Ace said, holding up his hands in an "I give up!" gesture. "And I thank you for it."

"Plus, I've got a *real* fine antenna for fools," Tiger acknowledged Ace's gesture.

"Damn, girl. I just bet you do!"

"ALL BUT one of the houses already got buyers," Buddha said. "All they need is a mortgage commitment, and So Long's got that part wrapped."

Everyone looked up. No one was all that interested.

"And the other's going to closing."

Seeing the flat facial expressions, Buddha realized the next move was his. Only Buddha never made a next move.

"So what's our next move, chief?" he asked Cross.

"Yellow to Orange."

"Like those dumbass 'terrorist' alerts?"

"Yep. Once we turn the baby gang's turf into a Red Zone, the curtain'll drop into place. And stay there."

"EXACTLY AS I tell you, yes?"

"You were right, no question," Cross answered So Long. "You caught East Garfield Park on the come. Now all kinds of people are talking investment schemes in the same neighborhood."

"The real estate people are very stupid. And very impatient, too. They say everything is location. But location, that means *nothing*. You know why? Because men are always the same, no matter where they 'locate.' They are always, how you say, 'measuring,' maybe? Who has the biggest—"

"Yeah?" Cross said, clearly not interested, speaking even as his mind replayed a movie. An old movie, always carrying the same message:

Muñoz held his already bloodied machete in both hands. He watched Cross approach, breathed deeply, and flung the machete into the wooden floor, where it quivered as if in its own death throes.

"You always wanted to know, didn't you, Cross? Any coward can fight with weapons. Only a real man fights with nothing more than his own hands. And now we see, yes?" Muñoz snarled, as his entire body flowed into a hand-combat crouch.

"No," Cross answered, pulling the trigger of his .45. The heavy slug took Muñoz in the stomach, knocking him to his knees.

Standing over Muñoz, who was writhing on the floor in horrific pain but still clawing at his sworn enemy with his hands, Cross carefully emptied the magazine of his .45 into the dying man's skull.

"YOU KNOW what I mean, Cross. Only the words they use change. Like they are using different rulers."

"Sure," he answered, hoping his one-word responses would eventually give So Long the message. He exchanged a quick glance with Buddha, who shrugged his shoulders in a "Lots of luck!" gesture.

"Men come in off the ore boats, they go to a bar and boast about all the girls they had on the other side of the lake. Makes them big, see? And men from places where they wear suits to work, they always want to know who has the biggest FICO score."

"Uh-huh."

"The money . . ."

"We had a deal, So Long."

"Yes. Good deal for you, right?"

"How's that matter?"

"Matters to me because we could do this again. Maybe many times. But, first, you have to make that block safe. Like you promised," she reminded the man who never negotiated.

"It's coming," Buddha said, stepping in before Cross said something wrong. *When it comes to So Long, the boss writes the checks, but I'm the one who has to make good on them.*

"Soon?"

"Drop me off at the next corner," Cross told Buddha.

"WHY CAN'T I play, too?"

"We need a gang, Tiger. An anonymous gang. You . . . stand out too much."

"A fight's a fight."

"There isn't going to *be* a fight. We're building a fire-break, that's all."

"So you want a bunch of guys who look like you?"

"Meaning . . . ?"

"Nobody remembers your face, Cross. They remember a tattoo on your hand. Which you change anytime you want. I don't know how you got that tiny little blue thing that shows up here," she said, tapping a long fingernail on the orbital bone under the urban mercenary's right eye, "or how you make it show up and then go away, but it's the same kind of trick."

"I still don't see—"

"An 'anonymous' gang? With Ace and Tracker and Buddha? What are you going to call it, the Deadly Diversity?"

"Nobody's going to see—"

"Rhino's too big to forget. And *nobody* forgets Princess."

"Don't worry about it. I got a plan."

"Some plan. The only part I've heard so far is no women allowed."

"You're giving me a headache, Tiger."

"Now, *that* I could fix," she said, standing up and holding out her hand.

"HERE'S THE thing," Cross told Rhino. "We never figured on Ace wanting one of the damn houses."

"We?"

"What's that mean?"

"You just said it yourself, Cross. If Ace hadn't wanted one of the houses for his family, we weren't going to do anything, were we?"

"You mean besides some street sweeping?"

"Yes. That was the deal you made with Buddha's wife."

"That was before I had everything checked out. Turns out that the only buffer we'd ever need for that, it's *already* in place. The block So Long targeted, it was never disputed turf. Nobody's moving on it from either side, east or west. And now that the block is filling up, the real estate people are selling a lot of stuff nearby. The people moving in now, they wouldn't know gang territory from their Michelin Guides, so that's one neighborhood that *is* going to change. No way yuppies are gonna live in a neighborhood that doesn't have some special name. You know, like 'Andersonville' or 'Bucktown.' If it wasn't for Ace's family, we wouldn't have to do a thing."

"So we'd be screwing So Long?"

"Somebody should."

"Cross, you're never going to be a good role model."

"I'll get over it, brother. In the meantime, let's get this 'gang' of ours put together."

"IT WAS Tiger who put me on the right track," Cross told the crew. "No way we could look like a gang, *any* kind of gang."

"So what we supposed to do?" Ace said. "Walk around in sheets and hoods?"

"Yep."

"What?!"

"You say 'sheets and hoods,' what's that mean? Klansmen, right? This isn't about race relations in Chicago, it's about us all looking the same. Only way to do that is under some white *sheets*, see?"

"I'm not being no kind of—"

"It's a *disguise*," Rhino said, his squeaky voice penetrating the fog.

"Camouflage," Tracker added.

"And now there's no reason why I can't—" Tiger began, before Cross held up his hand for silence.

"We're not going to be Klansmen. That wouldn't be scary enough for what we want. Plus, it might encourage some of those Aryan idiots to try a copycat move. That's the last thing we need. We're not looking for any kind of racial nonsense—what we want is terror, not territory."

"That *sounds* good, boss. So we're supposed to be—what? Arabs?"

"Come on, Buddha. You think I don't have a plan? How's this work for you? Remember that Zodiac Killer out on the West Coast years ago? They never caught him, right?"

"Whoever he was, he's probably under the ground by now."

"Sure," Cross acknowledged. "Doesn't matter. What made him so terrifying was that he was a *random* shooter. A psycho who couldn't stand people having sex in front of him. Like that 'Son of Sam' maniac. That's what terrorism is—you don't know what's coming, but you're sure it's coming *back.*"

"Terrorists, they hit anywhere. Maybe within a certain city or whatever. But who ever heard of terrorists who only work certain blocks?"

"What's your point?" Cross replied to Tiger.

"You're going to just roam around Chicago and blast people? I don't think so."

"We could find plenty of legit targets a few streets over."

"Some people *need* killing," Ace said.

"But we won't have to go that far," Cross said. "We just have to make a few dents on either side."

"So we *are* going to wear sheets?"

"No. Just hoods. Like this," Cross said, pulling out a crude drawing of a man in a white shirt, worn long and outside his pants. The man was wearing a black hood, with a white quasi-astrological sign on the forehead.

"That looks like Sweetie!" Princess was excited, but whether pleased or enraged was hard to tell.

"Sweetie is a purebred Akita," Tracker said quietly. "But not from Japan. Only American Akitas have a black head on a white body."

"I don't care where he's from," Princess said, his voice close to breaking. "The black portion is called a 'mask,'" Tracker continued. "So it is as though your dog was sending us a message . . . a technique we had not considered."

"Yeah!" Princess exclaimed, the trace of sadness instantly erased, replaced by his back-to-normal voice of childlike enthusiasm.

If Cross was bothered by the implication that he got his plan from a dog, it didn't show on his face.

"I DON'T like this much, boss," Buddha complained.

"What now?"

"We got the best car for this kind of work there ever was. But now we're all wedged into this . . . stupid thing."

"It's an Escalade, brother. Plenty of room."

"It's a *stolen* damn Escalade. So no way the owner isn't going to report it stolen. Even with the switched plates . . ."

"It's not stolen until he *says* it is. And he'll never know. We just borrowed it from the Valet Parking lot. Tiger's going to make sure the owner doesn't leave the club before two in the morning."

"Yeah, *there's* a good choice. She's likely to make sure the sap doesn't leave the club at all."

"Buddha," Cross said, his voice only lightly tinged with impatience, "we can't use the Shark Car. It's too valuable to risk. This way, we have all kinds of options if the wheels come off."

"What? Just pile out and make a run for it?"

"It's less than half a dozen blocks, brother. You can run that far. And who's going to chase us?"

"I still say—"

"One more block," Tracker warned, taking up his position by the rear passenger window.

Buddha downshifted, stomped the gas pedal to the floor, then slipped the shift lever into neutral as he removed his foot from the gas and killed the headlights. Despite his protests, he had prepared the drive-by car for its mission: tires pumped up to fifty PSI to decrease rolling resistance, with a quick coat of dull matte "dust" sprayed over the wheels, and the brake lights disconnected.

The claret Escalade coasted soundlessly into the next block. It was virtually invisible—all the streetlights had long since been disabled by the moronic random gunfire of the mini-gang that believed this was a way of showing face. An absolute requirement for all genuine gangstahs such as themselves.

"My side," Cross whispered. "Three on the steps of the yellow house, white jackets—"

"Acquired," Tracker responded.

The Escalade rolled on past, leaving one less gangstah on the steps—the one who had immediately dived inside the house when he saw the two on his right drop.

Buddha was already back on the throttle.

"SO WHAT did we get out of all that, boss?"

"We're not dealing with hard-core bangers here. Sure,

they're willing to shoot, but they're not fighters—it's not like we just invaded the projects."

"Still . . ."

"All we want is to push the buffer zone back a few blocks. Shouldn't take a whole lot more of this to persuade whoever's left."

"So you want me to just circle around and—"

"Yeah, why not? It's not like *that* side is gonna warn the other side. The car's already set for work, and we have to get it back before too much longer. So let's get it done."

"PRINCESS WANTED to come," Rhino squeaked from the back seat.

"It's not time for him yet."

"I know. But . . ."

"You know the plan, brother. First, we take out a couple on each side. Whoever's easiest. Okay, that's done. Half done, anyway. Next, we let them get a look at the black hoods. And if that doesn't do it, *then* we use Princess."

"*Use?*"

"What's your problem?"

"I just . . . I guess I just don't like the way that sounds."

"That is how Cross speaks," Tracker said. "He is only saying that each of us possesses skills which should be put to their best and highest use."

"As a decoy?"

"No. You are being unreasonable, Rhino. Would you be the best among us to scale a building?"

"I . . . Yeah, okay, I get it. But sometimes I just feel like we've all been used enough. No matter how good we might be at one thing or another."

"You want to—what—retire?" Cross spoke from the front seat.

"Well, we *could*, right?"

"I'm not an accountant."

"And you're not married to So Long," Buddha said, half under his breath.

"We signed on for this one," Cross continued. "So we have to finish it. After that, if you and Princess want to—"

"I wasn't saying anything like that, Cross," Rhino interrupted, his voice more a rumble than his characteristic squeak. "You and me and Ace, we made a pact. Have I ever not kept it? And, anyway, this job got a whole lot better than just money when Ace said he wanted one of the houses for himself."

"I know," Cross said, almost gently. "But I've got my obligations, just like you. We *share* those, right? And one of them is to keep Princess alive."

"What does that have to do with—?"

"That maniac would probably want to jump out of the car," Buddha cut in. "And even if he didn't, that cannon of a pistol he carries around would empty a graveyard. Couple of dead bangers taken out with nine-mil slugs, who's gonna investigate much past that? Occupational hazard. That's if it even gets reported. But a .600 Nitro Express? They'd hear *that* all the way downtown."

"Princess could—"

"Back to 'silent approach,'" Buddha said, purposely mocking the fact that the police would never go into gangland without lights blazing and sirens wailing, making sure everyone had plenty of time to stop their shooting and start running.

The Escalade entered the block in the same mask-mode it had used to slide into the territory of the other gang.

"Four on the far-left corner," Rhino said, peering through night-vision glasses.

"Try counting them now," Buddha said seconds later, putting his silenced, night-sighted pistol back on the seat as he wheeled the big Cadillac around the corner.

Neither of the two corner boys still alive saw the car depart—they were lying prone, facedown, just like the dead youths next to them.

"ABOUT TIME," Tiger snarled at Cross. "If Princess wasn't such a sweet boy, I would have had to do . . . I don't know *what* . . . to keep him from going out."

"Thanks."

"Sure. And next time, I get to—"

"If not, the time after. The job is to scare them off, not *kill* them off."

"Off is off."

"No. No, it's not. We start filling up the streets with bodies, the cops are going to have to do something, even if it's only to get in our way. We have a plan; we're staying with it."

"*You* have a plan."

"Right. I have a plan. You want to work with this crew, my plan's the *only* plan. You want to go your own way, that's your choice. *Always* your choice."

Tiger glanced from Tracker's flat eyes to Buddha's uninterested ones. Finally, she shrugged her shoulders. But even that move didn't change a single man's facial expression.

Maybe I'm losing my touch, Tiger thought, laughing inside herself as she contemplated such an impossibility.

"NOT A sound from my side," Ace said.

"Nothing in the news, either," Rhino added.

"News? Means what, bro? Newspapers, radio, TV . . . ?"

"All of that," Rhino explained, tapping his laptop. The custom-made job was scaled to the monster, weighing in at a svelte fifteen kilos. "Newspapers are disappearing. Even the ones that still publish, they all have online editions, too . . . which is probably what *started* them disappearing. Radio stations broadcast over the Net, and you can watch every TV channel there, too."

"Maybe they bury their dead?" Cross wondered aloud.

"Can't say for the Latinos, but a *name* crew would do that for sure. Only not like you mean."

Cross looked a question at Ace.

"If you in a gang with a name, they got to *maintain* their name. So, sure, they bury their dead, but not by dropping them in unmarked ground and pouring lime over the bodies before they kick dirt over them. No face in that. You *expect*, you're with a real crew, you get taken out, there's gonna be some . . . ceremony, like. Two, really. One for show: nice casket, speeches, flowers, invite his mother, limo to the cemetery. Hell, I've seen some so nice that it was enough to make a few of those stupid youngbloods in a hurry to get their own. The other is just for members—you know, pour out the 'X' on the cement with some wine, say a goodbye.

"Yeah. Only you're talking about a club with some history behind it. A name people recognize when they hear it—Vice Lords, Disciples, Stones, right? All the black crews, they pretty much do it the same way.

"Same for the Latinos. Don't know about the wine on the sidewalk, but they *really* go all-out on the ceremony . . . maybe even more elaborate than the Sicilians.

"But they don't recognize across the lines. The Puerto Ricans and the Mexicans don't mix. They'll try and one-up each other when it comes to show. The Marielitos, they seem to fit in anywhere if there's a need for enforcers. MS-13, they always leave their trademark—and it's pretty hard to haul a body away if it's been hacked into pieces. But none of that's on point here. The little crews we're dealing with, they got no name, and they're not about to challenge for one."

"What does that mean for us?" Rhino asked, genuinely curious. Although he'd done more time than either Cross or Ace—neither man had ever returned to more than temporary custody since they left so many years ago—he was the one of them who had never committed a crime prior to his first and meant-to-be-permanent incarceration. He had no concept of "gang" other than running with Cross ever since the master of subzero logic had kept him safe inside that last prison . . . and kept his promise to come back for him.

"If your whole crew is, I don't know, maybe a dozen members, tops, how are you going to bury two of them without advertising that you're down in strength?"

"True on that, my brother," Ace added. "That's why the

real clubs are always bringing in new recruits. Why they start them off so young, too."

"And they've got all kinds of incentives to put on the table—cash money, that's only part of it. What they put out there is the chance to snatch some respect. You can be ten years old, but if you're wearing the right jacket, nobody's gonna slap you around, take your lunch money."

"Uh-huh. But you got to put in work."

"So what's that gonna get you? Juvie?"

"Oh yes. That's the beauty of the system—you empty your clip, then you hand the piece off to one of the kids. Murder One, that's a couple of years for a peewee, but it's The Book for a teenager; all the jury has to hear is 'gang-related.' Could even buy you the needle, if one of your stray rounds hits a baby in a carriage."

"*Most* of their rounds are strays," Buddha said, disparagingly. "That's why they're all about the AK now. You don't have to be no marksman to hose down a block."

Rhino said nothing, but Ace caught his meaningful look and lobbed it back. "Don't be looking at *me*, now. 'Cause you missing the key point."

Rhino still did not speak, obviously waiting for the rest of the explanation.

"I'm no sniper. My kind of work, it takes one thing those long-distance guys ain't about to do. Get *close*. That's what I do. That's what I *been* doing. Ain't a fool out there don't know the Ace of Spades. Or how I come by that name. That's why I'm still in business. Most reliable game in town. You pay me, you *know* you're gonna get a body—the target's, or mine."

"You still hate them?" Cross asked the giant.

Rhino nodded.

"You still hate them *all*?"

"Yes," Rhino said, very softly.

"So what's changed?" Ace asked.

"Nothing," Rhino answered. "Nothing ever will."

THREE NIGHTS later, Cross entered Red 71 through the back entrance, working the rolling algorithm that changed the keypad sequence every twenty-four on auto-pilot. He walked into the back room soundlessly, but this was strictly from habit—if he wasn't stepping into safe ground there, no such ground existed in his world.

A low snarl so vicious that it would have turned a normal man's blood to ice and frozen him in place was just enough warning for Cross to dive, roll, and come up with his re-worked 1911 Colt .45 pointed. But before he could squeeze the trigger, he heard Princess scream, "No!" as the muscle-armored child tackled the kill-crazy Akita and took them both to the ground.

"You stop that, Sweetie! That's Cross. You know him. He's my *friend*. You can't bite my friends!"

The struggle was over in seconds. Princess kissed the beast on top of his head. "That's my *good* boy! That's my Sweetie."

Suddenly he noticed Cross had been ready to shoot. To Princess, there wasn't a lot of difference in the two possible outcomes. "You can't shoot my dog!" he warned.

"Yeah, I can. And if you'd been a second slower, I would have."

"If that's the way you're going to be, I won't bring Sweetie around here anymore!"

"Good."

The door between the beaded curtain and the back room slammed open as Rhino charged . . . then pulled up short when he realized the situation was, if not anyone's definition of "normal," at least quiet.

"Princess . . ."

"I know. I'm sorry. I only wanted to watch *Buffy* on the DVD. And Sweetie came with me. So when Cross just walked in—"

"You can't bring him back here."

"Don't worry," Princess sulked. "But I promised Sweetie I wouldn't leave him alone, so I guess I won't be coming back here at all."

"Nobody said that," Rhino told him firmly. "We'll fix something up so that anyone coming in the back will know if you're here. You *and* Sweetie, okay?"

"He's a real good dog, Rhino."

"Yeah, he's a prize and a half," Buddha said, his own pistol still in his hand.

Princess stood up, hugging the crazed Akita to his chest.

"Stop!" Cross snapped.

Even the dog was quiet.

"We can't keep this up, understand? We spent years building this place. It's our last-stand spot, remember? We have rules and regs. Nobody gets to change them."

"I didn't mean to—"

"I know you didn't," he said to Princess. "But I'd be just as dead as if you did, right?"

"No! I'd never let Sweetie—"

"Can you put the dog down, Princess?"

"Nobody's *ever* going to—"

"Put him down on the damn *floor*," Cross said, in a tone that would have done credit to Job. "Can you do that without him trying to kill any of us?"

"Sure! Just watch," the half-petulant child said, gently placing the Akita down. "Sweetie, stay!"

And the Akita did.

"I train him every day. He *loves* it. We have fun. I just . . . forgot about the back door. I'll never do it again. And he likes you, Cross. He really does."

"You know this how, exactly?"

"Sweetie told me. He likes everyone, especially you and Rhino and Ace and . . ."

"I didn't hear *my* name in there," the crew's driver said.

"Well, you're not as nice as the rest, Buddha. I mean, you're a swell guy and all. It'll just take Sweetie longer, that's all. I mean, he *already* likes Tiger."

"Yeah, well, he *is* a dog, right?"

AS THEY spoke, four men were navigating their way through the scrap yard surrounding Red 71, each dressed in some form of track suit, all carrying semi-autos at their sides, having been warned by their boss about the great variety of animals roaming at will.

"I don't see no dogs," one said.

"That ain't necessarily a good thing," another answered.

"What?"

"How you gonna shoot what you can't see?"

"What are they, invisible dogs?"

"Rocco, you'll never learn."

"I learned enough to make Captain."

"Yeah?" a third man said. "So how come you're still walking around with us?"

"I'll get it," Rocco said, grimly. "I'll get it soon enough."

"Then we'll be *your* crew, right?"

"Better hope you're not."

"There's the arrow," the shortest man said. His track suit was the most subdued of them all, navy blue, without a logo.

All eyes were drawn to the "1" in the "71" sloppily sprayed in red on the front of the concrete bunker. The "71" itself looked like the work of a palsied graffiti artist, the "1" trailing off to become an arrow. Pointing down.

"No guns," the shortest man said.

"We're supposed to walk in *that* place without—?"

"We're supposed to do what we're told," the shortest man snapped. "And Dominic was real clear—we walk in there with steel in our hands, we're not walking out."

The men started down the first flight of stone steps, as wet and damp as dungeon walls. There was no landing, just a turn into a second set of steps, which ended in the poolroom.

The tables were seriously old-old-fashioned: green felt, lit by individually hanging fluorescent lights. Wires ran across the top of each, piercing wooden disks that could be moved by a cue stick to keep track of the score for each player. The disks were natural-color oak, with every tenth one painted black.

Most of the tables were in use, but only a couple for shooting pool. The occupants ranged through every color, but no Rainbow Coalition symbols graced walls already covered with professionally lettered signs:

NO GAMBLING

NO SMOKING

NO FOUL LANGUAGE

An elderly man at the front desk was watching a small television, his chair tilted back and his feet up on an old milk crate. In that position, the green eyeshade he wore obscured his features.

"Hey!" Rocco said.

The elderly man gave no sign that he heard anything.

"Look, pal—" Rocco began, before the shortest man of the four pulled him away and took his place.

"What the hell are you—?"

The short man whispered, "The boss said no disrespect, remember? He said something else, too. You remember that?"

"Yeah, I remember."

"Okay, fair enough. You want to get tough with anybody down here, you're on your own. The boss said, anyone does that, they're not leaving. Me, I'm planning on leaving."

Rocco opened his mouth, then snapped it shut and stood off to the side.

"Pardon me," the short man said to the man behind the counter. "We'd like to speak to Cross."

"Cross?" the old man answered. "This place look like a church to you?"

"No. I mean, we need Cross—"

"You got vampires in your cellar?"

"You know what we mean, Pop. We're here on behalf of Mr. Costanza."

The man behind the counter adjusted his eyeshade to make it clear he was pointedly watching his little TV, no longer tuned to their station.

"Hey!" Rocco growled. "You hard of hearing, old man? We're from Mr. Costanza, okay? You tell this Cross that—"

"Maybe you should tell him yourself," Rhino squeaked, dropping a hand on Rocco's shoulder. His hand draped from Rocco's right pectoral, over his collarbone, and extended down to cover the trapezius muscle.

Three men turned around at the sound of Rhino's voice. Rocco didn't.

"No disrespect," the shortest man said, quickly. "Mr. Costanza said that Cross will know why we're here. If you could take us to see him, we'd appreciate it."

"Follow me," Rhino squeaked, as he snatched the top of Rocco's track suit and effortlessly pulled him off his feet, propelling the Captain-to-be forward. The poolroom went quiet, as all the men concentrated intensely on whatever they'd been doing, keeping their eyes down.

Rhino shoved Rocco through the ball-bearing curtain face-first. The others followed, parting the curtain carefully—the sound of metal on flesh was familiar to all of them.

They found themselves facing a table with two chairs that were both occupied. The backs of four empty chairs awaited. At a nod from a man on the other side of the table, three of them sat. None of them so much as glanced toward the corner where Rhino stationed himself, still holding Rocco.

"You're Cross?" the shortest man asked.

"What do you want?" a man with a bull's-eye tattoo on the back of his right hand answered.

"Uh, Mr. Costanza has a problem he needs a little help with. He sent us to explain it to you, see if you were interested."

"No," the man with the tattooed hand said.

"Just like that."

"Yeah. I know the name you dropped. Which is why you got back here at all. But nobody sends four men to deliver a message."

"Mr. Costanza doesn't go out much."

"Safer that way."

"That's not what I meant. I'm just saying, Mr. Costanza—well, you already know who he is—he wouldn't go anywhere without us. But he thought it would show more respect if we all came, see?"

"No. He doesn't want to talk on the phone, I get that. But I don't make house calls."

"How about some neutral—?"

"This is as neutral as it's going to get. If you brought enough cash with you for my consultation fee, I'll listen. If not, you all have a nice day."

"How much is—?"

"Five. But for you, ten."

"What's that supposed to mean?"

"Means you put ten grand on the table, we'll listen," Buddha answered.

"Yeah, I understand. But how come you doubled the price for us?"

"You didn't make an appointment."

"Mr. Costanza—"

"Should know better," Buddha finished the other man's sentence.

The shortest man didn't want to return without any message for his boss, but all he'd collected so far was a series of clearly intentional insults. He quickly ran through his options, finally said:

"How about if we came here to *make* an appointment?"

"To meet with who?" Cross asked, lighting a cigarette.

"Us. I mean, the four of us."

Cross took another drag of his cigarette, then said, "No."

"But—"

"We aren't going anywhere. But you are."

"I don't get it."

"You're going out. You're not coming back. Costanza wants to meet with me, he leaves the up-front cash in the rusted-out semi that stands at the entrance to the Badlands."

"Are you serious? The money wouldn't last ten seconds out there."

"I'll risk it."

"It ain't your risk. I mean, if you go there to pick up your money and it's not there, you're gonna—what?—think Mr. Costanza never had it left there for you? That's not right."

"One, you're not getting anything direct from Costanza. That's not how it works. Whose crew you with? Dominic's, maybe? Two, nobody will touch anything left in *that* semi's trailer."

"You're sure?"

Cross took a last hit off his smoke and ground it out in an obsidian ashtray—a gift from a man who knew and honored his ancestors, to one who neither knew nor honored his own.

"Yeah. All I need is a video of the cash, counted out right there, put into the envelope, and then into the trailer."

"You want us to make a *movie* out there?"

"I don't care what you do, or how you do it. A lousy cell-phone camera would be enough to handle what I just said."

"We'll make sure Mr. Costanza gets your message."

"Just make sure you get mine."

"Which is?"

"Don't come back."

"YOU BREAK anything on him?" Cross asked Rhino.

"No. He'll just have some bruises."

"When the rest of them see *those* bruises, that'll probably be the last time anyone ever takes that loudmouth's word for anything," Buddha said. "Nothing but gym muscles on his body, all the way to his tongue."

"He's not the one in charge," Cross said.

"I know, boss. But he was probably in charge of those four. The video from the front—he was the first one to step up."

"With his mouth, yeah. But it was the one in the blue outfit who got the job done. Costanza sent them over here, he'd use a buffer. None of those guys would be high enough. Doesn't matter, I still know what it means."

"What?" Rhino squeaked.

"Dominic's tired of waiting for the old man to retire. But he can't take him out without permission. And if he asks and doesn't get it, he's cooked. So he can't be seen coming in here—there'd only be one reason for that."

"He needs someone hit, how hard could that be?"

"Buddha, what he needs is a *plan*. It's got to look like the old man got himself done over something that's got nothing to do with politics."

"Politics?"

"*Their* politics. Even the oldest guy still in the game knows that *omertà* crap is only for the movies. They don't trust anyone. Why should they? Gotti was their god, but his closest pal rolled, didn't he? You want a deal, you always have to rat *up* the chain. So, if Dominic wants to pay us, it means he wants the whole thing staged. Either we come up with something that looks private—another man's wife, that kind of thing—or we let it be known that we did it."

"Let it be *known*?"

"Sure. What if, say, the old man hired us to do something—maybe hijack a load of powder—and he didn't pay us?"

"Only half of that works for me, boss. The Italians couldn't care less about some drug gang being ripped off, sure. No permission needed for that. But who's gonna believe that we put in *any* kind of work and didn't get paid in front?"

"Paid the money, sure. But what about the quarter-slice we had coming to us after they moved the package? Their mob *would* believe we'd like that deal. We don't traffic, that's known. So a big piece of change plus twenty-five percent of what the old man netted from selling it back to the same people we took it from, we'd take *that* deal. But if we never saw the last part of the payment, we'd *have* to drop him, right?"

"Right."

"That's just an example. Lots of ways it could happen. But it can't bounce back on Dominic; that's the big thing."

"I don't want to do that," Rhino said softly.

"That?"

"All these complicated things, all at the same time. All we could get would be more money."

"I'm not crazy about another war myself," Buddha added.

"There's not going to be any war," Cross assured both men. "By the way, where's Princess?"

"He said he was going to do something with Tiger."

"Shopping."

"Probably," Rhino said, shrugging his shoulders. "It wouldn't be the first time."

"Then where's that dog?" Buddha asked, glancing over his shoulder.

"Sweetie? He goes everywhere with Princess."

"What are they gonna do, leave him in the car while they go into stores and stuff?"

"What's your problem, Buddha?"

"Me? I got no problem. I was just curious, is all."

"Princess trains him all the time. That is one exceptionally intelligent animal. I looked up some stuff for Princess, and Sweetie was learning it pretty much as fast as I handed it over. If Princess tells him to stay in the car, that's what he'll do."

"Tiger lets him in the back of her car, that's her business," Cross said.

"Ah, she'd do anything that—"

"Walk soft," Cross cut him off, tuning into Rhino's frequency as he had from the very beginning, when they were both way too young to vote . . . all the way back to when Rhino weighed less than three hundred pounds.

"All I—"

"Buddha, use your head just once, okay? Can you think of a better way to keep your car from being stolen if you had to leave it in some parking garage for hours?"

"Now, *that's* the damn truth," the pudgy man said, clearly not offended. "Some of those parking-garage guys, they like to play with the cars. Check them out for money in the glove box, even play stunt driver, they get the chance. Tiger wouldn't even have to lock it. Just roll down the back windows, probably nobody'd even *park* next to it."

Cross could feel Rhino's temperature drop. The giant was a highly intelligent man, but his protectiveness about Princess sometimes overcame logic. Even knowing that Buddha had once saved the cage fighter's life wouldn't necessarily register if the Shark Car's driver let his barbed tongue cut too deep.

In the silence, all three heard the back door open.

PRINCESS ANNOUNCED his presence with, "Wait till you see what we got!" Even his prodigious strength was barely enough to carry the pile of boxes, ranging in size from micro to massive.

"You didn't get anything for yourself?" Cross asked Tiger, picturing a tall, wasp-waisted woman with tiger-striped hair and a body completely covered in white spandex prancing into a Michigan Avenue ultra-emporium with an outrageously muscled man who sported a turquoise tank top over fuchsia parachute pants. The man's eyeliner was midnight blue, his shaved head gleamed from a fresh application of moisturizer, and his makeup looked like the work of a professional. Tiger's black spike heels had orange soles; Princess somehow managed to make steel-toed combat boots work with his outfit.

"Of course I did. But Princess wouldn't let me—"

"That's good manners, right, Rhino?" the bodybuilder said. "Like you said: open the door for a lady, don't let her carry her own packages, same thing, isn't it?"

"Absolutely," Rhino squeaked.

"Damn!" Buddha said, impressed in spite of himself. "The two of you could out-spend So Long with one credit card tied behind your backs."

"Hey! These were all *bargains*," Tiger defended herself.

"Yeah? What was the total?"

"How would I know? It's not like I'm expecting a credit-card statement."

"Princess, you didn't use one of those cards we keep here, did you?"

"I wouldn't do that, Rhino. I know what those are for. I just gave the ladies cash."

"Ladies?"

"The ones who waited on us. Well, on Tiger, mostly—she picked all this out."

"How much did you—?"

"I still have money left," Princess interrupted, already on the defensive.

"Sure," Rhino said, dialing his voice to calm-down mode. "Don't worry about it."

"And you know what else? I got Tiger a present. A surprise. I was saving it for your birthday," Princess told the Amazon. "But I didn't know exactly when that was, and . . .

okay, well, anyway, here it is," he said, handing over a substantial-looking package wrapped so tightly in blazing blue fiber that it would take a skillful hand with a box cutter to open it.

Tiger looked at the package, then took it in both hands. "This is just beautiful, baby. I hate to even cut into it."

"Oh, that's all right. Buddha has a lot of it. For wrapping up the car when he wants to change colors."

"You used my . . ." Buddha's voice trailed off as he realized he was talking to himself.

"Open it! Open it!"

Tiger pulled one of her throwing daggers, gently worked the point under one corner, and slowly peeled the "skin" from the box. Then she carefully removed a heavy carton, opened that, moved aside a wadding of bubble wrap, and found the biggest semi-auto she'd ever seen. The five-pound pistol was a glistening gold color . . . and the entire barrel was done in tiger stripes.

"It's—"

"It's a goddamn Desert Eagle," Buddha said, holding his head as if a migraine were imminent. "Fifty-caliber, seven-round magazine . . . probably glows in the dark."

"That's *titanium* gold," Princess crowed. "They just got them in."

"Where's she supposed to carry that . . . thing?" Buddha asked sarcastically. "No way Tiger's gonna wear a shoulder harness. By the time she got past those—"

"I *love* it," Tiger told Princess, eyeing Buddha like a vulture watching a carcass, the *sooner or later* in her gaze unmistakable. "It's like this . . . sculpture. I can keep it on the wall, in my living room." Even in her spiked boots, she had to tug on Princess's hand to pull him down close enough for her to plant a smacky kiss on his cheek.

"I *knew* you'd like it!" the monster crowed. "See, I can shop, too!"

"Is it okay if we get back to business?" Buddha said, his voice a model of politeness. Which deceived no one in the room except the happy giant.

"WE'LL WORK it the way we always do," Cross told the others, now including Tracker, who had entered soundlessly. He was crouched next to the Akita, whispering in some language none of the others recognized. The Akita responded by lying down. Tracker scratched the beast behind one ear. Princess glowed with pride—all his hard work spent on socializing with Sweetie was clearly on display.

"We get paid by both of them? How are we going to sell that one, boss?"

"I'll handle the conversations. We need two shooters, which we've got, one distraction"—nodding his head in Tiger's direction—"and *maybe* some muscle . . . I'm not sure about that part, yet."

"Who am I supposed to distract?" Tiger said, midway between happy at being included and annoyed with her assigned role.

"Costanza. At the Double-X."

"You want me to dance every night until he shows up? You must be out of your—"

"We'll know when he's coming."

"Is that supposed to be funny?"

"Give it a rest, okay?"

Tiger sat down on the crate that the ever-gentlemanly Rhino had quickly dusted off for her. She crossed her legs and did her best to look slightly insulted. On Tiger, it looked more like a threat. Especially as she made a point of rewrapping the Velcro holster that held a pair of narrow throwing daggers around her muscular right thigh.

"Costanza can't be seen coming here. And he never knows who's watching—all those guys eat paranoia for breakfast. But he'll come to the Double-X. Maybe alone, maybe with one or two of his crew leaders. That's why I guessed that the ones we just talked to are in Dominic's crew—he's the closest to Costanza."

"That's when I—?"

"That's only if he *doesn't* come alone."

"Just lay it out, boss," Buddha said. "None of us are getting it so far."

"If you all can just be quiet for a few minutes, I will."

"YOU ARE certain?" a soberly dressed man in his sixties asked. His voice was just above a whisper, despite the total sweep for bugs performed every twelve hours by well-paid experts. In addition, noise-cancellation software was permanently programmed into the track which ran in an endless loop through the Bose CD player, placed between the two men on a face-level shelf.

"There are no other men that size in Chicago. Maybe in the world. And he talked in that squeaky voice he's supposed to have. And the tapes he gave me, I had our people look at them—they're not faked."

"How did he find you?"

"That I don't know. My *gumare* lives way out in Oak Park. No way anyone could have followed me, not in *this* city. I've been visiting her for a long time. Nobody knows, I'm sure."

"So . . . ?"

"So it's three-something in the morning. I'm walking to my car—not *my* car, the one I borrowed, just in case the feds are tracking my plates—when this . . . *thing* snatches me from behind. Grabs the back of my neck like it was a suitcase handle and *throws* me into a car. The car takes off like it was some kind of moving cloud—I couldn't hear the engine, and it didn't even bounce driving over those lousy streets around there."

"That is their car."

"Whose car?"

"Never mind. What happened next?"

"I never even thought about reaching for my hardware. Hell, I think bullets would have bounced off that monster, anyway. Then some guy in the front seat says he wants to make sure something gets to you, and I was the only man for that job. He hands me this package. The car comes to a stop. The back door opens by itself. He says, 'Out,' and you know the rest."

"You acted correctly. There are no options with those people."

"I don't know who—"

"Describe what you did after you returned to this place," the soberly dressed man instructed his underling. "Step-by-step."

"I came in downstairs. I took the package to the back. I had one of the guys cut it open. Carefully. For all I knew, it was a bomb or something, and I wasn't going to just hand it to you because some weirdos told me to—I don't answer to them.

"But inside was just these tapes. DVDs, I mean. I watched them, one by one, in the same order they were numbered. Okay, first I see four of Dominic's crew going into some building that looks like a concrete block. It's in a junkyard, and there's '71' spray-painted on it in red. Then they're talking to some old man behind a desk. Now they're in some room, talking to a guy with a big bull's-eye tattoo on—"

"The back of his right hand."

"Yeah! And they're saying that Costanza wants to meet with this guy about a job. Then it goes black. Next, it shows one of them—I don't know their names; they're not made guys, not if they're still in Dominic's crew—putting money into an envelope, and then putting the envelope itself inside some abandoned trailer. From a semi, but I couldn't see if there was a cab in front of it. That's it, except for the note."

"Yes. A very polite note: 'It is better to prevent a problem than to fix one.'"

"So Costanza's got to go?"

"Not yet. First, I have to speak with the man who wrote this note."

"You know who he is?"

"Yes. He is a man you can hire, a man with a crew of his own."

"Hire for what?"

"Anything," the older man said.

"THIS IS a strange place," the soberly dressed man said, looking out the side window of his personal car, a black BMW 7 Series, the long-wheelbase model. His most trusted lieutenant was in the front passenger seat, the wheelman was a high-ranker who normally wouldn't be playing limo-driver, but he never questioned the instructions he'd been given, considering who delivered them.

"Every place is strange if you don't know it," Cross replied from his position behind the driver.

"True. But why here?"

"So you can see the film wasn't faked. There's the semi-trailer, just ahead."

"You are the one called 'Cross,'" the older man said, pointedly looking at the tattoo on the back of the other's hand. "You work for money. How do you make money showing me that I have been betrayed? Why give me such a warning? How do you profit from this?"

"The pest control guy who comes to your house every month tells you there's rats in your cellar. You're not sure how they got in there, but you know how rats breed. So you tell him . . . ?"

"To exterminate them, yes. But this is something I can—"

"Handle yourself? Maybe. But you couldn't stop until you got all the way up to Costanza. Why call for a sit-down over that? And how could you be sure he wouldn't get tipped?"

"How can I be sure that you have not gone to some elaborate ruse to get me out here? Costanza does not have my position—which I have known for some time he wants for himself—but he has money."

"If Costanza paid me to do that job, you wouldn't be here."

"Hey, pal! That's Don Citelli himself you're talking to. You think you could—?"

The older man made a gesture to silence his lieutenant.

"You are correct. I would not be here. But not in the sense you mean. I would not be here unless I believed you wanted to talk, as you said on the phone. You may be armed. Or perhaps not. But the agreement was that I could pick you up at any place I chose. And that you would get in my car. So I am here. Not only because I believe you want to be paid, but because you have analyzed the opportunity Costanza's men brought to you."

"And because I can do something you can't."

"Yes?"

"I can take out Costanza in such a way that it would never be connected to you."

"How?"

"Trade secret."

"I should trust you, then?"

"Why would you not? You've asked around. Or maybe you already knew that if I take money for a job, that job gets done. Always."

"How much money are you talking about, here?"

Cross held up one finger.

"You cannot be serious."

"I'm always serious. How many times do you buy something that comes with a lifetime warranty?"

"You have an . . . unusual way of putting things. But that is far too much money for—"

"For total pest control. And don't waste any more of your time. If you don't want to pay the price, just say so, and we're done."

"You are a man who shows respect. I know you smoke. Yet when you step into another man's car, your nose tells you that no smoking is done in it. You could ask if I minded, but you don't do that. Instead, you don't smoke."

"This isn't a movie," Cross said, his voice devoid of inflection. "Say 'yes' or say 'no,' and I'll respect your decision. Either way."

"Half before, half after."

"I can live with that. But you sure you can?"

"What?"

"You take the deal, then Costanza's going to go. You won't know where, or how. But it will look like a personal thing, not business. If you're okay with anyone connected to you walking around with five hundred large, that's up to you. But anyone you trust that much, you sure you want to risk someone keeping an eye on him? Anyone seen with me, right after your enemy gets himself killed, that could make suspicious people certain their suspicions were justified."

"Would you mind stepping out of the car for just a few moments? You can smoke your cigarette, and I can confer with my people."

Cross responded by opening his door, stepping out, and closing it very gently—he knew that the BMW's door would finish the job on its own. He walked around the front of the car, giving all inside a view of him through the windshield as he strolled across the chopped-up concrete. Then he leaned back against a short stretch of chain link and lit a cigarette.

"We're here," a voice whispered behind him.

"You get better all the time," Cross said, dragging on his

cigarette so that even someone watching closely would not see his lips move. "I caught a tiny little movement—gold flash, maybe?—but nobody would even guess this place was occupied."

"That was Rico. New guy. Last time he'll ever wear that stupid chain."

"Just explain that I saw it, Condor. No more, got it?"

"Got it."

Cross had just snapped his still-burning cigarette away after the third drag when the front passenger window slid down.

"Okay, come on back," the lieutenant said.

In the back seat, the older man said, "You are as people say. My . . . friend in the front seat, he talks as if he is giving you orders, but you take no offense. Others might."

"Uh-huh," Cross said, his mind flashing on So Long's world-view of all men doing some kind of "measuring."

"We will have your money, all your money, tomorrow, before noon. Where should it be—?"

"You tell me. I'll take it from there."

"YOU COULD probably just blow the whole place up," said a man whose white-on-white shirt was in keeping with his suit and shoes—tasteful, and virtually screaming "custom-made."

"You're paying for a body. One body. You want to make sure none of the old man's regime come after you, that's a lot more money than we've been talking about."

"Yeah. I get it. And you just got your money. So now I'm going back to what I was doing. That girl with the stripes in her hair, me and her's gonna take a trip back to the VIP Room."

CROSS DISAPPEARED through the door behind his triangular table. He emerged in the club's backroom "office."

"We already have the old man's money locked in. And Costanza's. Half this job's already as good as done—Costanza's never coming out of the VIP Room. The others, you got their routine down?"

"Yeah, boss. Only thing is, Tracker's gotta drive, not me. This works the way it's supposed to, it's gotta be all OTC nines. Tracker's better than me at long distance, but this's gotta look like some stupid banger's drive-by—the old man always walks down the same alley before he goes into their place, through the back way."

"A drive-by in an alley?"

"Yep. No reason it can't be done, we use the right car."

"Which you have?" Cross said, knowing that Buddha would go to great lengths to avoid letting anyone but himself behind the wheel of the Shark Car.

"Right outside. The thing's a slug, but it can run on the batteries only—won't make a sound. Finally found some good use for that green crap."

"How much time—?"

"We leave now, maybe a two-hour cushion."

"Do it," Cross said.

"YOU GOT the most perfect ass I've ever seen in my life," Costanza said to Tiger. "But I'll get around to that later. First, you gotta do me right, understand?"

"Oh, baby, I'm gonna do you *perfect*," Tiger purred, licking her lips as she dropped to her knees in front of the man with deadly ambitions.

THE MORNING news—courtesy of the online issue of the *Trib*—was all about a "drive-by gone wrong." Apparently, the head of the Chicago syndicate—the word "Mafia" was no longer used without "allegedly" crowding it practically off the page, and the night editor frowned on any waste of screen space—had been killed by a group of young black males driving a 1990s-era white Oldsmobile Cutlass with oversized rims. Four men had been hit, three fatally.

Later issues made reference to the "apparent assassination" of Costanza, and the "shotgun murder" of his "underboss," a man known to the authorities as Dominic Tedesco. Several other as-yet-unidentified individuals were also murder victims, three of them taken out with a bomb planted under their car.

GANG WAR BACK IN CHICAGO!

. . . screamed the headlines the next day. The police said everything was "under investigation," but all the reporting sources made it clear that the description provided by the sole survivor of the drive-by was not being taken seriously.

If the mob wanted to bring back the good old days, it

wasn't exactly a police priority—not a single citizen had come under fire.

"They're too busy blasting each other to come anywhere near our zone," Cross told the crew. "Time for Phase Two."

"YOU STILL down with this all the way, Hector?" Cross said to a man behind the wheel of an egg-yolk-yellow '54 Buick Century coupe that had a fortune invested in slam-to-the-weeds airbags and a sound system mounted in the trunk that could cause permanent auditory damage at fifty feet. The man was a short, thick-chested Mexican with a Zapata mustache and streaks of gray in his neatly combed jet-black hair.

"There is no choice," the man replied. "We have our lives invested in our houses."

Cross knew those two houses had been acquired by a lifetime of the only work available for Hector, his wife, their three sons and two daughters, and, someday soon, the many grandchildren they all seemed to be racing to produce. Both houses were typical Chicago two-flats, one purchased many years ago, the other fairly recently. Hector and his wife had patiently waited for their next-door neighbors to default on a mortgage they never could afford, and watched from behind their bedroom curtains as the family had simply walked away from the place when their frantic phone calls to the "bank" had gone straight to an answering service. The difference between "Press One" and any other recorded option was nonexistent. They all came out the same way: "Pay up!"

Even more patience was required when the house was listed as "in foreclosure," but lenders were no longer willing to write the bogus loans that had collapsed the real-estate market . . . not without the government guarantees that had enabled them to take such "risks."

But Hector had known where to call if he wanted to borrow cash. And that he was obligating himself beyond the lien on the second house if he did. As he told his gathered family: "There is no choice."

"It's just a scouting mission," Cross now told him. "We need to see how they react to showing the flag."

"There will be no shooting?"

"Not unless they fancy a slow-moving target."

"But you do not think so, yes?"

"I do not think so," Cross agreed, making no reference to the back seat, where Tracker and Buddha watched from their respective windows.

The low-rider rumbled past the blocks, Mexicali hip-hop accenting ground-pounding from the uncorked mufflers.

"Showing," Buddha said.

"Got 'em."

Five seconds later, Tracker whispered, "Showing *only*," as another member of the mini-gang lifted his unbuttoned denim shirt to display the butt of a pistol in his waistband.

"*¡Haga fila!*" Buddha shouted out his window. "Get in line!" he translated for Tracker's benefit. "It's what you say when somebody threatens you—kind of telling them that you hear that kind of bullshit all the time. Spanish? Sure. But not Puerto Rican—Central American, like you'd hear in one of the spots where MS-13 is dug in deep."

"Another run?" Hector asked when they were well past the target blocks, approaching his own neighborhood. "I promised I would return this car in three hours."

"No, this was plenty. We want them aware they're being checked out. And confuse them, too. That's why Buddha yelled what he did: MS-13 don't do drive-bys, the Latin Kings don't speak south-of-the-border Spanish, and there's no real low-rider culture out here . . . not yet. We need to move them back, but they're not going to try going into claimed turf. And now, on their own turf, they don't have any idea who's *staking* a claim."

"They are like toothpaste in a tube, now, Cross. So where *could* they go?"

"Away," is all Cross said. And all the result he wanted.

"HAD TO snap off a couple," Ace reported to the assembled crew. "The bangers around here, they don't shoot like they do in L.A."

"What difference?" Buddha asked, genuinely curious.

"West Coast gang boys, they roll past a rival block, they just start blazing. Not looking to take anyone out—although they *will* do that if there's anyone who doesn't know enough to get down—just showing that they got heart. What *they* call heart, anyway.

"But on *my* side of town, they don't play that. They patrol, okay? Work the borders. Another gang flashes colors, they shoot. And that's to kill, not some spray job."

"So it doesn't matter," Cross explained. "Whichever gang took fire, all they'd really know is it was some *other* gang."

"They will be more alert," Tracker said.

"Alert for what? We're not going in any gang car, not on either side of *those* blocks, right?"

When no one responded, Cross handed out white sweat-shirts and black hoods with computer-generated admixtures of astrological symbols stencil-sprayed between the eye-holes.

"Hey, I didn't get one! I get one, too, don't I?" Princess demanded.

"Just me, Tracker, and Buddha on the Latin side; Ace and whoever he wants to use on the other."

"I got just the right boys," Ace confirmed.

"Why can't I go, too?" Princess demanded again.

"I can't go, either," Rhino told him. "We're both too big. That's something people might remember."

"So what's your excuse for me?" Tiger said, hands on hips.

"Same one," Cross told her. "Only you're a different kind of big."

"Very nice."

"It is," Cross said, without a trace of sarcasm in his voice. "And, Princess, we've got a *special* job for you."

"I bet," the huge man-child sulked.

"You and Sweetie," Cross added.

"Really?"

"Swear to Satan."

"You hear that, Sweetie," the hyper-muscled man said, dropping to one knee so he would speak directly into the dog's ear.

The Akita made a chesty sound.

"See?" Princess said to Tiger. "He understands words, just like I told you."

"I guess he does, baby."

"You're not thinking of—?"

"When Princess and Sweetie go, you go, too," Cross silenced Rhino.

"Want me to put on an apron, make sure the place is nice and clean when the men come home from work?" Tiger snapped.

"You're supposed to be in on that part, too," Cross answered. "But if you want to put on an apron when we get back . . ."

"You are a pig. You might even be King of the Pigs."

"Being honest doesn't make me a pig."

"That's true—you've got plenty of other qualifications," Tiger said, maintaining the distance between them in the presence of others, as she always did.

"YOU GONNA need a car?" Buddha said to Ace.

"I could *use* one, but only if you put it together. Otherwise, it's easier to just snatch one over my side of town."

"We'll build both cars," Cross said. "We want them to look the same, like they were part of a fleet."

"Matching outfits," Tiger said to Princess. "See how much fun we're missing!"

Before Cross could again start explaining that Princess would be needed for the final stage of his plan, the Amazon stuck her tongue out at him, grabbed Princess's arm, and walked them both out of the room, the Akita at their heels.

THE PROPRIETOR of the junkyard lived in his place of business. The deep-backed booth at the front gate had a bathroom, a cot, four mismatched sets of wooden chests of drawers, a large flat-screen, and a full rack of DVDs.

When he saw the Shark Car pull in just after dark, the proprietor purposefully went back to scanning his magazine—a combination of nude, nearly nude, and provocatively dressed young women, all handling some kind of firearm.

An hour later, Cross entered the booth.

"Taking two Town Cars. And we need a few hours in your shop."

The proprietor silently handed over a set of keys. The man with the bull's-eye tattoo on the back of his hand frightened him in a way he couldn't explain, even to himself. *What's the problem?* he asked himself . . . not for the first time. *He pays cash, never argues about the price, and he's been taking stuff out of here for years, with none of it ever bouncing back on me. He's even polite about it. But I heard stuff about him . . . .*

"GOT TOWED away because they weren't worth fixing," Buddha said, walking an inspection tour around the two cars. "It's not even worth swapping other engines and transmissions. This one could use a brake job, and both of them have no-tread tires and lousy shocks."

"We don't need them for more than—"

"They don't *run*, boss. We could borrow a couple from Oscar's garage. Black Town Cars are all he uses for that fleet of his."

"You mean take them?"

"From the back of the lot, sure. It's not like there's any night watchman to worry about."

"There's dogs."

"So we mist 'em, big deal."

"We only have a few hours, Buddha."

"No problemo, jefe."

Rhino caught Cross's eye, nodded his agreement.

"SAME SETUP as always," Buddha said, as he passed the glowing sign:

ALL-STAR LIMOS ☆ THE CARS OF THE STARS!

"Oscar *tries* to keep them all on the road, but there wouldn't be enough calls this time of year. Weather's too nice, and prom season's over. We won't even need the mist, we do this right. The back is nothing but old chain link with some half-ass concertina running around the top. And those cameras are just sorry fakes."

"Roll around the back," Cross said. "I know you can muffle this one down to a whisper, but we don't want to start up those—"

"Who said anything about starting them up? Let us handle this, boss. You take our car—we'll meet you back at the junkyard."

"You worked it out?"

"Yep."

"I'll just move back and cover you."

"Sure," Buddha said, turning toward the back seat of the Shark Car. "You guys all set?"

"Yes," Rhino answered, speaking for the others.

BUDDHA, TRACKER, Rhino, and Princess poured out of the Shark Car. Tracker held a long-handled bolt cutter; Princess held Sweetie's leash.

"You stay, now," Princess said. "Be a good boy."

Rhino knelt, grabbed the bottom of the chain link, and pulled gently. "We won't need to cut our way in," he said.

"Gonna scratch the hell out of the cars, but what's the difference?" Buddha said. "All we need is something to prop the fence up a few feet."

"We can just push them out," Tracker said.

"You and me?" Buddha said, incredulous at the idea of physical labor of any kind.

"Me and Tiger," Tracker said, nodding his head in the direction of the Shark Car, where Tiger had been sitting on Cross's lap to save room. The Shark Car was designed to hold the entire crew, but that was before Tracker and Tiger had been added. Even with Ace absent, Rhino and Princess reduced its carrying capacity considerably. And Tiger herself was much bigger than Ace.

"READY?" Buddha whispered.

"Just like when we do curls," Rhino said to Princess. When Princess grunted his assent, Rhino added, "Wait for Buddha."

"Go!"

At Buddha's signal, Rhino and Princess each pulled the

chain link loose from the bottom and kept pulling until a nine-foot section was the height of Princess's chest. Tiger and Tracker followed Buddha through the opening.

The pudgy man opened the door of a Town Car and hissed, "Keys inside." He pulled the gearshift out of "Park," and released the e-brake. Tiger and Tracker braced themselves, one gloved palm on the headlight cluster, the other closer to the center. Without exchanging a word, they used their legs to push the Town Car out through the back of the fence where Rhino had elevated it to shoulder height. *His* shoulder height. The car passed through without a scratch.

All three returned and repeated the same procedure. When the second car cleared the obstacle, Rhino and Princess slowly let the fence down. With Tracker and Tiger now behind the wheel of the two just-liberated cars, Princess and Rhino shoved them from behind until they were well clear of the lot.

"Sweetie, come!" Princess called softly.

The black-masked Akita hopped into the back of the Shark Car. Then three cars motored away from Oscar's place of business.

"**CHANGE OF** plans," Cross said to the proprietor's back. "We're not taking anything except a couple of sets of plates. When we come back, we'll have two more cars. Don't try playing around with the VINs, just get them crushed."

"I won't have a crew until—"

"Morning, I know. Your records are going to show the

two Town Cars sitting in your shop now were the ones crushed. You're just crushing four instead of two. I'll be back later to pay whatever that costs."

WORKING AS two teams, the crew had the stolen Town Cars covered in masking tape quickly.

"Just the bottoms," Cross told Buddha. "The tops have to stay black."

"You get outta the way, it'll get done quicker."

"YOU KNOW where to leave the car?"

"Yeah. But why don't you tell me another three, four times, me being such a dimwit and all."

"Ace will get you and the others back."

"I *understand*," Tiger said, making it clear that her patience tank was down to fumes.

"Let's ride," Cross told Buddha as he climbed into the front seat of the Town Car. Tracker had the back seat to himself.

TWENTY MINUTES later, Buddha pulled the Town Car into an empty spot at the curb. All three men pulled the black hoods over their heads.

Two blocks farther down, Tracker said, "Six of them. Right side."

"They have to see the outfits *first*. Once we start popping, they're gonna be running and ducking."

"How long a look they need?"

"Doesn't matter, as long as we start shooting before they do," Cross said to Buddha. "Watch them close."

The Town Car came to a smooth stop right in front of the six young men, all wearing jeans that sagged at the waist. They immediately flashed their warning sign—pulling their matching pseudo-silk jackets aside to display their pistols—a choreographed maneuver it had taken them weeks to master.

Cross and Tracker exited the Town Car, standing with their arms folded across their chests. Buddha took up a position behind the left front quarter panel, standing erect so his outfit was visible.

The gang froze at the strange sight. Before their leader could finish his "What the—?" sentence, Cross and Tracker extended pistols from the loose sleeves of their robes and opened fire in the gang's general direction. Four went down, two ran off.

The Town Car motored calmly away, as if it had just dropped off a fare instead of a message.

THE SECOND Town Car rolled up to the junkyard. Ace got out and walked over to the garage.

"Man, I don't see how those fool boys ever hit anything," he said. "I couldn't use my scattergun—too trademarked—so they gave me a Glock. I couldn't hit a damn elephant with that thing. But so what? All those fools are gonna remember is some men in these weird black masks opening up on them. I don't think any of them are ever gonna *forget* it, in fact."

"Casualties?"

"Probably not," Ace answered. "Couple got hit, though."

"Two on our side," Buddha said.

"Meaning the two you shot in the head?"

"Boss, you didn't say otherwise. I just free-fired, but . . . it's hard for me to miss, you know?"

"Yeah. Okay, everybody in our car, while I square up with the guy who owns this place."

"HOW MUCH do we owe you?"

"Is a grand okay? I mean, you know, it's four runs through the crusher and—"

Cross tossed a dozen hundred-dollar bills held together with a heavy paper clip onto the man's desk.

"In case you want to give any of your workers a tip," he said.

When the proprietor looked up, there was no sign of the Shark Car. Only then did he count the money the man with the tattooed hand had thrown his way.

"TOMORROW," Cross said, back at Red 71. "At Ace's house. The one on So Long's block, I'm saying. Say oh-nine-hundred—all the reports should be in by then."

"I'll take you and Princess," Buddha said to Rhino.

"And Sweetie."

"Of course," Buddha said to the muscleman, as if no other thought had crossed his mind.

Tracker and Ace both got in their own cars and moved out.

"So you're gonna take me home?" Tiger asked Cross.

"Right now?"

"When, then?"

"Whenever you say."

"That's a good boy," Tiger mock-purred into his ear, as she straddled him.

"THEY WENT to the ER," Rhino told the crew the next morning. "So the gunshot wounds were reported. That's on the Latin side. On the other side, there's nothing. Either they've got their own doctors or—"

"They're still running," Ace finished Rhino's sentence. "They got a good look at the outfits and all, but no way they take what we hit them with for white boys. They're gonna figure it's one of the major players, going on the down-low. Which means they already got the only warning they're gonna get."

"The ones you guys hit," Rhino said, nodding at Cross, "two were DOA. The others said it was some kind of Klan group, only with black hoods. One even said he saw some kind of markings on the hoods."

"You feel safe here?" Cross asked Ace. "Safe enough for Sharyn and the kids to move in, I mean. The heavy work's already done."

"Safe from *my* side, no doubt," Ace affirmed. "I can get

the word around that this whole block is off-limits in a couple of days," he went on, taking an ace of spades from his shirt pocket.

"Good enough. So now we wait a couple of days, then we seal the deal."

"So Long said nobody was backing out."

"Not *that* deal, Buddha. The buffer zone's only secure on one side, far as we know. So we stay around until we're sure. And I know just how we're gonna get that done."

"VERY NICE lady," K-2 said to Cross two days later. "So . . . polite. I know you told us not to take any money from her, but she just stuffed it in my jacket when I wasn't looking. Here it is," the Maori said, handing Cross a wad of bills.

"Keep it," Cross said. "Divvy it up with the others. Sharyn's not going to say anything to Ace. And neither am I."

"YOU UNDERSTAND?" Cross asked Princess. "All you're going to be doing is taking your dog for a walk."

"Sure!"

"Leave the pistol here, Princess."

"But . . ."

"You're just warning them. We'll be close by, but we don't want any noise that doesn't sound normal."

"It's the only way," Rhino assured him.

"Can Tiger come, too?"

"No," Cross said quickly. "We want them to run, not root them to the ground."

Tiger actually blushed.

"Okay," Princess said. "Let's go."

"SO FAR, empty," Tracker said, from his position high on a telephone pole. Too high for anyone at ground level to see that the goggles he wore were telescopic in one lens and a normal piece of plastic in the other. Anyone glancing his way would be looking at a repairman, so using the handset wouldn't draw a second glance, either.

"He's on the block itself?"

"Roger. Walking slow."

"Okay, just—"

"Action!" Tracker spoke calmly. "Hold your positions. No danger. He'll be off the block in less than—"

"We got him," Cross said.

"WHAT HAPPENED?"

"I was just—"

"He's asking Tracker," Rhino explained.

"All I could see was three of them. The Akita nailed one in the thigh. If it hit the femoral, he's going to bleed out right there. If not, he's going to need a lot of surgery—the dog tore off a big chunk.

"One of them took off faster than Usain Bolt. The third, Princess grabbed his wrist and threw him against the side of a car. He didn't get up. Probably won't."

"They yelled a bunch of stuff, Cross!" Princess immediately went on the defensive. "And I didn't do anything. It's just words, like you always tell me. So me and Sweetie were just walking. But then they ran up on us. They had knives. I thought they were going to hurt Sweetie. So I just grabbed one of them. When I looked for the next one, they were all gone. Then I saw the one that Sweetie bit. It was self-defense! They had those knives and—"

"Fools bought a ticket without checking the schedule." Buddha chuckled. "Didn't know the next stop was Dodge City."

"You did a perfect job, Princess," Cross reassured him. Turning to the rest of the crew, he said: "If either of those two never make it to the ER, so what? I can't wait for them to tell the cops that, this time, it was a *dog* they saw wearing the black hood."

"LET'S PUT it this way," McNamara said, taking another sip of his blazing-hot Dunkin' Donuts coffee. "You're not exactly on the side of the angels, Cross."

"Meaning what?"

"Whenever you do the right thing, there's always something in it for you."

"What's in it for me sometimes is doing a favor for a friend."

"I don't know what you're talking about," the hard-faced man other cops knew only by reputation. And that reputation was only magnified each time another story made the rounds.

"Sure" was all Cross said, reminding the cop he'd

known for years that the long-distance round that ended
the career of a predatory pedophile a while back had nothing to do with either of them. The predator had traded his
intimate knowledge of a kiddie-porn ring for a lightweight
sentence in a minimum-security federal prison, complete
with plastic surgery and a full set of ID to match. His last
kill had been the only child of a young couple whose home
McNamara had visited, patiently listening as they sobbed
out the pain of their loss. The fact that the grieving father
was a cop was the kind of coincidence nobody would ever
explain.

"You know, I was talking with the detective who inter-
viewed a couple of really out-there bangers last night,"
McNamara said. "Those kids must have huffed a *lot* of paint.
What a story: invaders with black hoods over Klan robes.
Okay, so maybe some local skinheads were up to no good.
But then they really went off the rails: now it's a *dog* wearing
the hood."

"What's next, space aliens?"

"*Nothing's* next. I don't know how many that gang
started with, but every one of them is going back to wherever they came from. As far away from that spot as they
can get."

"I don't blame them. That rocket the aliens rode in on,
next time it might have hit wherever they operate out of."

"Buddha *does* love fireworks."

"The Fourth is coming up. And we're all patriots."

"What's up with the new look, Cross? I've seen that one
before," he said, pointing to the back of the mercenary's
right hand, where a lightning-bolt slash had replaced the
bull's-eye tattoo. "But that thing on your cheek, how did you

get it to—? What the hell? I could swear I just saw a little blue . . . something flare just below your eye."

"Probably just the sunlight—I haven't changed anything. You getting bored, Mac? I heard you retired from fighting."

"Just taking a breather."

"Through what's left of your nose? You think a torn meniscus, no rotator cuff in your shoulder, and that titanium U-bolt that's keeping your neck straight, all that's going to heal by itself?"

"I can still—"

"I know. That's the problem. You look at the other guys competing and you say, 'I can beat them with nothing but my left.' You probably can. But you're willing to risk spending the rest of your life in a wheelchair for . . . what? Another gold medal? You've retired that trophy, Mac. Nobody's going to beat your record and you know it."

"It's not about records."

"I know—you just like fighting. And you call some of *my* guys crazy."

"I was *going* to say, I can still *train* fighters."

"Any money in that?"

"Probably not. But you never know."

"Yeah, you do. You got a lot of candidates up for the kind of training you'd put them through?"

"Not yet."

"The old days *are* the old days, Mac. Remember when you used to spar with Princess?"

"That I'd never do again. He could go five fives straight, twenty-five minutes, no rest, and he'd have plenty left. But you can't train a guy like him—you'd have to *un*train him first. Even with full pads, a helmet, and him wearing those sixteen-ounce pillow gloves, he almost killed me. I hit him with one of the best ridge hands I've ever thrown in my life and he didn't even flinch. I'm not sure you could stop him with a handgun, never mind *any* kind of strike."

"I know."

"He just doesn't get the concept of rules, Cross."

"Why would he? You know what kind of fighting he was doing when Rhino pulled him out."

"Yeah. Yeah, I do. Put him in some 'MMA' fight and he'd be arrested for homicide."

"There's no chance of that. Rhino tells him 'no' and that ends anything he even *thinks* about doing. Which is a good thing, because his idea of having fun is sometimes . . . felonious. But he's not in this for money, either."

"Neither of them, I know. This 'Tracker' you added, he's off the radar. Must have worked for the government."

"I did that. So did Buddha."

"That was a long time ago."

"Yeah. And they shred all the documents after twenty years, just like they say."

"You know what I mean. The woman—'Tiger,' right? If she's got another name, it doesn't show up."

"She's got—"

"The name she used when she visited you in the MCC? Funny, that name belongs to a baby girl. Stillborn, thirty-some years ago."

"What are you talking about, Mac? I was never in federal custody."

"I know. Like I said, you're not always on the side of the angels."

Cross felt the burn on his cheekbone, so he bent forward

and lit another cigarette to hide what he'd never convince McNamara was a bit of reflected sunlight. "So why am I here?"

"Because Ace owns a house now."

"No, he doesn't. Ace? Come on."

"You think all cops are stupid? Okay, so his woman, Sharyn, *she* owns a house. Not very far from where a lot of mayhem has been going down the past few weeks."

Cross hit his cigarette a second time. "Chicago PD's got a Gang Protection Unit now?"

"You're a laugh riot, Cross. But if there *was* such a unit, they wouldn't have a lot of gangs to protect. Not on either side of this house we've been talking about, anyway. Men wearing hoods, no way to make an ID. But that dog, if anyone—"

"Who? Animal Control? Where would they look? Besides, we've got a lawyer all ready with a SODDI defense."

"What's a—?"

"Some Other Dog Did It," Cross answered, with no change of expression.

"So—what now?"

Cross took a deep drag from his smoke, and snapped it out the side window of McNamara's white Crown Vic.

"It's done," he said.

"That right?"

"That's what you wanted to know, isn't it?"

"It'll do," McNamara said, starting up his car as a signal to Cross that their conversation was over.

CROSS WAS alone with Tiger in the back office of the Double-X. "Something's going on," he said.

"What?"

"You remember that job I got shanghaied into? The one where you visited me in the MCC?"

"I'm not likely to forget that."

"That . . . brand they put on me. The little one right—"

"Here?" Tiger said, touching the spot with a blood-red fingernail.

"Yeah. I don't know what I'm even saying with 'they.' It's not like I ever actually *saw* anything."

"You told me—"

"That wasn't a thing, Tiger. It was a . . . presence of some kind. We tried to put a name to it, but there isn't any."

"Well, it's gone now."

"No, it's not. That little blue thing, you can *see* it when it shows up. I can't, not even in the mirror. But I can *feel* it. And I felt it when I was talking with Mike Mac this morning. Twice."

"You don't think—?"

"It's got to mean something. And that 'Taylor' girl, she was on somebody's payroll, no question about that. Only we never got to ask her."

"You should have put me on it."

"On Arabella, you were the perfect choice. But that 'Taylor' girl was on a *lot* of payrolls, I'm thinking."

"More than the feds?"

"I'm . . . not sure. They'd be the logical ones, sure. They don't know what went wrong on that last operation, but they know I'm the only one left they could question about it."

"What about me? Or Tracker?"

"You hired on, remember? Probably got told some fairy tale to get you to do it. And they would've made the money good enough, too. But you weren't *there*. Not when it . . . happened. Blondie and Wanda, either they've been pumped and dumped—which is my best guess—or they're still on a payroll, only further down the ladder. Percy, that guy's barely human, but he'd be loyal to death—he'd tell them everything he knew. Which would tally with anything *any-one* could tell them, right up to the moment they sent me in."

"So they'll need a handle this time? To get you to talk to them, I mean."

"No," Cross said, lighting a smoke. "Those guys color outside the lines all the time, but what could they use? Prison? I've been there. They couldn't keep me when I was a kid, and I got a lot more resources now."

"But if you make it out, what then? You couldn't take your people with you."

"I wouldn't let them. I could disappear, but where would I hide Rhino and Princess? Buddha and Ace, they're tied to Chicago. They could get money to me, and I wouldn't need any more than that to stay invisible."

"They could lock you down so deep that—"

"Sure. And that gets them . . . what?" Cross said, hitting his cigarette lightly again. "They already know any story I felt like telling them, it'd slide right past their polygraphs. And there's no such thing as escape-proof. If one guy can build it, another guy can break it."

"Maybe . . ."

Cross took a last, quick drag, rubbed out his cigarette in the crystal ashtray on the desk. "There's one thing they can never stop me from doing, Tiger. One thing I can always do, no matter what."

"Tell me," the Amazon said, her eyes telegraphing that she really wanted to know.

"I can die trying."

"YOU THINK those . . . you think they want payback, boss?"

"I told you what happened down in that prison basement, brother. If . . . whatever it is wanted to just take me off the count, they could do it anytime they felt like it."

"But when that little thing on your face turns blue, you can feel it burn, right?"

"Yeah."

"A message, maybe?"

"I think it's more like a GPS, only a million times better. No matter where I go, they can find me. Fingerprints, mug shots, they're way past stuff like that."

"Maybe *that's* the message."

"Maybe. . . ."

"What, boss?"

"If that's the message, I got it. I hope you're right, Buddha. But it just doesn't . . . feel like that's it. I can't tell you any more than that—I don't know any more than what I said."

"Many died inside that prison," Tracker said, speaking slowly, as if working out a problem as he went along. "Whatever was doing the killing, it might have been random at first. But as it worked its way to where you and the others were waiting to try and capture it, there was no more random. A *choice* was made."

"You're saying, it made a decision to let me live?"

"It seems so."

"Why the hell would it—?"

Tracker shrugged at Buddha's question, indicating he'd already said all he had to say. All he knew.

The three men were silent for a long minute. Then Princess burst into the back room of Red 71.

"Buddha! You said we were going to go racing again. As soon as that other thing was over. You promised!"

Buddha took a deep breath to emphasize his patience.

"Sweetie wants to go, too!"

"Naturally."

"Can't we go—?"

"Princess," Cross said, gently, "you know there's no daytime racing."

"Well . . . Sure. But it's been—"

"Saturday night's the money night," Buddha explained for at least the tenth time. "That's when the cops are busiest, handling heavier business. And the racing, it's flash-mob style now, too. The location doesn't go out until an hour or two before."

"This is Thursday," Princess said.

Buddha again took a deep breath.

"So maybe this Saturday, huh, Buddha?"

"Fine," Buddha snapped. "This Saturday, okay? But not until at least after midnight."

"That would be Sunday, then."

"Will you—?"

"That's right, Princess," Cross cut Buddha off, possibly averting a disaster. "But people who go out Saturday night still think it's Saturday even when they stay out real late, see?"

"Oh. Then we'll be here at midnight on Saturday, right, Buddha?"

"Swell."

"WHAT THE hell am I supposed to do with—?"

"Just take him along. What's the big deal?"

"No big deal at all. Unless somebody 'starts something.' Then I'd need a few rounds from a ten-gauge tranq-out gun to slow down that maniac. And that dog . . . damn!"

"They don't have to get out of the car."

"But they *could*. And don't even *think* about me bringing Rhino, too. He might calm down the psycho, but I'm adding—what?—another half-ton of weight. Which nobody's gonna credit me for."

"You don't have to *win* the damn race, Buddha."

"They don't play for fun out there, boss."

"It's just money. We've got plenty. Tell you what: you put up a G—that's plenty, right? I'll pay it myself. You win, keep the cash, and just pay me back what I put up. You don't, forget about it, okay? No way you can lose a dime."

"Boss, it's gonna *cost* a lot more than a grand just to run. I got to rewrap the car—somebody might recognize it."

"How much?"

"There isn't enough," Tracker said.

Cross turned his head slightly in Tracker's direction.

"Amen," Buddha said.

Cross didn't change position.

"It is not in Buddha to lose," Tracker said, quietly. "Cheating to win would work for him. But cheating to lose, that would not be in Buddha's spirit."

"Just say a number," Cross sighed.

"That's okay, boss. Tracker just gave me a great idea."

THE SHARK CAR rolled into the gathering on the outskirts of the Badlands, now wrapped in a coat of pearlescent orange, with tiny fish scales embedded to catch any ambient light.

"When do we—?"

"Will you *please* remember what I told you? I got to *make* a race before we *get* a race. You know I got to talk to people to do that. And you know what *you're* supposed to do. Okay?"

"Okay," Princess said, just short of sulking. "But we *are* gonna—"

Buddha was out of the car and moving toward the gathering before Princess could finish whatever he was going to say.

"WHO YOU think you're talking to, some fool who wants to race on TV?" Buddha said to a tall man who was standing at the front of a refrigerator-white Mustang, arms crossed to emphasize his heavy-investment biceps. "I'm supposed to believe this is your daily driver, right? Why? Because it's got plates on it? Sure. Those headlights pop right out, don't they? How else are you gonna feed those turbos you got under there?"

"I don't run a lot of boost, so I can drive to work and all."

"You got your laptop boys handy—you can dial up any boost you want. And those fittings out back, say you're *not* gonna snap in a set of wheelie bars before you go? And that means leaving *on* that boost; otherwise, you wouldn't need them."

"I'm not trying to get over on anyone," the man said. "My car is *known*, pal. Where's yours?"

"Right over there."

"That? The orange one?"

"Yeah."

"And you want to go for . . . ?"

"Whatever you show."

"I can show five G's, if *that's* what you want."

"If that's all you *got*, sure."

Buddha walked back to the Shark Car, with the Mustang man and at least a dozen others in his wake.

"How much does that thing weigh?"

"Over seven."

"Get the hell out of—"

"Well, that's with me in it. And my passenger."

"That must be some passenger."

"Tap on the window," Buddha invited. "See for yourself."

The Mustang's owner took up the challenge, tapping the window with the knuckles of his right fist.

The glass zipped down.

"Hi!" Princess said, extending his hand.

The Mustang's owner stepped back, not interested in letting whatever in hell *that* was grab his hand. Then a warning growl came from a black-faced beast that popped its head out the same window. The entire crowd moved back.

"Want to see more?" Buddha asked.

"How about the engine?" the Mustang man said, as he hastily walked around to the front of the Shark Car.

"How about *not*" was Buddha's reply.

"I should just take your word for—"

"My headlights work," Buddha said, neglecting to mention that the DOT Xenon beams draped in an "eyebrow" pattern surrounded hubcap-sized paint peelers concealed behind blacked-out mesh. "There's no wheelie bars out back. So just assume the worst. I'll tell you this much—there's no turbo under the hood."

"Uh-huh."

"No replacement for displacement."

"And you got no bottle, either, right?"

"Got three of them," Buddha said, calmly. "A one-fifty, a two hundred, and a three."

"Jesus H. Christ," one man said. Quietly. And with genuine reverence.

"You wanna do this or not?" Buddha said.

"You leave on all that nitrous, you're gonna fry those tires," one of the other men said.

"Appreciate the advice," Buddha said. "But I didn't come here for advice—save that for your video games."

"For five grand, I get how many lengths?"

"Don't be stupid," Buddha told the Mustang man. "Just because I didn't see the trailer that hauled your ride, you really think I'm blind enough to miss that you're running a total lightweight? Yours is back-halfed for sure, maybe even a tube-chassis car. Think I didn't glom the Plexiglas? Or the missing wipers? Plastic fenders, right? So you've got turbos hauling *maybe* a ton. I got a street car, three-plus times as much weight as yours. All real, all steel, and all wheel—drive, that is. Like the man over there said, I can't *leave* on all those shots I'm packing, and I'm supposed to give *you* lengths?"

"We go on the flash," the Mustang man said grimly.

"Sure. Only we go on, say . . . *his* flash," Buddha said, off-handedly pointing at a young man standing in the gathering crowd. A man in a neon-blue jacket that matched his Mohawk.

"WHAT'S THAT for, Buddha?"

"I'm dialing in the splitter."

"Huh?"

"You remember when we stopped before? When I went out back, behind the car?"

"Sure!"

"I got a quick-change rear. Anything between 4.56 and 2.04. But that won't help if the blastoff hits all four wheels equal, okay? So—what I'm doing is dialing it so eighty-five percent goes to the rear wheels."

"Like . . . balance, right?"

"Yeah. *Just* like that."

"Buddha, do you think any of them recognized Condor?"

"Because of that Mohawk? Nah. They'll think I just picked someone who looked like they couldn't possibly be one of *his* boys. You know, because I didn't want the starter to be on his side."

"But Condor, he'll be on our—"

"Really?" Buddha cut off the man-child, even as he realized sarcasm would just bounce off Princess. *When am I gonna learn?* he admonished himself. For at least the hundredth time.

CONDOR STOOD between the two lined-up cars, a large-lensed HID flashlight in his fist. He flashed it once to the right, watched as the Mustang's driver held up a fist, indicating he was ready to go. As the Mustang's turbos whined to an ear-damaging peak, Condor flashed the light again, took Buddha's acknowledgment, and stepped back a few paces.

The Shark Car opened its muffler bypass. The ground-shaking rumble of its 14.5-liter Hemi flowed out, bouncing off the bodies of the spectators.

"*Da-amn!*" one young black man exclaimed, as if shocked. Had those standing near him known he had already placed a bet on the disguised Shark Car, they might have been suspicious. But since they'd been stunned into silence themselves, the possibility never occurred to them.

"What's that button for? The one on top of the—"

"Trans-brake," Buddha said, his eyes focused on a point at the very top of the dashboard.

Before Princess could ask another question, a tiny orange dot flared. Buddha released the trans-brake a microsecond before Condor's flash blazed.

While the Mustang still had its front wheels in the air, Buddha was a good three lengths ahead, and pulling.

The outcome wasn't close. The young Chinese man holding the videocam at the finish line wasn't asked for a replay—even the most fervent supporters of the Mustang didn't waste their breath.

A lot of money changed hands.

"YOU JUMPED!" the Mustang man yelled.

"No, *you* jumped," Buddha said, without raising his voice. "Only you didn't know it was off a cliff."

The murmuring of the crowd made it clear that any claim that Buddha had left early wouldn't get any support.

"My five grand—"

"You mean *my* five grand."

"Man, I *know* you cheated. I've got a—"

"Nine-point-five car, right? Maybe a shade under? And you just had to grab some big air, too. You brought a butter knife to a mortar fight, pal. Get over it."

Princess suddenly jumped out of the Shark Car, holding the snarling Akita on a chain that would have anchored a cabin cruiser.

"What's wrong, Buddha?"

"Seems like this guy thinks we cheated."

"We did not!"

"I know, Princess. Just calm down, okay? He knows better now." Turning to the Mustang man's backers, the always underestimated man said, "Right?"

One of the Mustang's crowd pulled away his denim jacket, making certain Buddha could see the butt of his semi-auto. But before he could launch into a speech, Buddha's pistol was out, its laser sight flaring red between the man's eyes.

"Seriously?" the pudgy man said, his black-agate eyes scanning the crowd for any takers.

A man a few years older than most of the crowd tossed an envelope of bills at Buddha. The Shark Car's driver snatched it out of the air without taking his eyes off the crowd. Or his laser sight off the gun-showing fool's white T-shirt.

He backed toward the car, telling Princess to come along

with his dog. The car exited in a sound blast, leaving a crowd of dazed men, many of whom would later remember side bets with some teenagers—teenagers who had disappeared as quickly as the randomly chosen boy with the blue Mohawk.

"You shorted him, right?" the Mustang driver said to his backer.

"Yeah. *That* would have been a smart move. If I'd known you were gonna go against the Shark Car, I would've stayed home."

"The what?"

"Ah," the older man sighed, "never mind. I wouldn't have known myself, unless I was a lot closer. That paint job . . ."

"What are you talking about?" the Mustang's driver said. "No way that guy could have fixed the race."

"Didn't have to," the old man said. "That car . . . I don't know what they have in there, but those guys, they always play for keeps."

"Who? What guys?"

"Look," the old man said, "I'm only gonna say this once. That driver, that's Buddha. And that monster with him, that's Princess. The dog, that's a new one on me. But here's the bottom line: do *not* mess with any of them, ever."

"Who the hell are—?"

"The Cross crew. Ask around, you'll get the joke." The man waited a couple of seconds. Then he shrugged his shoulders and walked away.

A few seconds later, the sound of police sirens ripped the night.

THE BACK door of Red 71 shuddered on its hinges as Princess charged into the back room, just a step behind the black-masked Akita.

"We won!" he announced. "You should've seen it, Rhino. Buddha was so far ahead of that other car—"

"Damn waste of time," Buddha told the others. "Race was for five large. After all the money I had to throw around, I *maybe* netted a couple a hundred."

"You wanted to do it," Cross reminded him, not looking up from the board where he and Ace were playing some form of chess, using no pawns.

"Yeah. Yeah, I did. But what I really wanted to do was test that wireless connector—you know, between the flashlight and the dashboard."

"Must've worked."

"Worked perfect," Buddha said. "But I didn't even need the bust. Like Princess said, it wasn't that close."

"So . . . ?"

"So I had to rewrap the car, and now I got to do it *again*, gotta refill the bottles, and—"

"You wanted to do it," Cross repeated, his eyes still on the board.

"And it was *fun*!" Princess added, taking no notice of the dour expression on Buddha's face.

DAWN WAS just starting to crack the Chicago darkness when Ace looked up from the board.

"Still a tie, brother."

"Always is."

"Where's the fool?"

"They're all out in the poolroom, except for—"

"Me," Tracker cut in, the first time he had spoken in hours.

"You know, I was raised to hate those damn things," Ace said. "Dogs, I mean. Those German shepherds they used on us down south . . ."

"You are not old enough—"

"To what, watch TV?" the slim man said to the Indian.

"Even then."

"I didn't have to see it *live*, bro. Older people did, and they passed it on. When I was coming up, pit bulls, you'd never see them. But every black man in Chicago, he'd seen those shepherds. Some way *too* up-close. And they passed that fear of them on, right down the line."

"The dog Princess has, he is not—"

"Man, I know that! But he kinda looks like a shepherd, don't he?"

"Same structure, perhaps. But they are known as *German* shepherds for a specific reason. Akitas were originally bred in Japan. Some speculate that the Axis could have been the—"

"I wonder if anyone really believed that, even back then."

"What are you saying, Cross?"

"I read a lot—"

"Man never *stopped* reading," Ace interjected. "Even when we were kids, locked up—Cross, he always had a book around."

"Here's the way I figure it would have played out." Cross spoke to Tracker, as if Ace hadn't interrupted. "The Germans had this racial-superiority thing, right? Well, you think the Japanese *don't*? If the Axis had won, one front would have fallen first. Maybe the Russians—they were the closest.

Maybe here, although it doesn't seem logical—Pearl Harbor was their best shot, and they missed with it.

"Okay, never mind that. Let's even say they *might* have tried to divide things up. But how long could *that* have lasted? The Germans were never going to leave Mussolini in charge of anything. And the Japanese were closest to everything in East Asia. Any way you slice it, sooner or later, they go after each other."

"Because each believed in their own racial superiority?" Tracker asked, frankly curious.

"No. I mean, sure, they each believed they were better—genetically, I'm saying—than any other race. But, more likely, they'd turn on each other because they'd just run out of people to kill. Even if they stayed united, they could hit Africa, but they could never *occupy* it. They'd be there forever, trapped—you can't occupy a jungle. The Middle East, now, *that* could've been a prize. All that oil. But, sooner or later, they'd end up with that same problem.

"Nobody learns from anybody else. The Russians laugh at us for trying to take over Vietnam. We laugh at the Russians for trying the same game in Afghanistan. The Chinese lay in the cut, laughing at both of us. But if they think the Japanese don't have long memories, they're as loony as that tool they made baby-king in North Korea. It used to be all about this 'arms race,' but there's probably more heavy-duty weaponry in Chicago now than anyone had on hand for World War II. And today, come on, who *isn't* nuclear?"

"Had they won, they would have killed each other," Tracker said, very quietly. "That is how the world will end. Not today, but someday. All it would take is for the wrong buttons to be pushed."

"Those buttons were pushed a long time ago, brother,"

Ace said. "I know you talking about the atomic stuff, but all that would do is speed things up. People—all of us people— we've been killing each other since we *were* people. Call it warfare, call it self-defense, it still means the same thing— you kill some of mine; I kill some of yours."

"It doesn't matter what you call it," Cross said, quietly. "The only rule is to hit first."

"And time it right," Ace said, reaching across the board with his fist for Cross to tap.

"YOU ALL moved out now?" Cross asked Ace.

"Whole family, yeah. I never liked my kids living in that place, but . . . you know."

"The whole city is shifting," Tracker said quietly. "When I first came here, there were more of my people in Uptown than on any rez. Now, mostly, we are gone."

"Why stay?" Cross said flatly. "There's no money here anymore. And there's casinos everywhere."

"That is bad money."

"Gambling is bad?" Ace said. "Since when? Come on, bro—you ever been anyplace where there *wasn't* any? You think it was just Vegas, then Atlantic City? My people couldn't live without those dream books for the numbers. And that thirst for rolling the bones, either."

"No. I say it is bad money because it makes us fat. Lazy, dependent, weak."

"I hear that," Ace agreed. "You guys get to call it a 'tribal allotment.' We call it what it is: 'Welfare.' Only don't nobody get well on it."

"When you're inside an electric fence, you don't have to see the barbed wire to know you're not leaving," Cross said.

"That's how my Moms got here," Ace said, just the faintest twinge of sorrow in his voice. "She had me, and her man left. So we went to the Welfare. You know what they gave her? A bus ticket."

"To raise a child alone in this city . . ."

"It's been done," Ace said. "But most just keep trying. You know, to make a family out of . . . whatever."

"How old were you when—?"

"Thirteen," Ace cut the Indian off in mid-sentence. "That sack of garbage, he beat on her one time too many."

"If you'd had a lawyer—"

"Like the one *you* had?" Ace half-laughed at Cross.

"That's over. Been over a long time."

"My Moms' been gone a *longer* time, brother. She didn't even get to come visit me. I thought—I was just a kid, you know—that maybe she was mad at me for what I did. By the time I found out she died just a few weeks after I stuck that 'boyfriend' of hers, I was already back on the bricks."

"And by the time we were ready to spring Rhino, you already were in business," Cross said.

"Ever since," Ace answered, again reaching his fist across the table. "And I'm not getting no gold watch when I retire."

"I AM here because we have another job," Tracker said, announcing his entrance the next night. It wasn't a question.

"Yeah. There *is* one thing I gotta take care of, back where I used to crib," Ace said.

"You're saying Big Luke's woman—she's still over there?" Cross asked.

"Yeah. And I got to make sure—"

"We only have the one house, brother."

"I know. And, big as that sucker is, it's got no room left. Kids got rooms of their own for the first time, you *know* they ain't sharing."

"Couldn't put those twins in the same house as—"

"Oh, you got that right. I got *three* boys, all of them old enough to get real . . . distracted."

"I apologize if I have been slow to understand," Tracker said. "But it is as if you are speaking in another tongue."

"Yeah. We kind of were," Cross said. "So let me run it down for you."

Clara would never know that keeping her girls safe was more than just her sacred calling; it had been a job for others, unknown to her, bought and paid for in the hardest currency there is.

There were five of them watching. Black teenagers with old eyes. Each already having proved impervious to every "rehabilitative" service the state of Illinois had to offer, from counseling to incarceration. Now they were a foul crew—wolves without the loyalty of the pack.

"Bitch packs a piece, man," one said. "Heard she shot one of the Disciples last year. Shot him cold. I cain't understand that—you'd think they'd be looking for payback, right? But . . . nothing. Maybe she got friends we don't know about."

"*All that's just talk,*" *another said.* "*But this much we know—she ain't going for no elevator jam.*"

"*All the time she been working, she got money,*" *another said.* "*Money in the house, too. I gotta get paid. She want to be stupid about that, too bad.*"

"*You see her girls? Them twins. That's what I want. Ain't nobody had any a that stuff.*"

"*Shut up,*" *their leader said.* "*Everybody get what they want outta this, we do it right. A vise, that's what we need here: come at her from both sides. Her apartment's on seventeen, right? We go up there, split into two sides, wait on the stairs. Soon's we hear that elevator open, we jump her. Take her down. Her keys won't help us—those girls keep the chains on from inside until they get the all-clear from Mama. So we make the bitch tell 'em to open the door. Then it's game time!*"

"*Bet!*" *one of the watchers said.* "*I'm gonna make them twins dance, man!*"

"*Let's move it. She making tracks now.*"

The pack split into two groups, cutting through the waste ground to reach the building before the woman did.

The leader and two of the others waited on the stairwell, their harsh breathing loud against the concrete. The leader leaned forward, opening the door a crack.

"*I can hear the cable. She be comin' soon,*" *he said.*

"*Freeze!*" *a voice whispered.* "*We hear* one *sound, you're* all *dead.*"

They turned slowly. The leader blinked at the sight of the whisperer, an unremarkable-looking white man, his back against the far wall. The dull-black Uzi in his right hand riveted their attention.

"*Hands up,*" *the man said. He walked over to the*

leader, who suddenly felt a clamp! *over the back of his neck, lifting the now terrified youth off the ground. Pain bolts shot along the leader's spine.*

"We're all going upstairs," the man holding the Uzi said. "To the roof. We're going to walk up the stairs. Nice and slow. One man's hands come down, you all die. Understand me? Die. I'm getting paid, bring you to the roof. I get paid the same, dead or alive."

The clamp released the leader, who slumped to the floor, hands still rigidly held over his head. He wasn't about to look behind him—whatever that clamp had been was something he didn't want to see.

"Walk," the white man said.

The pack was breathless as they stepped out onto the roof. The white man herded them over to a far corner. As they approached, they saw their two partners, standing with their hands high. Facing them, a blade-thin black man in a long black leather coat and a Zorro hat.

"Oh, shit!" the leader said. A visible shudder ran through his stocky frame.

The five pack members were herded into a row, their backs to the roof's edge.

The man in the Zorro hat stood before them, so finely balanced as to appear weightless in the roof's darkness. A leather thong was looped around his neck. At its end was a double-barreled shotgun, sawed off so far down that the red tips of the shells were showing.

"What they call you, boy?" he asked the leader.

"Dice."

"Dice. Yeah. Well, you just rolled snake eyes, boy. You know my name?"

"Yeah. I mean . . . yes."

"*Say it,*" *the thin man whispered.*

"*Ace.*"

"*You know how I come by that name, boy? You hear about me when you was telling stories in the dorms downstate?*"

"*Yes, sir.*"

"*Tell it.*"

"*They calls you Ace 'cause you the Ace of Spades.*"

"*Yeah, that's about right. You know what I do?*"

"*Yes, sir.*"

"*The ace of spades, that's the death card, right? Me, I make my living making other people dead. I'm a contract man, understand? I take the money, I take a life; you understand* that?"

"*Yes, sir.*"

"*Good. Now, listen. Listen real good. Listen the best you ever did in your lousy little life. That woman you was tracking? Clara? Well, somebody paid me money—good money. Told me make sure nothing happens to that woman. Nothing. Same for her girls, the twins. Get it? Now, you boys, you don't get no flak from the bangers round here. This dump ain't worth nothing now—city's gonna level it soon. So you king of this little hill. That's okay. You do what you do. But now* I *got a job for you. You want to work for me?*"

"*Yes, sir!*"

"*That's good. That's real good. Now, here's the job. You watch that lady. The way you* been *watching that lady. You watch them twins, too. And their crib. Anybody acts like they* might *be trouble, you take them out. You understand what I'm telling you?*"

"Yes, sir."

"You been watching her; I been watching you. I don't know what you see in her. Me, I see something in you. And what I see is potential. *So—you do this job right, there's work for you.* Hard *work, understand? Hard work pays hard cash. You got the heart to do it? I don't mean smoke some sucker in a drive-by. I mean walk up to the man, put the piece in his face, drop the hammer, and make him dead?"*

"Yes, sir."

"You want to learn how *to get that work? Steady work? You want to drive nice, dress nice, flash nice?"*

"Yes, sir."

"Then pay attention. First thing, you always get the money up front." The blade-thin man's left hand went into a deep pocket. It came out with a thick roll of bills, wrapped in rubber bands. *"This is four thousand dollars in centuries. That's a G apiece. For doing what I told you. A contract, understand?"*

He put his left hand forward, almost in the stocky boy's face.

"Take it and we got a deal. That's your word. In this business, your word, that's your life."

The stocky boy took the money, ignoring that a thousand dollars apiece would have been five grand, not four. Maybe the deadly creature standing before them couldn't count, but there wasn't a doubt he could kill.

"Now I'm gonna give you something else," Ace continued. *"Something even more valuable than the green, so listen* close *now. Which one of you wanted to rape the girls?"*

Silence covered the roof. Dead silence.

"I ain't gonna ask again. Anytime you got a pack like yours, you got someone in it got himself a sex Jones. Now, the thing about that is, sex fiends ain't reliable. You can't trust them. Their word is no good. You get dropped, they be the first to roll on you. Now, which one was it?"

Nobody moved.

"I guess maybe it was all of you," the blade-thin man said in a tone of deep regret. "Too bad."

"It was Randall!" the stocky boy said. "He wanted to do the twins."

"Motherfucker!" one of the boys hissed. He was a tall, well-muscled youth, wearing a black-and-silver Raiders jacket.

"You Randall?" Ace asked.

"Yeah, man. But I was only playing. I ain't gonna rape nobody."

"That's right," Ace said, nodding at Cross. The white man slid forward so quickly Randall had no chance to move before he was hooked in the stomach with the same hand that held the Uzi. The youth grunted as he doubled over. Cross spun sideways and snap-kicked him off the roof.

One of the other boys turned away, to vomit against the wall.

"You got paid," Ace said. "Anything happen to that lady or her girls, nobody gonna die as easy as that punk just did."

Silence.

"Now you know why I gave you four grand, not five. Like I said, one apiece. Give me your cell—not the damn phone, fool, just the number. You get the same pay—one thousand American dollars—every single week. Not apiece,

to split four ways. I call you, tell you where to come, pick it up. Got it?"

The black man seemed to vanish as his words were still hanging in the humid air.

THE CTA bus rumbled to a shuddering stop at the fringe of the ruins that had once been a fully occupied Housing Project. The front doors clacked open, and a tall black woman stepped to the sidewalk. She was dressed in a dark raincoat over a nurse's uniform, the white stockings and shoes a dead giveaway, even in the black night.

Adjusting her shoulder bag for maximum protection against a snatch attempt, the woman turned toward the cluster of mostly empty towers a quarter of a mile away. She walked past the bus-stop bench, her carriage proud and erect despite the exhaustion that suffused her body. She didn't even glance at the slumped-over figure of a man, sensing rather than seeing the near-empty bottle of cheap wine clutched in the bum's slack hand.

"Tough working two jobs, isn't it, Clara?"

The woman whirled sharply, her eyes X-raying the seated bum as she shifted one leg behind the other to brace herself—either to run if she could, or to fight if she couldn't.

"Cross?"

"Sit down," the bum said quietly. "Have a talk with an old friend."

The woman took a tentative step forward, eyes wary. "What happened to your face?" she asked, peering into the darkness.

"Just a little help from the makeup department, Clara. It's me."

"How would I know that?"

"Come on, Clara. You recognized my voice on the phone. You knew I'd be somewhere around here tonight. And you caught my voice again after you got off that bus."

The woman's hand slid into the pocket of her coat. Stayed there.

"Lots of people can do voices," she said.

"Big Luke always said you were a hard woman."

The woman blinked rapidly, tears very near the surface. But her hand stayed deep in her pocket.

"Even when you were a little girl, he told me. One night, we were talking. Just before we went in. Talking to kill the fear, you know what I mean? He told me about your pink party dress—about how you wore it to church one day and people were whispering behind their hands about it. How you just stared them down, backed them away, all their fake-Christian nastiness. He said he knew he wanted to marry you right then."

The woman took her hand from her pocket, walked over, and sat down next to the bum. Her nose told her the truth—whatever the man was, he was no wino.

"I still miss that man," she whispered.

"He knows. He knows what you're doing, how good a mother you are to the girls. What sacrifices you make for them."

"You believe that? You truly do?"

"I do. He's watching," Cross said, thinking, *Somebody sure as hell is,* as he felt the burning sensation high on his right cheekbone.

"I feel that, too, sometimes. That's why I never even thought about . . ."

"I know."

"I know things, too, Cross. I know about you. Things I hear. Who's watching *you*, then?"

"Damned if I know."

"You might be close to the truth with that, Cross."

"Uh-huh."

"I have all his letters. From over there. I read them, all the time. Read some of them to the girls. He wrote to them, too, you know. Separate letters he wrote, even though they're twins. Like he knew they would be different. I was pregnant when he went over. He never saw them."

"He sees them now, Clara. Sees you, too. Days at the Motor Vehicle Bureau, nights at the hospital. No vacations. No fancy clothes. Every penny for the girls."

"I keep them safe, Cross. It's hard lines here. Even the gang-bangers have walked away from the projects now—what's left of them, anyway—but I can't pass up the rent. I been tempted. Many, many times. But there'll never be a man for *me*—I'm waiting on Big Luke, and we'll be together again soon enough. But having a man for . . . protection, you understand?"

"Yes."

"But I go it alone."

"You want to move out, yes, Clara? Out of here. To a safe place."

"That's what I've been saving for. But the girls go to school, that comes first. That's our way. Me and Luke's, I always tell them. You finish college, make something of yourselves, *then* you go out and earn some money, buy your Mama a little house someplace."

"It's time now, Clara. As you sow, so shall you reap."

"The Word of the Lord? Cross, that's blasphemy in your mouth. I told you, I know what you do. Some of it, anyway."

"Same thing I did over there. With Big Luke."

"My man died serving his country," she said, head back, eyes flashing. "I knew he wasn't gonna get no medals for it. He wasn't still in the army, but . . ."

"It was just another war," Cross said, lighting a cigarette. "And I never had a country to serve."

The woman made a face. "I don't allow cigarettes in my house. Not liquor, either."

The man snapped the cigarette away without taking a drag.

"It's time for that house, Clara." He reached into his voluminous coat, took out an envelope, handed it to her. "There's a piece of paper in there along with the money," he said. "It's got names, photos, addresses, Social Security numbers, dates of birth, copies of signatures. They're all going to have to renew their licenses within the next few weeks. All you have to do is make sure each one gets registered as an organ donor."

"Why do you . . . ?"

"You don't want to know, Clara. You worked your whole life, now harvest time is coming. The crops are ready to come in. Take the money, buy your house. There's enough there. More than enough. I'm just planting my own seeds, that's all."

"Couple of Luke's letters, he talked about you, too. He said you didn't care if you lived or you died."

"He told you the truth."

"And he cared so much. He had so much to come back to. You didn't care. But you came back and he didn't. Why is that?"

"I don't know."

She reached over, took the envelope, put it in her pocketbook.

"Goodbye, Clara."

"Goodbye, Cross."

"HE'S ON the top of the list," the white-coated intern said into the pay phone in the basement of the hospital.

"You're sure."

"No doubt about it. He gets the next one."

"Kiss your student loan goodbye," a voice told him.

A PHONE rang in the living room of a modest home in Merrillville, Indiana. It was snatched on the first ring by a pretty woman whose face showed the etched lines of living with death hovering just below the ceiling of her home.

"Yes."

"It's time," a voice said. "You remember where to meet?"

"Yes."

The woman put down the phone. "Lois, come in here," she called.

A teenage girl walked into the living room, a paint-daubed artist's smock covering her to her knees.

"What is it, Mom? Did they find . . . ?"

"Not yet, darling. I have to go out for a while. You watch your little brother. And say a prayer, okay?"

The girl nodded. Stood patiently for her mother's kiss.

The woman drove quickly to the parking lot of a local diner. She pulled into an empty slot in the back and started to roll down her window. Before it was all the way down, she saw a man detach himself from a motorcycle and start toward her.

He approached, leaned against the car, his face hidden from her eyes.

"He's on the top of the list," the man said.

"We waited so long."

"You sure you want to go through with this? It's expensive. And they might find a donor on their own. Maybe in a real short time."

"He doesn't *have* time," the woman said. "What good's a house if one room will always be empty?"

THE MAN was so old that even his expensive cologne couldn't mask the stench of the impatient grave. A silk suit hung limply on his wasted frame. A two-carat blue-white perfect solitaire flickered in the neon light, sliding down his bony finger toward the knuckle as his palsied hand trembled.

The black stretch limo was parked in an alley behind the bar, the old man seated in the cavernous back seat. Bodyguards flanked the limo, standing outside.

The chauffeur's partition was closed.

The door opened, and a man climbed inside and seated himself across from the living skeleton. One of the bodyguards closed the door behind him; it made a noise like a bank vault.

The two inhabitants of the back seat sat in silence, both waiting.

"You are very good," the old man finally said, his voice a reedy imitation of a human's. "You have patience. Respect. The old ways. Too bad you were never one of us."

"There aren't enough of you left," the other man said.

"Yeah, that's true. Less of us all the time. This . . . thing you got to do, it ain't for me. Rocco, he couldn't take me down. Too many buffers. But I got people I got to protect.

" 'The Accountant,' he calls himself. Like he knows it all. But he *don't* know. The big thing he don't know is that *we* do. The indictment is sealed, but we got a little peek inside. He turned. Rolled over like the cowardly dog he is. Figures he'll take a couple a years in a Level One, play some tennis, come out, and start over."

The other man stayed silent.

"You got everything you need?"

"Rocco Bernardi."

"Then it's done, Cross?"

"We got two things left, then it's done."

"Here's one," said the old man, handing over a thick envelope.

"Watch the news," Cross said, stepping out of the limo into the night.

A PHONE buzzed in the guard booth at the gates to a mini-mansion in the lush suburb of Winnetka.

"Front gate, Anthony speaking," a smartly uniformed man answered.

"Have Bert bring the coupe around to the front."

"Yes, sir," Anthony answered, nodding over to another uniformed man, next to him in the booth. "Right away."

The other man took a holster and cartridge belt from a hook, strapped it on, and walked across the manicured, floodlit lawn to a four-car garage. He pressed a transmitter on his belt and the garage door rose. The interior was as brightly lit as an operating room.

The man opened the door of an anthracite-black Bentley Continental GT, its flanks gleaming under endless coats of carnauba. He started the car and sat patiently, listening to the muted purr of power. Then he slowly backed out to the circular driveway in front of a white brick two-story house and vacated the driver's seat, leaving the door open.

A man came down the steps to the car, moving with an air of moderate caution. He was dressed in a conservative midnight-blue suit. His brilliant white shirt set off a red-and-blue tie in a tiny diamond pattern that rippled in the glare of the floodlights.

"Everything okay?" the man asked.

"All quiet, Mr. Bernardi," the guard said, touching his cap with two fingers. He maintained his position even as the Bentley shot away, firing a barrage of marble chips from the driveway at his ankles.

The big coupe turned at the next corner, heading for Chicago's downtown, the Loop. Its driver punched a single button on the cellular phone in the console between the bucket seats, and lit a cigarette while the phone rang through the speaker system.

"Hello . . . ?"

"It's me. I'm on my way."

"Oh, good, honey. I was wondering when—"

"*Don't* wonder, bitch. That's not your job. I'll be there in an hour, tops."

"I'll be waiting, honey. I—"

The man who called himself "The Accountant" broke the connection.

As the Bentley rolled onto a winding stretch of road, a young woman in a wheelchair watched from a darkened room lit only by the sickly amber glow of a computer screen. She lifted a pair of infrared night glasses to her eyes, touched the zoom, zeroed in on the license plate: "ACCT 1."

The young woman dropped the night glasses to her lap, wheeled herself over to the computer. A few lightning-fast keystrokes opened a small window in the upper left corner of the screen.

"?" appeared in the window.

Her fingers tapped keys; "Rolling" appeared on her screen. She hit another key and the screen went blank. One more keystroke and her hard drive began reformatting. She immediately turned to a new computer and booted it into life.

In an office on a high floor of the Sears Tower, a man turned from another computer screen and picked up a telephone.

In an after-hours joint on the West Side, Ace felt a vibration in his shirt pocket. He took out a small box and glanced at its liquid-crystal display. The blade-thin killer walked through the club, into a back room where a man was watching television. He turned from the screen at Ace's approach, waiting. When Ace nodded, the man got up and walked out the back door.

A city ambulance was cruising the Dan Ryan Expressway. A round-faced Hispanic woman was driving, her hair spilling out from under her cap. A lanky white man with a prominent Adam's apple was in the passenger seat. Their radio was quiet. A *b-r-r-r-ing* sound filled the cab. The lanky man took a mobile phone from his shirt pocket and flipped it open. He didn't speak.

"Alert," the phone said into his ear.

The lanky man nodded at his partner.

"TELL CACASO he has a deal," the man in the Bentley was saying into his cellular phone just as the door to the truck bay of an abandoned warehouse at the edge of the Badlands slid up.

A car flowed out into the night—an anonymous city-camoed sedan that no one was ever sure they had actually just seen. A pudgy man was at the wheel, guiding the massive vehicle delicately with his fingertips.

"I got him on the scanner," Cross said from the passenger seat. "Probably the *federales* do, too—they like to keep track of their assets."

Buddha said nothing, piloting the Shark Car through the Warehouse District on the Near South Side, heading toward the Loop.

Cross pulled a burner cell from a shoulder holster, hit a number.

"How close?" he asked.

"He's on the Drive," a voice came back. "Maybe ten minutes. Fifteen tops."

Cross pushed another button on the cell phone, waited for the telltale hiss of acid being released, and tossed it out the window.

"He's going to his girlfriend's, Buddha. So they'll have a couple of his boys out front, to cover him. It has to be on the turn-in, okay?"

"Sure, boss."

The Bentley kept well within the speed limit. The driver talked on his phone, making deals with his mouth. And making plans in his head. The sleek custom-painted car turned off Lake Shore Drive, heading to the Gold Coast apartment where his mistress waited.

"He's about two kliks away now, Buddha. Stay sharp."

The pudgy man made no acknowledgment.

Cross hit a number on another phone. In the cab of the ambulance, the lanky man didn't speak, just listened:

"Going down" was all he heard.

"Hit it!" the lanky man told his partner. As she stepped on the gas, he picked up his radio.

"We're going out of service for a personal. Fifteen minutes; acknowledge."

"You're clear," came back the dispatcher's voice.

"Let's hit the Gold Coast, Zee," he said. "There's a little Afghan joint not far from there I want to try."

"Remind you of old times?" The woman smiled.

The Bentley motored along, its smug driver never noticing the anonymous Shark Car moving in from a side street.

"Got him?" Cross asked.

"Locked," Buddha said, focusing.

"Harvest time," Cross said, adjusting his shoulder belt.

As the Bentley slowed down for the corner, the Shark Car took it broadside, knocking the heavy coupe into a line of parked vehicles at the curb. Cross slid from the car, looking dazed, his hands empty.

Bernardi bounced from his coupe, unhurt. And angry. As Cross approached, the informer's fists were balled, and his face was a mottled pattern of red and white.

"You stupid hillbilly sonofabitch! Look at my car."

"I'm . . . sorry, man," Cross muttered. "Look, I got insurance. Really. See . . . ."

Cross reached into the pocket of his coat. The sneer vanished from Bernardi's face as the silenced semi-auto came up. The first shot took away the bridge of his nose. Cross walked over, cranked off two more rounds into the man's head, one in each eye. The Shark Car was off the block before the doorman at the fancy building a block away had finished dialing 911.

"DAMN! You hear that, Zee?"

"Yeah. Let's go!"

Less than a minute later, the lanky man was back on the phone.

"We're coming in, got one down."

"Trauma team?"

"You can try, but there's no way he's gonna make it, looks *real* bad. But his license says he's an organ donor. May not be too late to . . . you know, with all head wounds. We've got him iced down—maybe they can save *something*."

"You're clear to fly, come on."

"ETA under two minutes."

The ambulance piled into the hospital lot. The body was wheeled out on a stretcher, rushed straight into the OR. Then the surgeons went to work.

THE PHONE rang in the woman's home in Merrillville.

"Mrs. Layne?"

"Yes."

"Please come right away. A casualty just arrived, too late to save him. But he was an organ donor, and his heart's in perfect condition. We've done the blood-typing, and it appears to be an ideal match. We've already started surgery on your husband."

"It's the miracle!" the woman cried out, as if she had known it would come.

"CLARA TOOK the money?" Ace asked, just the barest whiff of suspicion in his tone.

"Sure. I told her it was Big Luke's. Money he gave me to hold, a long time ago."

"Well, he *did* that, right?"

"Uh-huh."

"We *spent* that money. And a lot more. All on those punks we paid to keep Clara's place safe."

"That's right."

"No way you were holding *that* much, bro. I don't know what else Big Luke was into, but—"

"Pretty close," Cross admitted. "But, yeah, it was running low."

"So where'd the money for Clara to buy that house come from?"

"I invested what was left."

"Sounds like you bet on a long shot."

"Yeah. Just like when Buddha goes drag racing."

"THAT IS your calling card, is it not?" The speaker was sitting in partial shadow. His shape was slender, his voice transcontinental.

"Calling card?"

"Your—I am not sure how to say this—perhaps, your 'motto'?"

"I still don't see—"

"One shot, one kill."

"You mean, is that what people said about me?"

"If you will."

"It's what I was known for, but my name was never put out there."

"There?"

"In the World."

"We are not . . . ah, pardon me. Let me summarize, then. If you will, you had a certain reputation of . . . military service, but that reputation was only among your comrades. Certainly not . . . publicized, am I correct?"

"Pretty much," a medium-sized man with heavily muscled forearms answered. The iris of his left eye was a very slim circle of a blue so pale it was almost white, making its light-gathering black pupil appear greatly enlarged. "Only, how do you know anything like that? You're not—"

"Surely you understand that not all military personnel wear uniforms."

"What *I* understand is that I had a drink in a bar with a gorgeous woman. And I woke up here. Wherever this is."

"Sometimes, it is necessary—"

"What's necessary is that I see someone in the chain of command. Someone that I know—not someone who wears campaign ribbons, or talks right. Someone I know personally. Like my CO."

"Unfortunately—"

"Linton, James Thomas. Sergeant. Seven oh seven four nine one one."

"You are hardly a prisoner of war, Mr.—"

"Linton, James Thomas. Sergeant. Seven oh seven four nine one one."

"There really is no point in this."

"Yeah. Yeah, there is. See, I gave you my right name. And you act like you already knew my MOS. But if you did, you'd know the serial number I just gave you isn't a match."

"That isn't our concern."

"Your concern is that you want me to dial someone long-distance."

"Well put."

"Linton, James Thomas. Sergeant. Seven oh seven four nine one one."

"I see. So an off-duty assignment, one that pays extremely well for less than a few hours' work, that doesn't interest you, Sergeant?"

"I know what 'extreme' means to people like you."

"Like me?"

"Like you. I'm supposed to buy that you're CIA or something like that. But with that accent . . . Never mind that if the spooks wanted me to do a job they'd just order me, not put money on the table . . . . You picked the wrong guy."

"You are forcing me to . . . offer other inducements."

"Save your breath. I already know I'm dead. So I figure, whoever you want dead, the best way to serve my country is to let you just get on with it."

"There are worse things than death."

"No, there're not. Just longer ones. And you're not going that route, anyway."

"You know this . . . how?" the shadowed man asked.

"You can't torture a man into the kind of shot you need made. Oh, you use enough of . . . whatever you've got, you could probably make me pull a trigger. But nothing you do, nothing you threaten to do, could make me hit the target. And you'd never know, would you? Maybe some of your torture tricks might damage some nerve endings, mess with my eyesight . . . something like that."

"You are correct."

"I get another medal for that?"

The faint light that shielded the shadowy man went black.

CROSS WALKED past the man with the green eyeshade. As he reached the upper flight of steps leading to Red 71's front door, the brand on his cheekbone burned so sharply he had to draw a breath.

He sat down.

The burning decreased.

He started to walk back down in the direction of the poolroom. With every step, the burning decreased again.

By the time he had pushed through the black-beaded curtain and was seated behind his makeshift desk in the back room, the burning was gone.

Even rubbing the spot where he'd first felt the warmth didn't bring it back.

"HE WAS no use to us." The voice of the man who had been shadowed when talking to the military sniper came through the Sat-phone's speaker.

"So you . . . ?"

"Eliminated any problem that might be associated with this," the shadowy man finished the sentence, looking out through the bunker-slit of a thick-walled structure the same color as the sand on which it sat as he spoke.

"Always the best way," the voice agreed, less than a second before the bunker was hit by a drone missile.

THE MAN seated in the back of a strip joint in the Near North section of Chicago was the heir to an empire awarded to him by those with the power to do so. He hadn't expected such an opportunity. Still, he had to be cleared by the National Commission of any complicity in the deaths of both Costanza and his boss before the prize was awarded. He had not been present when that decision was made.

"I don't believe in luck," one of those Commission members said.

"Nor do I," a much older man agreed. "But that doesn't mean one man cannot profit from the mistakes of others."

"I still say—"

"All respect," the older man interrupted. "But if Damiano was skilled enough to orchestrate the near-simultaneous deaths of Citelli and Costanza, and did so in such a way that nothing pointed to him, Damiano would be *molto pericoloso*, would he not?"

"How could he know he'd be the one we'd tap?"

"If we picked a different man, and something happened to him, that'd be Damiano's suicide note," another man added.

"Damiano asking to hit this Cross guy, may be the same thing? I mean, why come to us? Whoever he is, this Cross, he's not part of our thing."

"Damiano, he'll have some story to tell, no matter what," the younger man said.

"So. We are agreed, then?" the older man asked a question that none present took as such.

THE SEATED man faced an audience of three men, who were also seated. Each of them had a man standing just to their right shoulder. The man in the center of the three had two men behind him. Neither of those men's hands were visible—they weren't there to light cigars or fetch drinks.

"This town's been full of contract men since way before

I was born," the man in the center said, softly. "But none of your people could find a single one willing to take on the job, is that what you're telling me?"

"I wanted the job done a certain way," the subordinate said. "*Only* that way. The closest anyone could get to the door of that Red 71 place is almost three-quarters of a mile away. And it's not even a level shot—they'd have to be shooting down. That's why I had to reach out so far."

"To *Afghanistan?!?*"

"Yes. This guy, the one we wanted, we only knew about him because his spotter—that's the guy with the range finder; he measures the wind, elevation . . . stuff like that—he talked too much. He was putting it around. The war was about to be dialed back, big-time, so him and his partner, they were, you know, looking for work."

"So?"

"That guy, the shooter I mean, he couldn't deliver."

"Not a man to ever use again."

"No one ever will."

"Yes, I understand. So you are saying, we have made no progress?"

"I think we kind of have. This guy—Cross, he's called— he's a contract man. Best there is."

"That's the guy you asked permission to hit?"

"Yes. Because, see, we found out he already *had* a job. And the deal with this guy, he takes your money, you get what you paid for. Period. He's strictly an outsider. He'd take money from anyone."

"So?"

"So the guy he was paid to hit," the subordinate paused for effect, "that was you."

"*Me?* How could that be? Before all that . . . craziness started, why would I be on anyone's list?"

"It was *after*," the subordinate said. "But once we found he'd been hired, what I wanted to do was hit this guy—Cross, I'm saying—before he could make a move. That way, you'd be safe, no matter what. And we'd have plenty of time to deal with . . . ."

The room went silent. "You're crazy!" the subordinate sneered, to no one in particular. "What am I now, a fortune-teller? How could I have—"

"Nobody said it was you, Damiano," the man standing behind the left shoulder of the man sitting directly across from the subordinate said, very calmly.

"Until just now," the man standing behind his right shoulder added.

"WE KNOW you already got paid," the phone-voice said. "This is just to tell you, the man who paid you, he's not going to need proof-of-performance."

"Ever?"

"Ever."

"I've got friends in high places, now?"

"People told me you had a strange sense of humor," the phone-voice said, just before the connection was cut.

"WHY THE front door, boss?"

"Got to test something, Buddha."

"You want me to go out first?"

"If this works, nobody's going out at all," Cross said, touching high on his right cheekbone as he spoke.

"SO WE'RE DONE."

"Unless you want to keep paying those punks to keep an empty apartment safe?"

"Come on!"

"And they're not like most over that side of town, are they?"

"Meaning . . . ?"

"They see you coming, they don't run, they step to you."

"True."

"So, the way I see it, you owe them one more payoff."

"They always come all together, bro. Four of them."

"You drive—they know your car, right? Let Tracker and Buddha do the rest. We don't need any noise when we finish this."

"I won't even leave my—" Ace stopped, startled at the playing card he'd just pulled from his shirt pocket. He turned the card in Cross's direction.

"What the hell is this?"

"It's an ace."

"Yeah. Supposed to be *my* ace. So how'd it get turned into the ace of hearts?"

"Got me." Cross shrugged, feeling the near-invisible blue brand burn against his right cheekbone.

"I don't like it," Ace said, very softly. "You don't think that those . . . ?"

"That's not the question, brother. You're thinking, could . . . whatever was here before . . . could it come back, yeah? Me, I'm wondering, did it ever leave?"

"You're not wondering," Tiger said.

All eyes turned toward the Amazon, but she was done talking.

TWO NIGHTS later.

"I want to show you something," Tiger said to Cross. The two of them were alone in the back of Red 71.

"I wish you would."

"Stop it! I'm not playing now. You know what a relay camera is?"

"Picks up whatever it sees, and passes it over to a storage box. That way you can keep it running twenty-four/seven. The top security companies use them, so they're not over-writing their own data."

"Not exactly a bodega cam."

"No. Those have to keep their tapes ninety days. If there's nothing on them, they just hit the 'Restart' button. They aren't exactly high-def to begin with, and after they're on the third or fourth overwrite, whatever they pick up is just a jumble of black and white. Cops hate them."

"Why?"

"Because they end up looking for some dark-faced man in a black hoodie—guy could be anything from Greek to African, and even *that's* useless if the stickup artist pulled a bandanna over his face. There's no scale, so they can't even narrow down the guy's height. But the local TV stations will run the tapes—you know, that 'Have you seen this man?'

crap—and when the cops don't find the guy, people think they're not doing their job. There's tapes of two-bit 'gangsters' jumping over counters, pistol-whipping some poor bastard. Looks ugly. And it is, I guess. Still, those tapes, they're really not much to go on.

"But you know those nature shows? Where they set up a relay camera and just let it run, sometimes for weeks, or even months?"

"Sure."

"You know how they make them real small now? The lenses not much bigger than the eraser on a pencil—you can plant them just about anywhere."

"Tiger, what's with all this? You got something you want to tell me, spit it out."

Tiger ran both hands through her thick, striped hair, stretching like the big cat she was named for. Cross recognized the gesture. Not an attention-attracting move; it was a sign that the Amazon was in warrior mode, measuring the enemy's strength, computing the odds.

Cross lit a cigarette, saying nothing.

He was already stubbing it out when Tiger said, "We found something."

"We?"

"Me and Tracker. Remember, we were on the team that brought you in to get a specimen of . . ."

"Yeah. But I didn't pull it off."

"You sure?" Tiger said, very softly. She planted one haunch on the edge of the man-for-hire's desk, a solid cypress plank that was balanced between a pair of wrought-iron sawhorses, and extended a long talon to tap Cross's face just below his right eye. "Up close, I can see it."

"That blue thing?"

"No. That only happens when . . . Well, I'm not sure what sets it off, but you know what I mean."

"Yeah. I can feel when it burns. But I don't know what . . . activates it."

"It just looks like a tiny scar now. Nobody'd ever see it unless they were looking for it."

"I still don't see where you're going."

"Be patient," Tiger said, a smile flashing across her lips so quickly that Cross couldn't be sure it had ever been there.

"I am," Cross said, pointedly.

"There's a wall over on the South Side. The whole side of a building. Pretty much all that's left of that building, actually. Ace showed it to us. It's kind of a mural for graffiti artists. No gang tags. So nothing to *over*tag."

"Okay. So . . . ?"

"So what Ace told us was there *used* to be tags. All Vice Lords, but different sets, you know?"

"Sure. That's more West Coast crap—every few blocks, there's something like another division of the same army. Gangs get so big, they start to subdivide. Supposedly started in Compton, but you can't trust the wire on that. So you got Crips breaking into smaller units—48th Street Crips, like that. But here, even that's not enough. Gangster Disciples may be the father, but it's got a whole lot of sons: Maniac Gangster Disciples, like that."

"Right. But Ace showed us this wall. Like he wanted us to verify what he saw. Only it wasn't there."

"Slow down, girl. Ace brought you over to show you something, but there was nothing to show?"

"Yeah. And Ace, he's the last guy on the planet to start seeing ghosts. That's where we got the idea for the camera."

"Just show me," Cross said.

THE WALL had once been whitewashed, but time had faded it to a shade of ecru that seemed to blanket certain parts of Chicago. Parts known to be don't-go-there dangerous.

The DVD that Tiger was playing showed all kinds of ghetto artistry. Not tagging, more like murals. Mostly portraits and scenes.

"Martin Luther King on the same wall as H. Rap Brown—haven't seen those two together before. Look like the same artist did them both to you?"

"It was the same artist," Tiger said. "No secret about it. We talked to her ourselves. She said it was a 'spectrum mural.' Nobody bothered her while she was working."

"Who was watching her back?"

"Nobody, is what she said. She's not affiliated, and she wasn't flying colors while she worked."

"That's a *lot* of work."

"Took her a little more than two months, working every day."

"Neighborhood girl?"

"Born and raised. But she's not an artist, she's an architect."

"So she could be earning some real coin . . . ."

"Yes. Only she worked on that mural every day—I mean *every* day—and she didn't have a night job."

"Somebody was paying her bills?"

"I guess so. But she was living alone. By choice. I thought she was about twenty-two—but she's damn near forty. Long-distance biker—bicycle, I'm saying, no motor—and she's spent a *lot* of time in a dojo. Girl's got legs of steel."

"Black girl?"

"Mixed, I think. Not just her skin shade, her hair."

"You get Rhino to run her?"

"All checks out. This girl—Antoinette—she's all about off-the-grid stuff. Her building, where she lives, it looks like about what you'd expect in that neighborhood. But there's a solar collector of some kind on the roof. Rhino said she *owns* the building, but there's no account with any utility. No bills for electricity, gas, phone, Internet—nothing. He was impressed . . . and you know what it takes to impress *that* man."

"What? He wants to put one of those solar things on top of Red 71?"

"Ask *him*."

"Tiger . . ."

"Tracker said you were very still inside yourself. He said he never knew a white man to be like that. How about you just relax for another few minutes, let me tell this my way, all right?"

Cross lit another cigarette.

"Okay," the Amazon said. "Let's add it up. This girl—and she's a *pretty* girl—works on that mural every day. Nobody bothers her. Nobody even . . . I don't know, it's like she's got protection everybody knows about, but it can't be that. Like I said, she's not *with* anyone.

"Now, here's the thing. Ace said there was a gunfight right across from the mural one night. Not late at night, just when it was getting dark. None of the bangers got hit, but a little girl took one in the back of the head as she was running for cover.

"Just as Ace was coming back, first light, he sees a pair

of playing cards on that wall. *Huge* ones, covering the whole mural. Two cards: ace of clubs, jack of hearts."

"Painted over what that girl was—?"

"*No.* That's just it. It was kind of like a hologram. Ace said he could see right through it."

"The girl—this Antoinette—she show up later?"

"Yep. And went right back to work. The cards, they were gone. Like they'd never been there at all."

"Ace doesn't see things. He doesn't drink, doesn't smoke, wouldn't touch drugs."

"I know that."

"So that's why you mounted the camera?"

"Right."

"And . . . ?"

"See for yourself," Tiger said, softly. "It's just about to come up."

The screen was still filled with the mural when a pair of playing cards materialized over it, just as Ace had described to Tiger. This time, it was the ace of hearts and the jack of spades.

"Stayed just like that for almost ten minutes," Tiger said. "Then it just . . . disappeared."

"Same time?"

"Yeah. Like it was filling in the crack between night and dawn."

"Got a date on that thing?"

"Of course."

"Anything happen that night?"

"Anything . . . ?"

"Violent deaths."

"Not in that neighborhood."

"But . . . ?"

"You remember that puny little 'Führer'? The one that ended up with a long sentence for plotting to kill the judge who sentenced him? The original sentence was nothing to start with, but he turned it into an all-the-way with *that* move."

"Yeah. But that was—"

"Few years ago, I know. But he put together some 'followers.' He's locked in PC, but that Web site what's left of his 'storm troopers' put together claimed he was secretly running the AB from Inside. He went from a terrified little twit to shot caller. Magical, huh? Only that was pure Internet baloney. Still, *somebody* didn't like it much."

"He got—?"

"Not him. That little group of play-Nazis. The ones that put up that Web site. They had a storefront. And I mean *had*."

"Bomb?"

"Nope. Five people—two female, three male, none of them over twenty-five—all got shot in the head. What the papers love to call 'execution style.' The shooters sprayed 'AB' over everything in there—walls, computers, posters. They got so carried away, they even sprayed all over Hitler's picture."

"What happened to the Web site?"

"Nothing, Rhino says. But it hasn't been updated since that night."

"So where's the connection?"

"I don't know, okay!"

"Sssshhh, girl. There's nothing to get worked up about."

"Really?" Tiger said, reflexively touching the knives in

her holster. "I'll buy that. I'll buy it the minute you explain how Ace's calling card changed color. How did the ace of spades turn into the ace of hearts?"

Cross felt the spot below his eye burn, as if in answer to the warrior-woman's question.